Praise for Sharon Gwyn Short's first novel, ANGEL'S BIDDING

"Private detective Patricia Delaney is a '90s sleuth who uses computer databases as well as old-fashioned gumshoe savvy to solve a baffling murder in the fast-paced and intriguing ANGEL'S BIDDING. Sharon Gwyn Short's debut effort is sure to win readers to this new and lively series."

> —KATHY HOGAN TROCHECK
> Author of
> *Every Crooked Nanny* and
> *To Live and Die in Dixie*

"I can think of very few debuts more promising, or more satisfying, than Sharon's (and Patricia Delaney's) in ANGEL'S BIDDING."

> —WILLIAM J. REYNOLDS
> Author of *The Naked Eye* and
> *Things Invisible*

By Sharon Gwyn Short
Published by Fawcett Books:

ANGEL'S BIDDING
PAST PRETENSE
THE DEATH WE SHARE

THE
DEATH WE
SHARE

Sharon Gwyn Short

FAWCETT GOLD MEDAL • NEW YORK

A Fawcett Gold Medal Book
Published by Ballantine Books
Copyright © 1995 by Sharon Gwyn Short

All rights reserved under International and Pan-American Copyright Conventions. Published in the United States by Ballantine Books, a division of Random House, Inc., New York, and simultaneously in Canada by Random House of Canada Limited, Toronto.

Library of Congress Catalog Card Number: 95-90431

ISBN 0-449-14916-1

Manufactured in the United States of America

First Edition: December 1995

10 9 8 7 6 5 4 3 2 1

To my family: David, Katherine, Gwendolyn.

With thanks to: Dr. Stephen England and Dr. W. B. Ashcraft, for medical advice. And to Wendy Gray and Joey Bates, for musical advice.

Several hymns are named in this novel:
Rock of Ages, Cleft for Me; words by Augustus M. Toplady (1776), melody by Thomas Hastings (1830).
When I Survey the Wondrous Cross; words by Isaac Watts (1707), melody by Lowell Mason (1824).
Amazing Grace; words by John Newton (1779), Early American melody.

> *"A prima donna dies no less than three times: First go her looks, that is death number one; then her voice, that is number two; and finally the death she shares with the others."*
> > *Lillian Nordica, opera singer,*
> > *as quoted in*
> > The Last Prima Donnas
> > *by Lanfranco Rasponi*

Chapter 1

What first struck Patricia about Carlotta Moses was her absolute stillness.

Carlotta stood at the window, holding back the drapery. One would expect her slender, pale hand to tremble under the weight of the heavy sapphire material, her thin body to quiver with the tension of her rigid pose. Yet Carlotta was as still as a statue: long, ivory neck; sharply sculpted chin; slightly parted lips; deeply carved eyes. Even the folds of her black skirt hung perfectly still, as if not so much as a draft in the room would dare to disturb a thread of Carlotta's outfit.

Did those unblinking eyes really focus on the snow whirling and gathering outside the window? Patricia Delaney wondered. It did not seem possible. Carlotta had been standing thusly—straight, unwavering, silent, not even the slightest breath seeming to move through her—ever since Howard Eismann, Carlotta's husband, had directed Patricia into the library of the Eismann—

1

Moses estate—nervously explaining that both he and Carlotta, as well as Carlotta's son, Quentin, and her daughter-in-law, Wallis, were eagerly waiting for Patricia.

And yet, while they fussed over her—taking her coat and hat and gloves; offering her tea or coffee, which Patricia declined—Carlotta never moved from her position at the window. Had Carlotta been so entranced by the frozen view, as she "eagerly" watched for Patricia, that she herself had frozen in place? Patricia smiled at that thought. Carlotta Moses, retired, world-renowned operatic diva and movie star, with thousands of adoring fans, would wait for no one.

Patricia knew this because she counted herself among Carlotta's fans, although she was a generation removed from most of them. Her father, Joseph, had always loved opera, particularly as performed by Carlotta, and had shared his love of it with all six of his children. Yet Patricia, the youngest, was the only one who had grown to share that love. From years of hearing and reading about Carlotta Moses, Patricia knew a considerable amount about her: her rise to operatic fame; her marriage to a movie director; their failed attempts to have children followed by the adoption of Quentin; the tragic death of her first husband in a boating accident; her second marriage to Howard Eismann many years later; her retirement from the operatic stage and her debut on the movie screen; and finally her retirement from the movie screen and her subsequent, gradual withdrawal from the world. In four years Carlotta had not been known to leave her home in Indian Hills, a wealthy town east of

Cincinnati, Ohio. What Patricia did not know yet was why she had been summoned by Carlotta.

Patricia Delaney was an investigative consultant specializing in background searches on individuals for companies, organizations, and sometimes other individuals. Normally, her clients came to her office in Alliston. Charles Leiber had called her the previous morning, introduced himself as Carlotta's attorney, and requested that Patricia come the next morning to the Eismann–Moses estate. Patricia had accepted the assignment immediately.

Now she surveyed the little group gathered in the library, all but Carlotta seated in a grouping of sapphire-blue Queen Anne sofas and chairs just inside the perimeter of a large Persian rug. The furniture, rug, and draperies offered the only color in the room; the library was otherwise all mahogany flooring and paneling, and leather-bound books.

Patricia wondered who read them. Howard—who sat on the edge of a sofa, one hand fussing inside his gray suit jacket, searching for some pocket or another, the other hand sweeping nervously through his thick white hair? No, she imagined him with a stash of Western paperbacks. Wallis—who sat on the opposite sofa, toying with one of the many gold chains that perfectly accented her plain, black cashmere dress? No, for her Patricia selected the latest contemporary fiction bestseller, and perhaps a fashion magazine or two. Quentin—who sat next to his wife, flicking a surely imagined bit of lint from his impeccable navy trousers, and then another from the impeccable burgundy sweater? No, for him Patricia imagined a thick biography or historical tome.

Patricia resisted the urge to look again at Carlotta while trying to imagine her moving away from the window to reach for one of these books. . . . But again, no. This library was simply a setting for Carlotta; Patricia could not imagine a secret reading pleasure for Carlotta; she was too much, in Patricia's mind, the image of the diva as shown on the stage, in the press. It seemed unreal to be here, with the great Carlotta Moses actually standing by the window—or perhaps that really was a statue, and the real Carlotta would come sweeping into the room any minute now. . . . Enough, thought Patricia. She had finally started to warm up after coming in from the cruelly cold January morning; she was ready to get to work.

Patricia looked at Howard. "Mr. Leiber telephoned me yesterday morning, telling me he had gotten my name from a contact he has in the Schultz, Moore and Bell law firm." Patricia didn't explain that Jay Bell was also the leader of the Queen River Band, a classic rock-and-roll band in which she played drums on Tuesday nights at Dean's Tavern in Alliston, a southeastern suburb of Cincinnati.

"Mr. Leiber said that you and your wife were very eager for me to come here this morning to assist you with a problem. Why don't we start with a general description of it? Then I'll probably ask a few questions, get a few more specifics, and we'll see if it is the kind of work I handle."

"Oh, I'm sure it is the kind of work you handle, Ms.

Delaney. When Schultz, Moore and Bell recommended you, we knew—" Howard started.

Quentin stirred restlessly. "Actually, I'm the one who contacted our family's attorney about this problem. And of course you'll handle it, Ms. Delaney. We need your full attention immediately."

Patricia looked at Quentin. "Mr. Leiber did not inform me," Patricia said crisply, "that I would be considering"—she paused to silently underscore that last word—"taking on a case for the whole family."

"Oh, but it concerns all of us. Very much. Me at the museum, our daughter, not to mention Carlotta's reputation—" Wallis's words rushed out, then stopped abruptly as Quentin clenched her knee.

"Please, Wallis, we need to explain the situation rationally to Ms. Delaney, and then I'm sure she'll understand."

Patricia smiled. "Patricia. Just Patricia, is fine. And I would like to start with hearing what Mr. Eismann has to say."

She looked at him. Howard rubbed his florid cheeks, then clasped his hands in his lap. Despite his brilliantly white hair, the expensively cut gray wool suit, the silver-framed glasses at the tip of his nose, his manner reminded her of that of a scared little boy. He reached a nervous hand into his jacket again, this time pulling out a small bottle with which he struggled until Wallis took it from him, murmuring, "Please, let me. . . ."

"As you can see, Patricia"—Quentin snapped off the final syllable of her name—"my stepfather is not well. He has a heart condition, which this situation has worsened. He will answer your questions, as will Mother, assuming she feels up to it, but first let me explain to you what has happened."

He cleared his throat and continued. "Two days ago my mother received a telephone call. Actually, our housekeeper, Marcy Bergamore, took the call, but it was for Mother. The caller introduced himself as Wayne Hackman. Does the name sound familiar?"

Patricia considered, then shook her head. "Should it?"

"It should if you follow television tabloid shows."

"I go for renting the occasional *Thin Man* movie—or maybe a Disney classic—myself."

Quentin proffered his first true smile of the morning and seemed to relax a little. "I have to admit, I'm rather glad you don't watch the TV tabloids."

"Why did this Wayne Hackman call your mother?"

"Hackman is a so-called reporter for this syndicated hour-long show called *Flash*. He told Mother that he was working on a show about her."

Patricia frowned as she considered Quentin's statement, unable to imagine Carlotta Moses agreeing to an interview on a TV tabloid show, or to imagine why anyone from such a show would be interested in her. Carlotta's life had been lived publicly since her operatic debut in 1945, and her life had been lively but devoid of the disgrace on which such shows tended to feed.

"Why is a show like *Flash* interested in your mother?" Patricia asked.

"The reason is—" Quentin started, and then stopped abruptly, gasping. His face contorted in a sudden spasm of strong emotion. Anger? Fear? The expression was difficult to classify as Quentin struggled to regain his former composure.

Wallis had finished her ministrations with Howard, who sat quietly, hands fallen to his sides, eyes shut. Now Wallis turned her attention to Quentin. "It's all right, darling—I know it's difficult," she said, holding and stroking his hand.

"The reason this Wayne Hackman wanted to talk with my mother-in-law," Wallis said, looking at Patricia, "is that he'd been contacted by someone claiming that as a young woman Carlotta had a son, and that she'd given him up for adoption when he was nearly four years old—just before her debut."

Patricia rubbed a finger across the white diagonal scar on her chin as she considered the ramifications for Carlotta and her family if such a story were true. The biological son, and any of his relatives, could want money from Carlotta, or favors, or—even more distasteful, perhaps, to Carlotta—an actual relationship. Many of Carlotta's fans would not believe the story, even with irrefutable evidence, but some would, even without evidence of any kind. To at least some degree, Carlotta's reputation would be damaged, and by extension, so would her family members' reputations. Carlotta and her family could easily absorb a loss of money, but a damaged reputation . . . To this diva, and apparently to her family, there could be no worse loss. No wonder they each acted as if suffering from varying degrees of shock.

Patricia wondered briefly why this person—or the alleged son—didn't contact Carlotta directly. But the answer came to her quickly; Carlotta, although beloved for her remarkable talents on stage and screen, was not known for personal warmth. The contact or the alleged son—were they the same person? Patricia wondered—would be instantly rebuffed. If money was the goal, more would be gained by going through a show like *Flash*.

"Did Hackman say anything about what kind of proof this person has?" Patricia asked.

Quentin looked at her suddenly, sharply. "Proof! There can be no proof! Maybe Hackman made this all up for his own reasons! Or this is just some deranged idiot's idea of . . ."

Hackman might not have proof, Patricia thought, but he certainly had at least a little something to go on. Patricia knew enough about tabloid television to know that only a bit of fact was needed as the basis for embellishment. Pointing this out to Quentin, however, did not seem likely to calm him.

"Quentin, presumably you want me here to provide some expertise to help with this situation," Patricia said. "That means I am going to have to ask a few perhaps uncomfortable questions of all of you."

"Yes. Sorry. No, Hackman didn't suggest any proof."

"Just a moment; I need to take a few notes on this." Patricia had brought two cases with her, her briefcase and a smaller case carrying her small but powerful notebook computer. She opened up the notebook computer on her lap, powered it up, started up the word-processing package, and tapped in a few notes. Later, back at her office, she'd transfer the notes to her desktop computer.

Patricia finished tapping and glanced up at Quentin.

"All right. Hackman didn't offer anything helpful, did he, like the name of this contact? Or what connection the contact supposedly has with Carlotta?"

Quentin frowned. "What do you mean?"

"It would be helpful to know if Hackman's contact is the person claiming to be the son, or someone else, perhaps someone who has reason to want to hurt your mother."

"No, he gave no clue about his contact. He asked Mother if she would agree to be on the show. Of course she said no, and of course he knew she would. He only asked because that way he'd be able to state that Carlotta had been contacted and refused to comment. These so-called journalists. They take a shred of information and try to make it appear to have more significance than it actually does. . . ."

"Hackman has created a problem for you," said Patricia. "But if there's no proof to support his claims— not even a shred of it—couldn't your attorney threaten to sue the producers for slander or libel?"

"We thought about that. But that would draw attention to this, and believe me that's something we don't want. My mother's reputation needs to be protected, quietly, from this lie getting any attention at all," Quentin said.

So her instinct about the family's defensiveness of its collective reputation was on target, Patricia thought.

"What about counterproof then? Surely a physician could examine Carlotta and testify that in fact she'd never had children."

Quentin looked as if his sweater collar were suddenly threatening him with asphyxiation. In the brief moment of silence that followed, Patricia heard a note, middle C, being struck on a piano in a nearby room, followed by the major and minor scales played rapidly in succession: C major, A minor . . .

"No, my mother would never agree to something so . . ."

"It would be pointless, of course, anyway," Howard said.

Patricia startled and looked at Howard; she'd almost forgotten about him. He was now busying himself with preparing a cup of tea, as if of course he'd been listening all along to the entire conversation; and perhaps, thought Patricia, he had.

"You see, Carlotta was pregnant several times before and lost the babies. This is why she and her first husband had to adopt Quentin. But a physician could not truthfully say she'd never carried children, or that she could not have possibly carried one to term, given it up, had a bit of bad luck later, then chosen to adopt— although, of course, that's not what happened." Howard stirred his tea, then tapped his spoon against the rim of his cup. The pianist in the nearby room was on to F major, then D minor.

"And at any rate, Quentin is exactly right. Carlotta would never agree to have such an exam in order to defend herself from something of which she's not guilty." Howard took a sip, frowned at the cup, then dropped in another sugar cube.

"But we wish to guarantee, as quietly as possible, that this show not take place," Howard continued.

"And that's why we've contacted you," said Quentin. He had fully regained his composure now, and again wanted to take charge of the conversation. "We want you to find this . . . contact"—he spat out the word as if the unnamed person were unworthy of being recognized as human—"and let him know we're willing to pay him. Plenty of money. Far more than he could get out of that ridiculous show."

"You want me to track him—or her—down; don't assume this person is male. Then you want to buy this person's silence?" Patricia asked.

"We're not buying silence about something that is true. We're not asking to cover something up. We're simply paying him to back off with this ridiculous story. Or her, as you so correctly point out. Whoever it is, surely money is what this person wants, anyway. . . ."

"You're offering yourselves up for blackmail!" Patricia said.

Quentin suddenly turned red, his face again contorting with emotion, this time obviously rage. "What choice do we have? If you don't want to do it, then I'm sure Leiber can find us someone who—"

"Now, Quentin, please calm yourself," Wallis said soothingly.

How long before Wallis cracked from constantly playing the comforter? Patricia wondered. But, still, she appreciated Wallis's intervention. Patricia would not have liked hearing what she thought Quentin had been about to say, or his implication that her services were easily duplicated.

"No time is good for such a problem, of course, but now is particularly awful," Wallis said. "Have you heard of the Carlotta Moses Museum we're developing in Lebanon?" The scales continued in the next room—B flat major, G minor.

"Yes," Patricia said quietly.

"You have?" Wallis sounded surprised.

Patricia smiled. "Yes. I did a little research yesterday afternoon, in preparation for today's visit, to see what recent news I could find about your mother-in-law."

Actually, the research had been a simple matter of tapping the name "Carlotta Moses" as a search term in a news database and reviewing the results. Patricia had also looked up the property records for this home and searched for records for Quentin and Wallis, in public property records also available in a database. Quentin and Wallis had no real estate locally, but owned a rental property in New Mexico.

The unnamed pianist in the adjoining room progressed to the E flat major and then C minor scales.

"Carlotta recently inherited the home in which she spent her later youth, a home in Lebanon, which is a small town about twenty miles north of here," Patricia said to Wallis. "The place had actually belonged to her stepfather, Douglas Powell, and had passed to his sister, Violet, and after her death a year ago to Carlotta. Now the home is being renovated to house memorabilia from Carlotta's career, and you are serving as the director. Profits from the museum will be used to create a scholarship fund for musicians. Am I right in guessing that you are the one who sent the information to the local newspapers, to get some publicity well in advance of the museum's opening this spring?"

A flat major, F minor.

"Yes. I'm the one who sent the information out,"

Wallis said. "I have a television interview this afternoon, and I'll do even more publicity as we get closer to the date of the opening. It's important that the opening goes well, for several reasons. . . ."

"One reason is that our daughter, Ashley, will be making her debut at the opening," Quentin said.

A flat major, F minor.

"Debut?"

"Yes, her singing debut," Wallis said.

D flat major . . . and the beginning of B flat minor . . . and then the scale stopped midway.

Suddenly a note, middle C, was struck repeatedly and loudly on the piano in the adjoining room by the unnamed pianist. A brief bit of silence was followed by a woman's voice then singing this note with *la*. The note was sung tepidly, but the voice gained strength as it started up an arpeggio. On the top note of the arpeggio, the voice wavered, then gained a little strength as it worked its way back down.

It was as if the singer beginning her vocal exercises released Carlotta, for suddenly she turned from the window.

Carlotta looked directly at Patricia, who held her gaze, unwavering. "What do you know of me?" Carlotta asked, her words spoken evenly, precisely, directly.

The first answers that came to mind were the most obvious—you're a world-renowned soprano and movie star, Ms. Moses, a superstar who, even though living within these walls for the past four years, draws attention easily with just a simple press release, a superstar who has lived most of her life with unquestioning adoration from innumerable fans—fans like my father, Joseph Delaney, who sees you as superhuman.

But these answers were too obvious, and Carlotta's direct, unwavering gaze told Patricia that they were also not the kind Carlotta was looking for.

Patricia drew in her breath slowly and evenly just as she did at the start of her morning meditation sessions, sifting quickly through all that she recalled her father telling her about the great Carlotta Moses, all that she herself had read about the great Carlotta Moses.

"For the first year of your formal training," Patricia finally replied, stating each word distinctly, "you insisted upon practicing breathing, more than learning specific music. You practiced the art of controlling your breath, your diaphragm, your lungs. Three hours of breathing exercises in the morning, two in the evening. You insisted upon this, and continued doing extensive breathing exercises, because, you said in an interview in 1975, just before you retired from opera and moved on to acting, and I quote, 'besides gaining a base of physical strength, necessary to support the voice in performing the most difficult arias, it taught me to temper and focus my passion for music, to discipline the passion so that I could then direct that passion at the audience.' "

Patricia stopped, and forced herself to keep looking, unwavering, at Carlotta. Finally, Carlotta smiled slowly and then moved past Patricia. As she did so Patricia caught a scent of a jasmine perfume. A surprising fragrance for Carlotta, she thought, far too simple for so complex a personality . . . but then some things, such as a woman's scent, would not be captured in an interview stored in a database. Carlotta sat down next to Howard.

"Excellent answer, Ms. Delaney. Only a fan would know this about me. I'm assuming you are a fan?"

Patricia smiled. "I am a fan. But I am here as an investigator."

"Yes, yes. The call from this Hackman. The poor timing what with the museum opening in a few months. Ashley's debut. My first time out in public in four years."

Carlotta smiled at Patricia's surprised look. "No, they didn't get to that, did they? Yes, I'm going to the museum opening. It's my museum, after all. Let me ask you, Patricia, if you know another quote, from another great singer. Lillian Nordica said it. . . . I read it once. . . . 'A prima donna dies no less than three times: First go her looks, that is death number one; then her voice, that is number two; and finally the death she shares with the others.' Do you know this quote?"

"No," Patricia said.

"Well, I've died the first two deaths. And before I reach the death we share, I've little left to enjoy but my reputation, and I won't have it destroyed, especially not by a two-bit reporter with a crackpot story. I'm going to devote myself to the museum, to helping Ashley get her start in music. So, then, Patricia, are you taking our case or not?"

Patricia smiled. Finally, somebody in the room wasn't assuming that she would take the case. She suddenly liked Carlotta, liked her directness, even her undisguised egotism, and no longer felt put off by her eccentric behavior at the window. "Yes," Patricia said, "I'm taking the case."

"How do we start, then?"

"The best way to proceed is to first establish if this Wayne Hackman actually did place the call. It's possible that someone—maybe someone working on the museum, someone working here, someone you used to work with—is disgruntled or jealous and simply trying to cause you grief or discomfort," Patricia said.

Carlotta laughed dismissively. "One always has one's enemies, of course." Then she looked a little sad. "But no. It's been too long since I've been on stage or screen for me to have any active rivals now."

"And anyone else in your family?" Patricia asked.

"I retired about three years ago, left the business in Quentin's hands," Howard said, "and I can't imagine anyone wanting to hurt me, certainly not in this way."

"I run Eismann Furniture Stores now," Quentin said. "We returned here after Howard's retirement."

Eismann Furniture Stores sold very expensive, very exclusive furniture in the Cincinnati area. Patricia could not recall any negative press about the privately owned business, but she made a note on her laptop computer to check it out.

Patricia looked at Wallis. "Can you think of anyone, now or from the past, who'd want to harm this family in this way?"

Wallis shook her head quickly. "No. I'm working on the museum by myself—well, with Carlotta, of course, but, I mean, there are no other employees right now, except the crew that's repainting and wallpapering, but they're just for hire temporarily, and there's no one from where we lived before, in New Mexico. . . ." Her voice trailed off as Quentin gave her a sharp look, quietly sending a message that apparently Wallis understood as a request for her silence on the subject of their lives in New Mexico.

Patricia tapped some more notes into her laptop computer, including one to thoroughly check into the backgrounds of all of Carlotta's family members. Perhaps there was something one of them had overlooked; perhaps there was something one of them didn't want to admit in front of the others.

Patricia looked up at Carlotta and Howard. "I think I should check into the backgrounds of your household staff, and regular visitors as well."

"Why?" asked Howard. "We just have the housekeeper, and I can't imagine she—"

"How did Hackman get your telephone number? It's unlisted, isn't it?"

"Yes," said Carlotta.

"Then either he used an investigator to dig it up for him, or he knows a few investigative techniques for finding unlisted numbers, or he's contacted someone who knows you. It's just a possibility, and it's a good idea anyway to check out the backgrounds of your staff and your regular visitors, because if he's serious about doing this show, you can bet he'll be in touch with them to see if they'll go on it. If any of them have financial problems, they'll be more likely to go on."

"Well, there is the groundskeeper we have in the warmer months," Howard said.

"And the psychologist, working with you, Mother, what is her name—" Wallis stopped abruptly as Quentin suddenly squeezed her shoulder. Wallis looked at Patricia helplessly. "Just to help her prepare for attending the museum's opening," she added lamely.

Agoraphobia, Patricia thought. No one wants to put a name on the psychological condition into which Carlotta had slowly descended, and was now fighting to overcome. Were there any other problems this proud family wished to leave unnamed? Problems that might inspire someone with a slanderous bit of gossip to contact a television tabloid show?

The voice in the adjoining room, which had been practicing arpeggios all along, stopped abruptly. Carlotta suddenly sat very still, frozen again.

"I'll need a list of the visitors that come regularly, Ms. Moses," Patricia said quickly. "Any hairdressers, accountants—"

The voice in the next room shrieked in frustration, and several cacophonous notes crashed on the piano's upper register.

Carlotta looked at Patricia. "Howard can give you the details. When can we expect a report from you? In the next few days?"

"This is Wednesday, so let's see, I'll try to get back to you no later than Friday, but it depends upon—"

The middle C was played repeatedly again on the piano, and the voice took off again on its arpeggios, but with less conviction than the first time.

"Tomorrow. I want to hear what you've learned by tomorrow," Carlotta said firmly. "Now I must go help my granddaughter."

Carlotta stood and left the room. Wallis moved to

stand as well, but Quentin pressed her back. "Let Ashley be," he said. "She needs to learn from Mother."

"I know, but—" Wallis started. She looked at Patricia and smiled apologetically. "She's so nervous, Ashley is, but she can have a great future if she'll just—"

"The staff and visitors," Quentin said firmly. "We're supposed to list them for Patricia."

Howard smiled and gestured toward the coffee and tea service. "Are you sure you wouldn't like a beverage before we get too far into the list?"

Creating this list could take a while. Patricia was tempted to ask for her year-round favorite drink—iced coffee, sometimes with a shot of bourbon. Even with subzero temperatures and snow raging outside, the drink was tempting. But it would have to wait until the day's business was complete.

"No, thanks," she said to Howard. "Now, you mentioned a housekeeper and a groundskeeper. Let's start with them. . . ."

Chapter 2

Halfway between Cleveland and Columbus, Joseph Delaney pulled off of I-71 and, a few minutes later, into the drive-through lane of a Wendy's fast-food restaurant. As a rule, he avoided fast food, but he didn't want the effort of getting out of his car and going into a restaurant. It wasn't precisely that he was in a hurry. It was just that Joseph was afraid that if he went inside, he'd be tempted to telephone Margaret. And she'd say to him, "Oh, Joseph. What's gotten into you? Come on home and we'll talk about it." If he heard that, he'd turn around and drive back to Maine, instead of heading on to Cincinnati.

So he entered the drive-through, ordered a cheeseburger and a large coffee, then sat in his car in the parking lot, leaving the car running and the heat on. He started eating the cheeseburger without tasting it, then sipped the hot coffee, watching the steam rise from it and fog the inside of his windshield.

If only he hadn't driven through Cleveland, Joseph thought, if only he had at least listened to his head instead of his heart and not driven past the house where they'd raised all those kids—Joseph, Jr., and Sean and

Maureen and Ryan and Kelly and Patricia—he wouldn't
be having these doubts gnawing at his gut even more
ferociously than his hunger. He hadn't questioned what
he was doing the afternoon before, when instead of
turning left to go home from the violin lesson, he found
himself turning right, then getting on the highway, then
driving a few hours, telling himself he was just taking
a drive, that was all, then realizing he was too tired to
keep on driving, then checking into the motel, then
making the decision to keep on the next morning, then
deciding to head on to Patricia's.

Staying awhile at Patricia's was a good idea, he
thought, until he sorted out what to do next with his
life; Patricia was single with no kids and she was the
only one of his children with an uncomplicated life,
even if she wasn't the child who would be most happy
to see him. Yes, a visit with his youngest was a good
idea, he'd been thinking as he drove up the street to that
house, still feeling confident in his choice to take this
spontaneous break from his wife and his current home
and life in Maine. He'd had no doubts about it. Joseph
Patrick Delaney hated doubts.

And then he'd driven up his and Margaret's former
street in Cleveland, toward their former house, and suddenly there it was. He'd stopped and stared at it awhile,
the memories coming just as suddenly as the house had
appeared in his visual range, the memories coming all
at once, in no particular order.

Joseph and Margaret had always meant to move from
the tiny house, especially each time a new baby came
along. But they'd never seemed to find the time or
money, at least not until after his retirement two years

ago, when at last they'd moved to Maine, his favorite
state, and into a house that, without children, had more
room than they knew what to do with.

Now the house was a simple two-story row house
with white aluminum siding. Ten years into owning the
house, he'd built the one-car garage behind it to store a
new car, the first and only car he'd owned that wasn't
second- or third- or even fourthhand. For two months
the garage had actually held the new car, before all the
extra paraphernalia from the house and kids just over-
flowed, as if by a will of its own, into the garage.

Joseph looked at the wraparound porch, in front of
which Margaret had grown flowers; the little stoop they
called a front lawn; the side window where the girls—
Maureen and Patricia, at least, never Kelly, Kelly had
always been such a good girl—would crawl out and
jump down to the bushes late at night after curfew to go
out with their boyfriends; the front door that had been
decorated in black for a month after they learned that
their oldest son, Joseph, Jr., had been killed in Vietnam,
the black on the door making the white house look as if
its guts had been ripped out. And for a while they had.

The house looked the same, except the young couple
who had bought it had replaced the old white aluminum
siding with light blue vinyl siding. New white shutters
had been added. Joseph wondered if the woman—
who'd been pregnant with the couple's first child when
they'd bought the house from the Delaneys—had grown
flowers this past summer in the flower beds Margaret
had tended for forty years, or if she had time for that.
He seemed to recall she worked. But then Margaret had
too, teaching piano in their home. They'd needed the

extra income to help feed all those little mouths; Joseph's salary as a high-school music teacher didn't go far for that many.

When he realized he was weeping as he stared at the house, Joseph drove away. Halfway to Columbus, he stopped crying and realized he was hungry; he hadn't eaten since lunch the day before. Now, in the Wendy's parking lot, watching the snow whirl around outside his car, he found himself weeping again.

Joseph wiped his eyes and took another drink of coffee. Then he pulled out a map and started calculating how much time and how many miles he had left on this trip. Cleveland occupied the northeastern corner of Ohio; Columbus was in the center; Cincinnati in the southwestern corner. It had taken him, in this weather, roughly two hours to get halfway between Cleveland and Columbus. Another five hours and the luck of the Irish, he figured, and he'd be to Patricia's.

Joseph wiped clear the inside of the windshield and the windows, then started back toward the highway. He fiddled with the radio, then put in his favorite tape: Carlotta Moses, singing the role of the Countess Almaviva in *The Marriage of Figaro*. He had made the tape off of a record, badly scratched. But it had been the first recording of Carlotta Moses's work he'd purchased, and somehow that made even the scratches and skips seem magical. And right now Joseph Patrick Delaney needed something—maybe *anything*—to jumpstart his life again.

The music—Carlotta Moses performing in *The Marriage of Figaro*—was beautifully clear on the stereo system in Carlotta and Howard's bedroom. It was from a compact disk, remastered from the last recording Carlotta had ever made. *Figaro* had also been her debut. The first and the last of her music, thought Carlotta. She lay on the chaise longue, eyes closed, listening to the music.

But not, she thought, really hearing it. Physically, yes, she heard it. Yet it didn't reach into her, didn't fully pervade her very soul; it only went within her so far, and then stopped around an uneasy knot in the middle of her soul. The music entered but never filled her.

Some critics had contended that Carlotta was too dry, relied too much on technique, that she was a master of the precision of music, but not of the emotion. Publicly, she dismissed their criticisms. There were, after all, all the fans who felt her music did reach into their very souls.

And yet Carlotta privately knew her critics were right. And she knew why. It was because she could not hear music. And she knew why that was, too.

Hearing music, Carlotta's mother had said, was as much a gift as knowing how to make music. If you could hear music, she said, you became part of its transforming force. Music, she had said, was magic, because as it entered you, and you entered it, you transcended time and place, you became part of it, you became something more than you were.

And for a time, as a child, Carlotta had had the gift of hearing music. Mother, who was so happy and beautiful and wore the scent of jasmine, would tell her about a composer, or a piece of music, then put on a recording and they would listen until they stopped listening and began hearing, the music entering them, and them entering the music. Even after Father died, they had the magic of music. Even, for a little while, after Mother remarried, and they moved into the Powell house, they had the magic of music. But then music became forbidden in the house ... and then Mother grew sadder and sadder and finally took her own life ... and Carlotta was left there, in the silent, musicless Powell house ... and then somehow things started going wrong. ...

And after she left the house, she spent most of her adult life creating music for millions of people. But she had never fully regained the gift of hearing music just for herself.

Carlotta knew why, but there was no way now she could undo it. She could only listen, and listen more, testing her soul again and again with the music, hoping for the gift of hearing to return, for the music to again permeate her entire soul, for if that could happen, she would know that the core darkness had been washed away, that she had at last found forgiveness, perhaps even redemption.

The music came to an end. Carlotta remained still upon the chaise longue for a few more minutes, then finally aroused herself. She stared out the window. If only she could bring herself to leave, she thought, just for a little bit. Perhaps then she could bring about a solution to this wretched problem of the television man ... but no. It was impossible for her to leave. Her agoraphobia had started upon her return to the Cincinnati area.

Both she and Howard had grown up in the area, and had met briefly as young people, before Carlotta's move to New York. For Howard, the brief meeting had inspired a deep, passionate love for her. For Carlotta, the meeting was not memorable; already she was dreaming of a singing career, of breaking away from her music-less home life and going to New York. But Howard had always been a devoted friend, visiting and keeping in touch with her throughout the years and never, himself, marrying until one day, many years later, he surprised both himself and Carlotta by asking her to be his wife. She, in turn, had surprised both of them by agreeing.

But by then, Quentin and his family had moved to New Mexico, Carlotta's career was nearing its end, and Carlotta was dreadfully lonely. Carlotta married Howard, even though it meant returning to Indian Hills because of his business. She'd thought she could handle being back in the Cincinnati area, although she'd always resisted returning, even turning down engagements to sing with the renowned Cincinnati Metropolitan Opera.

The return to Cincinnati was a mistake. If she'd asked, Howard would have whisked her away to another home, anywhere she wished, as much as he loved Cincinnati. But then she'd have to explain why she loathed the area, and she could not do that. Not to Howard, not to anyone. Slowly, Carlotta found herself starting to withdraw from the outside world, until the withdrawal was severe enough to warrant a diagnosis of agoraphobia. It was part of her now, and although she wanted to overcome it enough to attend her museum's opening, she considered the disease her penance. . . .

Carlotta sensed a presence, turned, and saw Howard in the doorway, watching her. He was worried about her, she knew—the problem of that awful television man had left her exhausted and more withdrawn than usual. But she really did just want to be alone. And yet Carlotta was touched, as always, by Howard's absolute, unwavering devotion to her.

Sometimes she thought that she needed him as much as he needed her; after all, she could not bring herself to leave him, even though it would mean leaving Cincinnati. Partly, she told herself, it was because she knew that the agoraphobia would go with her, even if she could close her eyes and wish herself to Paris or Vienna or New York. But on a deeper level, she knew it was because she needed Howard.

Carlotta had lived all her life independent and aloof from others, only needing people to fill certain roles for her, not really caring who filled them as long as they were filled. But Howard, gentle Howard, touched her somehow, and the touching scared her. . . .

She started to look away, but then Howard smiled tentatively, waiting in the doorway of the expansive bedroom he shared with Carlotta. Then he reached in his vest pocket, removed the small bottle, put a nitro-glycerin tablet under his tongue, and returned the bottle to his pocket.

Carlotta watched the process, then forced her voice to be cool and even as she observed, "You've been taking more and more of those lately."

"Difficult times, dear. I'm fine; I didn't mean to worry you."

"I wasn't really worried. I was simply noticing."

"Yes, of course. There's enough else for you to worry

about, isn't there, poor dear, than my silly habits with my tablets?"

Carlotta smiled then, and held her arms out toward Howard. Over the years her reaching had become their symbol that it was all right for Howard to approach her. He rushed from the doorway to the chaise longue and sat down beside Carlotta.

She rested her head on his shoulder. "Dear Howard. You're always such a comfort to me. You always manage to make things right."

He stroked her hair lightly; he knew she didn't like a lot of pressure. "The visit from that investigator took a lot out of you, didn't it? Maybe we don't need her, if she's going to stir things up too much, unsettle our household . . ."

"No," Carlotta said firmly. "We need her to find whoever this person is making these—these ridiculous claims. Then we can pay the person off, and move on. I don't want anything marring the opening of the museum, or of Ashley's debut."

"Carlotta—dear Carlotta. Money doesn't always take care of everything."

Carlotta moved away from Howard, looked back up at him. "What do you mean?"

"What if this person doesn't want your money?"

"What do you mean? Why else contact this hideous television show?"

Howard looked away. "Maybe the person's after something else. Revenge, maybe, or I don't know—"

"Howard!" Carlotta's voice was sharp, reprimanding, yet she looked terrified, as if Howard had struck her.

"You don't think this person would, would really want . . ."

Howard took her hands in his, looked directly at her. It was difficult for him, she knew, to do this. He was risking her wrath, and that was something he hated— her sudden fits of temper, where she pushed him or anyone else away unequivocally. To take this risk meant he was very serious about what he was about to say. "Carlotta, my darling, I want you to know you can tell me anything. Anything. And it will not change my love for you."

Carlotta leaned close to him, her lips nearly brushing his. "And will it not change what you told me to convince me to marry you?" He had told her that if she would marry him, he would do anything, anything in the world for her, anything she asked him for. And she had asked him for many things, but never, so far, anything to truly test his promise.

"Nothing will change that," Howard said. "It's a promise I'll fulfill and take to my grave."

Carlotta nodded, smiling, pleased. Howard leaned forward to kiss her then, and she let him. Then she stood abruptly, went to the large bay window overlooking the gardens that led to the stable, gardens now covered with snow. She sank into the cushions in the built-in seat and stared out.

"Are you going to the home this afternoon?" she asked.

"Yes," Howard said. He was being dismissed. "I was about to leave. That's what I came to tell you. I'll send your best. And I'll bring back a full report, my love." He started out.

"No, wait!"

Howard turned to again look at Carlotta. She had turned from the window, her arms outstretched to him. He moved to her swiftly, both stunned and pleased by her sudden neediness of him. She had never called him back after dismissing him before.

He sat down next to her and enfolded her in his arms.

"You said I could tell you—ask you—anything—" Carlotta said. Her voice hitched on a sob.

"Anything, my darling," Howard said, and began stroking her hair.

Rena Powell, at sixty-nine years old, had skin so fair that it was nearly pallid; so dry that it appeared almost powdery. Her gray hair was combed back in a stiff bun. Rena's high cheekbones and prominent brow gave her a gaunt, even skeletal, appearance. Her pale blue eyes seemed to focus on nothing of this world. And yet, as she listened to music, she became, thought Kendra Allen, beautiful. Transformed. A shimmery sort of peace settled upon her as her eyes drooped nearly closed and an inscrutable smile came to her lips.

Kendra had just inserted a new tape of Yanni into the tape player. For a moment she also listened to the New Age music, a smooth melody line overlaying a repetitive rhythm. Then she wheeled over to the desk where Rena was ready to begin working.

"There! That should help us relax," Kendra said, trying to keep energy in her voice. After a long morning of engineering and computer classes at Wright State University in Dayton, about fifty miles north of Cincinnati, Kendra was exhausted, but she knew she had to

keep her appointment with Rena Powell at the Heartland Retirement Home in Lebanon—never mind the
long drive from north of Dayton to the northeastern side
of Cincinnati, a drive made worse by the awful weather.
Kendra had been working with Rena for nearly two
months, and her progress had been remarkable.

Kendra moved as close to the desk as her wheelchair
would allow.

"I readjusted the hand strap—it should be more comfortable now. Ready to give it a try?"

Rena nodded. Even that much communication was
remarkable progress since Kendra had first met Rena.
Rena had come to the home after the death of her aunt
Violet, who had taken care of her most of her adult life.

Rena lifted her right arm and placed her hand—what
should have been her hand—over the gray ball-like device. Rena's hands were deformed, the thumb and forefinger fused together, the other fingers barely more than
stubs.

Kendra's knowledge of Rena's background was
sketchy, but according to Betty Hanlon, director of the
Heartland Retirement Home, Rena had been born with
the deformity. Her condition was complicated by the
fact that as a young woman, she had suffered an attack
that had nearly killed her, and that had destroyed her
voice box. The attacker had never been found.

Rena spent her first several months at Heartland in
physical therapy. Her muscles had atrophied to the point
that she could barely walk or lift her arms.

Kendra learned of Rena during visits to her grandmother, who lived in one of the semi-independent units
of Heartland. Kendra had a degree in physical therapy,

but since her own accident—an automobile wreck that
left her paralyzed from the waist down—had given up
her practice. Now she was working on a master's in
biomedical engineering at Wright State University, and
was very interested in learning to make computerized
devices that would help the disabled.

Kendra wrapped the Velcro strap about Rena's hand.
"Is that comfortable?"

Rena nodded again.

"Try rolling the ball around the pad."

Rena did, jerkily, and the cursor on the computer
screen jumped around.

"Okay. That's better than before. You'll get more
control of it as you get used to it, and I'll keep adjusting
the device to work better." The device was a modified
computer mouse, redesigned to fit in the palm of Rena's
hand. Rena could not click the buttons on a conven-
tional mouse or track ball, so Kendra had devised a pad
with pressure points in the upper right and upper left
corners that, if Rena rolled the device over them, would
click on instructions on the computer screen.

Thanks to computer technology and a little innova-
tion, Kendra thought maybe, just maybe, she could
teach this woman to communicate for the first time in
probably over fifty years. But it was hard to know how
much this woman knew, how much was still in her
mind. Kendra knew little of the care Rena had received
from her aunt Violet, but she did know that Violet had
not sought outside help.

"Just a minute," Kendra said, "while I bring this program up. I've made a few adjustments to it, too." Her
heart was pounding extra hard. If she could just get the

right combination of software and physical device, then perhaps she'd have something that could help Rena. And others like her.

Kendra glanced at her watch. It was Wednesday, and Howard, Rena's brother-in-law—that's who the director said he was—always came to visit in the late morning. He was late. Maybe, thought Kendra hopefully, he wouldn't come at all. She didn't want her work with Rena to be interrupted.

Kendra had met Howard only once or twice. He always seemed uncomfortable, and only stayed a few moments. Kendra knew that Rena's sister—stepsister, actually—was Carlotta Moses. Kendra didn't know much about Carlotta, except that she was formerly a great opera star, that she never came to visit, and that she, or her money, was responsible for getting Rena into this place a year before. Howard, though, had made her uncomfortable the few times she had met him. He stared at her so suspiciously. It was hard to say how Rena felt about his visits. Her face became emotionless when he was around.

"All right now. I've changed the interface a little. Instead of lining up the letters like a keyboard, I've grouped them at the bottom of the screen—vowels here, most frequently used consonants here. If you need one of the lesser-used letters—like a *q*—you click on this button and a menu of those letters comes up. That leaves more area around the letters for you to click on—you don't have to be so precise where you point. And if you want a space, just run the mouse quickly over the right corner of the pad twice. Here, let me show you."

Kendra placed her hand over Rena's and guided her. Her ultimate goal was to make the software work with other software so Rena could use it, for example, with bulletin boards to communicate with others, and with word processing so she could write and print letters. But this was a long way off.

"H," Kendra said. "Now *I*. See? You click on the letters and the message appears above. Now you try."

Kendra slowly moved her hand away. Rena sat very still. Kendra held her breath. It was probably too complex, she told herself. And the mouse wasn't moving smoothly. . . .

And then Rena began clumsily, but eagerly, moving the mouse to make letters appear on the screen.

Kendra watched, clenching her hands so hard that her fingernails dug into her palms. Rena quivered. Neither woman noticed Howard Eismann suddenly appearing in the doorway of Rena's room.

For the first time in over fifty years the mute woman with the deformed hands was able to give a message to the world. As it appeared on the computer screen, Kendra suddenly felt chilled, even frightened. She had to read it over a few times, to make sure she was seeing it correctly.

She was.

The message said, simply, *i sing, i sing.* . . .

Chapter 3

The business of Patricia Delaney, Investigative Consultant, was located in a strip mall named—with the sort of cheerfulness only suburban developers seem to muster—Prosperity Plaza. On this Wednesday afternoon in January, however, the plaza appeared neither prosperous (Patricia's vehicle, a black Chevy S-10 pickup truck, was the only one in the parking lot) or cheerful (sleet mixed with snow was falling rapidly and freezing to the already iced-over lot). The sign in Alliston's Doughnut Shop best summarized the situation for all of the businesses in Prosperity Plaza—indeed, for most of the Cincinnati area—CLOSED DUE TO WEATHER.

But not, thought Patricia, the business of Patricia Delaney, Investigative Consultant. She had, after all, an immense amount of research to do on the Carlotta Moses case. Patricia grabbed her briefcase, mentally braced for the sudden blast of subzero air, then opened the truck door and stepped out carefully onto the iced lot. Even with the black fedora and black gloves, and though clutching the collar of her black-trimmed red coat close to her neck, she gasped at the painful blast of arctic air hitting her bits of exposed skin: wrists, face, ears. Patricia slipped as she tried to hurry, but managed to balance herself, then moved gingerly, slowly. Broken bones or torn ligaments she did not want or need.

Finally, Patricia made it to the entry of the two-story section that anchored the west end of the strip mall. The first floor of the section was occupied by the Alliston Doughnut Shop; Patricia had one of the four office suites on the second floor, her neighbors being an accountant, a family counselor, and an independent insurance agent, all of whom, she noted, were closed for the afternoon. Still, even on one of the worst winter days in southern Ohio in recent memory, Patricia smiled at the nameplate on her door.

Patricia let herself in the door and began peeling off her coat, hat, and gloves. As she did so the now-familiar feeling of coming into a home-away-from-home washed over her, providing as much a sense of relief from the cold as at last being inside. She had been in this office—and in business for herself—for nearly five years. Before that, Patricia had gathered the experience needed to go into business, and to get an investigator's license, by working three years at Adams Security and Investigations in Cincinnati. And before that, she had worked as a news reporter and editor at several midsized midwestern newspapers until she realized that she most loved the research and investigative aspect of her work and could do without the writing and editing. Now she was deeply involved in the work she loved best and saw as her life's calling.

Patricia's office was divided into two rooms. In the smaller back room she stored hard-copy files (red for active cases, blue for completed cases) as well as extra equipment and supplies. The back room also had a mini-fridge, always stocked with iced coffee and yogurt, a microwave, and a sleeping bag now too worn for Patricia's camping trips, but perfectly serviceable for those nights when she worked too long and was too tired to safely drive home.

In the front room Patricia met with clients; two comfortable visitor chairs were in front of her desk, on which she always kept a vase of fresh flowers, currently white and pink carnations. She'd repainted the walls a light buff right after moving in, and replaced the dull, white draperies with sky-blue mini-blinds, then hung several of her favorite nature photographs taken on hiking-and-camping expeditions—Patricia was an amateur photographer. A few plants also graced the room. Patricia hoped the fresh, simple decor helped put visitors at ease—or at least distracted them from noticing the awful shag carpeting, which Patricia had nicknamed "spilled taco," because of its mix of orange, yellow, and green fibers.

Patricia hung her coat up on the coatrack in the front room, then took her laptop computer to her desk. Turning on her personal computer, she smiled at the sound of the little gray box, as she called her machine, starting up. Several messages displayed quickly on her computer—standard system messages about available memory, and so forth—and then a final message appeared on the screen: *Seek, and ye shall find.*

Patricia hoped the day's message was prophetic. She had gathered her favorite maxims from the Tao Te Ching, the Bible, and other religious texts—even from the occasional fortune cookie—and entered them into a simple program that selected one saying randomly and displayed it whenever she started up her computer. She tapped the space bar to clear the message, then began the process of transferring the notes she'd taken at the Eismann–Moses estate to the personal computer on her desk.

The computer was the working heart of her business; Patricia's love for and dedication to research and investigation provided the soul. She rarely trailed errant spouses or watched thieving employees; she did not own a gun; and most of her investigating was into public information, available to a great extent on computer databases. Her expertise was of considerable value to her clients, who mainly wanted background checks on individuals (potential employees or mates) or other companies (potential partners or actual competitors). She sifted through the vast amount of available information to find the facts (XYZ Corporation's earnings), and left the sifting through the facts for the truth (XYZ Corporation is a good investment risk) up to her clients. Facts and truth, she discovered time and again, were very different commodities.

But the occasional case came along that made her curious about the truth, and Carlotta Moses's was such a case. Patricia paused from her work and tried to conjure the image of Carlotta Moses sitting across from her, as if she had come to Patricia's office in person, as most clients did. But she couldn't imagine Carlotta sitting there. She could only see Carlotta standing before her great bay window, holding back the sapphire drapery, perfectly still as she gazed upon the gathering snow, as if lost in her own world, yet all the while following ev-

ery word Patricia and Howard and Quentin and Wallis
had spoken, and somehow only freed to move after her
granddaughter, Ashley, in the adjoining room had suddenly begun singing.

Patricia shook her head to clear it, then brought up
the newly transferred notes on her desktop computer.
She had an extensive list of regular visitors and staff:
housekeeper, gardening staff, hairdresser, priest, granddaughter's accompanist, psychologist, attorney, doctor,
accountant. Howard had even been able to provide a
list, also fairly extensive, of staff who had either quit or
been fired. And, of course, Patricia would investigate
the backgrounds of Carlotta's immediate family members. There was not, she noted, any mention on Howard's list of regular visits from friends or former
colleagues. She'd have to ask him about such relation-
ships later.

Patricia saved the notes, then started a new file, out-
lining a strategy for the case. Research the people on
the list, plus family members. Contact Wayne Hackman,
see what she could learn from him. And learn more
about Carlotta's past, particularly about the time when
this supposed son was born.

Connections, connections, Patricia thought. It was a
matter of establishing the connections among the play-
ers she knew about, and the ones about whom she had
yet to learn. It was a matter of gathering all the little
facts, sifting through them to find the one big fact that
most concerned her client: who had called Wayne
Hackman claiming Carlotta had a son she'd rejected.
Carlotta would have to deal on her own with any truths
that might be culled from that fact.

And yet, Patricia realized, Carlotta herself had shown little involvement in finding out who had contacted Hackman. Quentin had contacted the family attorney, not Carlotta; Howard had provided the list of names for Patricia to research, not Carlotta. Carlotta had seemed receptive enough to Patricia, yet she had taken no initiative in getting help for her problem. Family members were doing the work for her. Was that, Patricia wondered, a natural result of Carlotta's withdrawal from the world? Because Carlotta always had people to work for her? Or because Carlotta herself hadn't really wanted outside help with this particular problem? And if the last was the case, was Carlotta holding something back?

Patricia pressed her lips together in a determined, almost stubborn line. Carlotta, or at least her family, wanted to know who had contacted *Flash* and made this allegation of a long-ago rejected son. Almost surely, the person was someone from Carlotta's past, someone who knew her before her debut. Even if it was someone Carlotta had yet to recall, had yet to name as a possibility, Patricia would find out who it was. That was, after all, what she was being paid for.

Patricia exited her word-processing program and logged into an on-line information service, one that specialized in information about television and movie productions. It was a simple matter to tap in the keyword *title* followed by *Flash*. Within seconds, a document giving the particulars about the show appeared on her screen, detailing all the producers, reporters, and other personnel. The database also gave the address and phone number for *Flash*.

Patricia checked her watch. It was 4:30 P.M., so in

California people might be starting back from lunch—no heavy snows there to keep people away from work. She tried the *Flash* phone number. It was busy.

Patricia printed out the information from the entertainment database, then exited it and entered a news database, and again searched on the word *Flash*. Within seconds, a list of results appeared. She selected a few to look through; one newspaper article discussed tabloid news shows like *Flash*, their popularity, and the traditional media's mixed reaction toward them: a feeling of contempt and a need to compete. Examples of *Flash*'s stories included one about a popular singer who was an alleged child molester, another about a big-name sports star's supposed involvement in placing bets on his own team. And of course there was the garden variety of shows about people in the public eye who were somehow involved in drug or alcohol abuse. There was little distinction between fact and truth; merely a seeking of just enough facts to report "shocking truths" that would increase ratings.

Patricia printed the article, then exited the database. She picked up her telephone and pressed the last-number-redial button. This time the *Flash* number was not busy.

A young chirpy voice answered on the third ring, "Flash Productions. How may I direct your call?"

"I'd like to speak to Wayne Hackman," Patricia said.

"Mr. Hackman is in a meeting. May I take a message?" The chirpy voice became crisp.

Patricia's lips curled into a smile at that. Of course he was in a meeting. It was a rule of life—the executives one needs are always in a meeting.

"I'm not sure if I should leave a message about what I know. . . ." Patricia let her voice trail off.

"You can just leave a number, then." The voice snapped from crisp to cold.

"Well—all right." Patricia gave her office number and her name, then added, "But maybe you should also tell Mr. Hackman that I have some inside information about Carlotta Moses. I know that he's working on a story about her, and it might be useful."

A silence followed. Patricia was about to say hello again, when the voice, now gone from cold to hushed, said, "Carlotta Moses? You have information on her? What did you say your name is?"

Patricia smiled again. "Patricia Delaney," she said. "I'm an investigator." Hackman would research her name—or have his own investigators do so—and find out that fact before calling her back anyway, so there was no point in trying to skip around the fact. "I work for Carlotta Moses, and I found out that Mr. Hackman wants to do a show on her. I have some information he can use—and the ability to get more. You've got my name and number?"

"Yes." The voice of many colors now sounded timid.

"Read it back to me."

The voice did so.

"Good. Just tell Mr. Hackman that my information comes with a price."

Patricia hung up.

It would be several hours, perhaps a day, before Hackman got back to her, Patricia thought. Information was an expensive commodity, and it didn't pay to look too eager at the bargaining table. It didn't pay to go unarmed, either. She'd spend a little time this afternoon doing a background check on Wayne Hackman.

Patricia went to the back room and got a pitcher of iced coffee out of the mini-fridge. She poured herself a glass, then got a red file folder from the supply cabinet. Might as well, Patricia thought, start a hard-copy file as well as the computer file for the Moses case.

Just as she got back to her desk, the telephone rang. She arched her eyebrows. Not Wayne, surely.

Patricia waited for the telephone to ring a few more times before answering. "Patricia Delaney, Investigative Consulting."

"Hi, Patricia. Dean. Staying warm?"

Patricia smiled, felt herself relax. Dean O'Reilly was the owner of Dean's Tavern, where Patricia played with a classic rock band, the Queen River Band, on Tuesday nights. She had met Dean about a year before when she started playing in the band. She had stayed late one Tuesday night, they'd started talking, and became, over time, friends. Now they were friends and lovers.

"Trying to—as long as my truck doesn't freeze up. I just had to negotiate the hills and curves of Indian Hills. Fun driving."

Dean let out a long, low whistle. "Indian Hills? Pretty swank neighborhood. Didn't know pickup trucks were allowed over there. Isn't there some sort of ordinance?"

Indian Hills was known as the home to the very well-off families of the Cincinnati area. "It's a long story," Patricia said.

"Why don't you come by the tavern and fill me in on the details?" Dean asked.

"Surely you're not going to be open tonight?" Patricia was surprised.

"Are you kidding? Close on the ever-popular Wednesday karaoke night? All my karaoke nuts disappointed?"

"All that cash not making its way to your register . . ."

Dean laughed. "Hey, what's a little snow? Besides, you should take a look out the window. The snow's letting up; the salt trucks should be out soon. But maybe we'll still get lucky. No one will be there except us— just you and me, a roaring fire, anything we want to eat or drink."

It was Patricia's turn to laugh. "Don't throw the blankets and pillows in front of the fireplace yet. I'll be there—but so will those diehard karaoke nuts of yours."

Patricia and Dean hung up, and Patricia decided to start researching the names on her list. She was particularly looking for financial problems—but other possible reasons as well—that might motivate someone to contact *Flash* with a story that would hurt Carlotta.

Several hours later her research into newspaper databases, legal records, and property records had revealed nothing of note about anyone on the list. The only mildly interesting information she'd uncovered, from several New Mexico newspapers, was that Quentin and Wallis Moses had invested unwisely in condominium construction. Quentin had left his job as a management consultant to oversee the project; Wallis had been the curator of a small, privately owned, but highly respected historical museum. When the condominium project failed, Quentin, Wallis, and Ashley left New Mexico and moved back to Cincinnati.

Patricia supposed the unhappy circumstances of their departure, and now being dependent upon Carlotta, could provide any of them with motives for hurting Carlotta. Perhaps Quentin chaffed under his mother's rule. Wallis might resent having left what was probably a beloved job. Ashley might detest being forced into the role of Carlotta's protégée—especially since, from what Patricia had heard, Ashley had little native talent or patience for the study of voice.

But why would any of them want to hurt Carlotta in quite so strange a way as contacting *Flash* with a story about an abandoned son?

Patricia shook her head. It seemed unlikely that anyone from Carlotta's present had made the contact. Someone from her past, then, from the time when the alleged son had been born—from the time before Carlotta's operatic debut.

Yet, Patricia thought, she knew very little about that time in Carlotta's life. Carlotta had revealed little of her personal life, especially of her early life, in interviews. Patricia resolved to search for and find all the public comments Carlotta had made about her early life. Then, at least, she'd have a basis to work from when she questioned her about it.

But before doing more research at the computer, Patricia needed to take a break and stretch—at least see what the weather was like now. She got up and walked to her window, overlooking the parking lot of Prosperity Plaza and the boarded-up, closed-down gas station across the way. At Christmastime, just a few weeks before, the station's lot had hosted a civic group's sale of Christmas trees and wreaths. Now all that was left was a forgotten wreath tacked onto the station's door. Beyond the closed gas station, rising up on a hill, Patricia could glimpse Alliston College.

The snow had stopped, but enough had amassed to blur the curves and edges of everything. That the snow had stopped only made the world seem finally frozen into utter stillness, utter silence. It was so simple to fall into such a state oneself, transfixed by the sight of snow erasing, blanketing, whitening, chilling. . . .

Suddenly Patricia shivered and pulled herself away from the window, thinking she had been like Carlotta for a moment. In that moment she knew how Carlotta felt, not wanting to leave the sanctuary she knew well to battle through the bitterness of the outside world.

For Patricia, it was a moment of seasonal madness, created by physically real coldness and snow. For Carlotta, it was year-round madness, created mentally after she retired from the stage and moved to Indian Hills with Howard. Patricia wondered, as she returned to her desk and computer to begin the background checks, what bearing, if any, Carlotta's agoraphobia might have on this case.

Chapter 4

In a perverse sort of way, reflected Maurice Horne, it was impressive how his young student managed to sing everything with a soft southern twang—hardly, he thought, the intonation intended by the composer whose piece she was currently butchering. Maurice stirred in his chair. He could no longer distract himself from Mitzi McCallister's awful rendering, even with surreptitious glances at the soft curves of her young body, bound in too-tight jeans and sweater.

Maurice brought his fists down onto the piano keyboard. Mitzi jumped at the sudden cacophonous crash, stopped singing, and stared wide-eyed at Maurice. Within seconds, her eyes welled with tears. Maurice sighed, closing his own eyes for a second. So quick to tears, he thought. No spirit, like Carlotta or Rena in the old days. Either of them would have stared at him dry-eyed and quietly defiant, awaiting his criticism. But then, just as Mitzi did not have the spirit of a potential diva, neither did she have the voice.

Maurice opened his eyes again, started to speak calmly, then saw that Mitzi was openly weeping. "What's wrong now?" she asked. Her speaking voice was more heavily accented than her singing voice, but when she spoke Maurice found her soft twang appealing, even inviting. He imagined reaching out, touching her hand.

No, he thought. Such impulses had gotten him into serious trouble in the past. He thought of her singing, and his irritation returned. Maurice cruelly mimicked her accent and her words: "What's wrong? What's wrong?"

He pounded the piano keyboard again before continuing in his natural voice. "You are singing a requiem as if you just heard it on a bar jukebox! You sing as if you've never had a lesson, and you've been coming here for what—seven, eight weeks! You don't breathe where you ought, then you gasp for breath in the middle of a phrase, like a cow huffing. Haven't you been doing the breathing exercises I taught you?"

Mitzi was no longer crying; she had calmed herself during his diatribe and was now staring at him coolly, as if she were studying him. Her new aspect made Maurice nervous. As a young man, he had been strapping, handsome, even imposing. As an older man, he had thinned to gauntness, and was now given to numerous nervous gestures, his hands constantly fiddling. Catching himself thumbing his earlobes, he quickly clasped his hands together in his lap. To Mitzi, he realized suddenly and with a new surge of anger, he must look ridiculous. "I asked you a question!" he shouted. "Have you been doing your breathing exercises?"

"No," Mitzi said coldly. "They're stupid. I came here to learn about singing, not about panting in rhythm."

"Proper breathing technique is one of the foundations

of good singing. You foolish girl, you want simply to leap on the stage with your raw, untrained voice and have everyone adore you. Your voice must be mastered by your whole body and mind and soul, even to the nuances of drawing breath—where are you going?"

Mitzi had grabbed her coat off the chair and was putting it on. "I'm leaving."

"You can't leave. You're not done with the lesson."

Mitzi started wrapping her scarf around her head and said, "You can't make me stay. And I am done with the lesson. And with you."

Maurice's heart tightened as he realized both that she was serious and that she owed him for this lesson as well as for the previous two. And he needed the money. He grabbed Mitzi's arm. "You owe me for three lessons. You'd better pay me."

For a second fear flashed in Mitzi's eyes. Then she easily broke from his weak grasp. "Me pay you? You shouldn't have gotten my hard-earned money for the first lessons. Tommy says I have a pretty voice. The people who come to the Stompin' Grounds on Friday nights like how I sing. I just came here to make my voice a little better so I can make something of myself—not to learn some highbrow music and some weird breathing stuff."

Mitzi was pulling on her gloves now and backing toward the front door of Maurice's small bungalow. Maurice was tempted to say how Mitzi's biker boyfriend Tommy undoubtedly liked that weird breathing stuff, but he forced himself to smile nicely. "I'm sorry, Mitzi. You do have a pretty voice. I just want to help you be your best. Let's sit down and talk about what you want to learn. . . . You want to wait until Tommy comes to pick you up, anyway . . . no need to leave in this cold weather . . ."

Maurice's charm was not working as it had so well in many past situations when his temper had gotten him into trouble. Mitzi opened the front door and stepped out carefully onto the iced porch.

Maurice's temper flared again. "Have it your way," he hollered out the front door after Mitzi, who was now walking as fast as she could along the road's icy edge. No doubt, he thought bitterly, she was heading to the Stompin' Grounds bar, where she'd find comfort with Tommy and the others encouraging her to sing something about heartbreak or lust or both. "You'll never amount to anything," he added, but Mitzi was far enough along that she probably didn't hear the words, while Maurice cringed reflexively after realizing what he'd said. He'd heard those words often as a kid.

Maurice shut the creaky door without bothering to lock it, and shuffled over to a couch in the small front room, which had become even colder during the scene at the front door. He settled into the lumpy couch, closed his eyes, and tried to figure how his father's shouted *"You'll never amount to anything"* had turned out to be such a bitterly accurate prediction. Maurice was seventy-two years old, living in a rented house on the outskirts of Franklin, Ohio, a small town known for a certain roughness. Franklin was north of Cincinnati, separated from the city's northernmost suburbs by a stretch of about twenty miles of farmland.

Even the furniture in the small house wasn't his—a lumpy, soiled couch and a lumpy, soiled bed fulfilled the "furnished" part of his rental agreement. The only large furnishing Maurice had brought with him to this home was his worn, upright piano.

Maurice had grown up in Cincinnati, aching to get away from his tyrannical father and his fearful, quaking mother. For a while it seemed his musical abilities and the breathing techniques he had developed for voice instruction would bring him success; he'd become a well-known music teacher in the area and become engaged to Nella Crouch, the daughter of a well-off banker.

But then his temper and lustfulness—sins his strictly religious father had preached against but never himself fully overcome—got in his way. Maurice lost Nella, lost his job. The United States became involved in World War II, and Maurice could think of nothing to do but escape to the front lines, half hoping for death to release him from his miserable life.

He had survived, though, returned to the Cincinnati area, and spent most of the rest of his life in sales or piano tuning or both, occasionally succeeding, usually failing, drifting from job to job. He'd married another woman, Ellen, who was prettier than Nella but not quite as witty or bright—shortcomings that, to Maurice's surprise, bothered him. They had a daughter, Valerie, and a son. Their son, Lyle, was born prematurely and lived only a few days. After that, Maurice became so bitter and angry—railing against the inequities of the world much as his father had done—that Ellen finally left him, taking Valerie with her to Alabama. Then Maurice moved from job to job in the area, keeping minimal contact with his daughter.

Maurice opened his eyes and was surprised to find that as he did so, tears fell from them. He wiped his eyes. Thinking about Lyle always did that to him. If the boy had lived, Maurice was sure his life would have been different. He'd have been a good father to a son, he told himself. Not that he hadn't cared for or loved his daughter, but a son . . . he'd dreamed, while in the war trenches, of having a son, of treating him kindly, of being the kind of father he'd always wanted.

But life had denied him the chance of even this dream, and Maurice could not get past the bitterness to find joy in his daughter, his wife, or his work. He'd drifted, until he couldn't get any sales job at all, and finally come to this small town three years before to try, for the first time in years, teaching voice again. His piano tuning didn't offer quite enough income.

Maurice met parents at local churches who were intrigued by the musical career he had invented for himself—setting it in France, drawing upon his dim memories of small towns he'd trudged through during the war—claiming he'd returned to the area in which he grew up to retire. He found enough parents who were so eager for music lessons and so naive that they didn't question his credentials, that at first he'd done fairly well. He had even pleased and surprised himself by actually teaching a few students something about singing.

But soon enough the old patterns reemerged in his life; he began frequenting bars, began losing his temper. Now his last student—found at a bar—had just walked out on him, owing him money. And Maurice desperately needed money.

Maurice shivered, drew his sweater more closely around his thin figure. He eased up out of the couch, flicked on the television in time for the noon news, then settled back down on the couch. As always, the television's sound, even set at a moderate level, seemed to fill and reverberate in the tiny house.

The typical stories were on the Cincinnati station—a bar fight resulting in homicide; sports; the weather. Then a feature report came on. A thin, nervous woman was introduced as Wallis Moses.

Upon hearing the last name, Maurice sat up on the edge of the couch, leaning toward the television. "The Carlotta Moses Museum in Lebanon," the woman was saying, "will serve not only to display treasures from Ms. Moses's glorious career, but will also educate visitors about opera in general. Profits will be put in a scholarship fund for voice students, managed by ..."

Maurice did not hear the rest of the report, distracted as he was by his own musings about Carlotta. He stood up, wandering from the room without even bothering to turn off the television.

Maurice ended up in the bedroom, where he sat down on the edge of the bed. Carlotta Moses, he thought. Carlotta and Rena. Maurice's gaunt face drew up in a sneer. The reporter would much rather interview him, Maurice was sure. The stories he could tell of Carlotta Moses way back when ... Yes, he was sure the reporter, and the viewing audience, would rather hear about that than a bland story about a museum in her honor.

Maurice shook his head. No, he had a better plan than that. Much better. Life would get better, he told himself. He was seventy-two, it was true, but he could still have many years left. One of his grandfathers had lived to a hundred and two; a grandmother to ninety-eight. There was still time to capture at least a little of the happiness that had eluded him.

Maurice turned on the bed, studying for a moment the box that sat in the middle, causing the bed to sag more than usual. The box held his few treasures. He was packing, getting ready to move on. To hell with Mitzi, he thought. In a few weeks he would have let her go anyway. And in a few weeks the money she owed him would seem like nothing, although in the meantime the money would have come in handy.

Maurice picked up a picture from the nightstand and studied it a few moments before adding it to the box. It was a photo of his grandson, Leonard, proudly wearing the cowboy outfit Maurice had sent him at Christmas. The gift had taken most of Maurice's resources for the month, but the photo, which had arrived in the mail a week ago, had made it worthwhile. Leonard grinned joyously, and Maurice could not help but grin back, this time with a real smile, at the image of his seven-year-old grandson. Maurice had been a poor father to his daughter; deep down he knew he'd have probably been just as poor a father to his son, had he lived. But now, if his plans worked out, now maybe he could be a decent grandfather to Leonard.

Maurice carefully placed the picture in the box. Then he opened the nightstand drawer, which contained mostly old letters, now yellowed and dry with age. Maurice sifted through them, not paying much attention to any of the items, until he came to an old program. *The Marriage of Figaro,* August 1945, starring Beryl Hysell . . . except Beryl had taken ill—cancer, it turned out to be—and her understudy, Carlotta Moses, had filled in for her, turning the opportunity into a grand debut. After that, no one talked of Beryl anymore, just Carlotta, the new diva. . . .

This memento made Maurice frown, made the anger surge within him again. He had just returned from the war and was spending a little time in New York before returning home, when he'd seen a brief article announcing that Beryl's illness would indefinitely remove her from the stage, and Carlotta Moses would take her place. Maurice had been stunned but delighted. This was the chance of a lifetime; if Carlotta gave him the credit he deserved as her first teacher, maybe he could start over again. He had found out where she was living, waited outside her apartment until she came back, tried to reason with her about giving him credit and a chance—and she had pushed him away, telling him she wanted nothing to do with him or anyone from her life in Lebanon, Ohio, ever again. But he had gone to her debut performance, anyway.

Now, if Maurice continued with his life as he was, he would definitely lose, lose even the chance of a relationship with his grandson. But he wasn't going to let that happen. He had a plan. He smiled at the thought of it. Now what, he wondered, would Carlotta say to that?

For a while Maurice continued to sit on the edge of the bed, contemplating his plan, still holding the dry, old program from Carlotta Moses's debut performance, still smiling. Then suddenly he sensed, rather than heard, movement in the small room.

He looked up.

A figure filled the doorway.

Maurice kept smiling, tried to fight back the jolt of fear that knotted his gut, that tightened his groin with the sudden need to urinate.

Distracted by the blaring television and his thoughts of Carlotta, Maurice had not heard the person come in, probably through the front door he'd left unlocked after Mitzi left. Maurice squinted, trying to identify the figure, but it was hopeless. The dimness of the room and the person's bulky winter coat, scarf, and hat made it impossible for him to tell who it was, even to identify the intruder as male or female. Still, he sensed, with the instinct of the hunted, that if he could peel away the layers of winter wear and see the person, he'd know who it was and why he or she was here. And he sensed that the reason would offer no reassurance.

"I'm not sure what you want," Maurice said. "Please, just tell me what you want—"

But then the figure moved forward, and Maurice saw the gun trained upon him. Reflexively, he clenched his fists, crumbling the opera program from so long ago into dusty bits. He opened his mouth to speak, but nothing came out. He was still gaping silently as the gun was fired.

A sudden shock slammed into Maurice's chest and exploded in pain throughout his body. A roaring filled his head as he launched back on the bed, sending his box and its sparse contents sprawling to the floor.

For a millisecond, the image of Leonard in his cowboy outfit passed before Maurice's inner vision.

Then there was darkness. And then, nothing.

Chapter 5

Patricia couldn't really denounce the singer on the stage of Dean's Tavern as off-key from the music from the karaoke machine. That would imply the blue-jeaned, black-shirted, tweed-jacketed, trim, mustached man straddling the microphone stand had selected one key and stayed in it.

At least, she thought, she could be amused in between cringes. The woman to whom the song was directed looked miserable, as her companions whooped encouragement at the stage and the man persisted with yet another chorus of "when a ma-yan lu-uves a woe-man . . ."

The closest this man would get to one key tonight, thought Patricia, would be when he started up his car, presumably with the woman by his side. Or maybe not. As he finished up the song and started back to the table, obviously quite pleased with himself, the woman took off in the general direction of the ladies' room.

Patricia took a long sip of her bourbon and iced coffee, stared off in the roaring fire, shook her head, and said, "This guy is awful. Someone tell me, why did I tell Dean that yes I thought a karaoke night would be good for business, especially on Wednesday nights. Better yet, someone tell me why I'm here myself on karaoke night."

" 'When a woe-man loves a ma-yan . . .' " Jay crooned.

Patricia looked away from the fire and shot a look across the table at Jay Bell, who was smiling, pleased with himself and his humor. He took another long drink of his beer. Patricia and Jay were the only other customers in Dean's Tavern.

"Now, Jay, we both know my feelings for you are on the purely friendly side. I'm just sitting here to keep you company on this cold winter's night."

"Now, Patricia, we both know I wasn't referring to your feelings for me. Point A, I am merely your dear friend, band leader, and occasional attorney, no matter how delighted I might be to be otherwise. Point B, I, being loveless, came out to this tavern on this awful night out of a desperate need to mingle with human companions."

Patricia laughed. "Sweet Saint Peter! Do you attorneys learn to talk like that in law school? Or is it just an essential part of the nature of someone who becomes an attorney?"

Jay grinned. "Both. Now, where is Dean, anyway? I'm amazed to find myself with the honor of your company. I thought he'd be sitting here with you beside this cozy little fire."

"He was. He went back to the bar so the bartender could get home before the weather gets much worse. I think he's about ready to kick out the group up front so we can go home, too."

"Ah, no wonder you're looking so forlorn. Perhaps it would cheer you up to tell me how your work is going lately. Did my colleague ever get in touch with you?"

Patricia looked down into her drink, swirled it around a few times, took a sip. "Yes. In fact I met with his client this morning at her home."

Jay stared across the table at her for several minutes, then finally said, " 'Oh yes, Jay. Thanks for mentioning my name to Charles Leiber. I always appreciate your esteemed recommendation. Why, without well-placed friends such as yourself . . .' "

Patricia laughed. "Sorry. I do appreciate your passing my name along. It's just . . ."

Jay waited. Patricia swirled her drink. "What?" he asked finally.

"It's just that this is going to be a complex case, I think."

"I thought you liked a challenge."

"I do." Patricia stared into the roaring fire again. She did like, even prefer, a challenge. And she should be pleased with how much progress she had already made in researching the backgrounds of the names on her list from Howard. But Patricia couldn't shake the sense that she had not been given all the facts known to her client, or that it was not going to be as simple as discovering the contact's name and delivering it up to Carlotta Moses for a quick and easy payoff. . . .

"Um, Patricia, excuse me, but could you join the rest of us here in reality land?"

Patricia looked up at Jay. "Oh, sorry. Yes, Jay?"

"I'd be happy to let you go off in your own thoughts indefinitely, my dear, but this man just came in the door and is staring at you. He's starting to work his way over here."

Patricia turned around—and froze when she saw the man approaching her table. There was no mistaking the identity of the tall, big man, with the shock of black hair only recently laced with gray, the stubborn set to the jaw, the mischievous green eyes and amused smile that was so like hers, the broad, only slightly stooped shoulders in the red-and-black hunting jacket. He was a bit more tired looking than he had been three weeks ago at Christmastime, that was the only difference. Except he was here, on her turf, without warning . . .

Patricia didn't get a chance to complete the thought before he got to the table and swooped her up in his arms in a huge, tight hug, making her ribs and shoulders creak like he always did with those hugs, smelling like the menthol-scented aftershave that he always wore, hugging her as if he hadn't seen her in years instead of weeks.

"Patty! You're looking great as ever. Still wish, though, you'd grow that hair out a little longer. You always had the prettiest curls of the lot."

"Dad. What are you doing here? And how did you find me here?"

Joseph Patrick Delaney frowned at his youngest child in the way that always used to make her behave, and now just mildly irritated her. "That's some kind of greeting from my own flesh and blood. And on a night like this that'd freeze the devil right out of hell."

"Dad!"

"Right. After I got to Alliston, I went to a gas station and called your home. You weren't there, so I thought I'd come here and see if Dean O'Reilly would tell me how to get to your house. You mentioned both him and this place often enough in your calls and letters home. So I called here and got directions."

"You called and got directions? And didn't say who you were?"

"No one asked who I was. And of course I got directions. You don't think I'd drive around in this damned near blizzard thinking I'd find you by pure instinct, do you?"

Patricia stared at her father. That's exactly what she'd expect. Joseph Patrick Delaney, admit to needing help? But then, never in her wildest imagination would she have expected that one snowy January evening her father would come strolling into Dean's Tavern.

"Well, now that you know how I got here, I wouldn't mind a whiskey and a place to sit. Are you going to ask me to join you or not?" Joseph asked brusquely.

"Right. Sorry," Patricia said. "Have a seat, Dad, here by the fire. No, here, take my seat, I'll move over one." She moved, and her father shed his coat and hat and settled into the chair. "Now tell me *why* you're here."

But Joseph was frowning suspiciously at Jay, who was gaping at both Patricia and her father, not sure, apparently, who to stare at most. An attorney and an Irishman just once removed from the homeland. If she snuck away and left them alone, Patricia thought, they might cancel each other out with their blarney, which might not be so bad, except then she'd be without a band leader and a father, and she had already purchased their birthday cards and organized them in month-by-month files for the year—a first-of-the-year ritual that proved, according to her friends, that she was obsessively organized. And what would she do with the spare birthday cards?

Patricia was unable to amuse herself long with the possibilities, for her father's booming voice started launching questions at Jay.

"So you're the young man. You don't look much like what I'd expected. Well, what do you have to say for yourself? Where are you from? How is your business?"

"Dad, this is Jay Bell. Leader of the band I play in. A friend, Dad, a friend."

Joseph looked at his youngest daughter and smiled broadly, showing his even white teeth, his eyes sparkling with humor even if he was tired. He took off his coat and said, "Sweet Saint Peter, my girl, how can I know your friends if you don't introduce them to me? I'm forced to jump to conclusions."

Jay burst out laughing. "So that's where you get that charming phrase, Patricia. You never told us how much like your dad you are; and you look so much alike, I mean given age and gender differences of course. . . ." Jay's voice trailed off as both Delaneys looked at him.

Patricia looked back at her father. "Okay, Dad, now tell me why you're here."

"Can't a father come visit his own daughter without getting the third degree? I'd thought you'd be overjoyed to see me, Patty."

Patricia cringed at her family's nickname for her. She'd expended considerable energy during her adult life trying to convince her family members—to no avail—to call her by her full name. "What's going on? Oh my God—is something wrong with Mom? Is Mom okay?" Patricia grabbed at her father's arm.

Joseph looked up at the stage, where the karaoke singer was crooning. "She's fine. What in Sweet Saint Peter's name is that? If that's not the most pathetic excuse for music . . ."

"It's just someone doing karaoke, Dad, someone singing the song to the prerecorded background. It's not meant to be serious music; not every bit of music has to be—"

"But Patricia, earlier you said—" Jay started, then stopped and slinked down a little farther in his chair at Patricia's withering look.

"Well, hmm, I believe I'll be taking my leave now," Jay said. "I guess I should say good-bye to Dean on my way out?"

"Sounds like a good idea to me," Patricia said, smiling at Jay as he left. Her family problems weren't his problems, after all.

Joseph looked with concern at his daughter. "You sound a mite grumpy, Patty. Is this weather getting you down?"

"No, no, it's fine."

"It affects some people like that, you know. Lack of light, all that cold. Now, I myself appreciate the rougher climates. Makes me think of the coast where my parents came from; they always said . . ."

Patricia sighed. Never mind that her father had never

been to Ireland, that in fact he'd lived his whole life first in New York City and then in Cleveland, until finally retiring two years before in Maine, of all places. Maine. While everyone else in his set was thinking of Florida or Texas or the Carolinas, Joseph Delaney was, of course, insisting that he and Margaret go to Maine, only because after a family vacation there years before he proclaimed it to be a lot like the coastal area of Ireland his parents were from, as if he were just off the boat from Ireland himself. In fact, he not only had never visited Ireland, he hadn't even been a twinkle in his father's eye until several years after his parents settled in New York. And he had as much Bronx in his voice as he did Irish brogue; the brogue was only picked up from his parents and became considerably thicker the more Irish whiskeys he drank.

Patricia waited for him to take a breath, then broke in, "Dad. Please. I've asked three times already. Now tell me what you're doing here."

Joseph stared back at the stage. "All right, then, Patty. I've left your mother. Temporarily, anyway. It was—sort of a spontaneous thing. And I came here because you're the least encumbered, and can take me in for a while while I figure out what I'm going to do. Assuming you'll have me."

The news hit Patricia as if it were a physically crushing force. She'd always thought of her parents as close, of their marriage as exemplary. "But—why? You can't be serious! Why? Why have you done this?"

Tears suddenly welled in Joseph's eyes as he heard the pain in his daughter's voice. He looked away. "I—I can't explain it right now." He looked back at Patricia abruptly, the tears blinked away. "It's between your mother and me. We'll work things out. I'm just asking for some room and board temporarily. I won't be any trouble." He smiled broadly, as a thick lock of his hair fell over his brow. He brushed it back, and Patricia noticed that—despite the bravado of his voice, despite the cheery expression on his face—his hand trembled.

Patricia stared at her father for a moment. She wasn't going to get any more information out of him, at least not tonight. She sighed. "Of course you can stay with me, Dad."

"Thanks, Patty. I knew you wouldn't let me down." He reached over and patted her hand.

"On one condition," she added flatly.

"And what might that be?"

"That you call Mother as soon as we get back to my place."

Joseph frowned. "I told you, this is between your mother and me."

"You said you left spontaneously. That means you didn't plan this, you didn't tell Mom where you were going."

"Now, what makes you assume—"

"How much luggage is in your car, Dad?"

Joseph looked into the fire, without answering.

"Right," said Patricia. "Just what I thought. Now, we're going to get out of here, go to my place, and you're calling Mom. I can't be distracted by worrying about Mom worrying about you."

"I haven't had a whiskey yet." Joseph's voice had just the slightest tinge of a pout to it.

Patricia sighed. "Fine. You can have a whiskey. Then we're going home, and you're calling Mother. Then you can stay at my place until whatever this is blows over—"

"It's not something that's just going to blow over."

"Okay, then you can stay at my place," Patricia repeated evenly, through gritted teeth, "until you decide what you're going to do next. But you're calling Mom. Understood?"

"I find it just a bit troubling that my youngest child— the only one of my flesh and blood with even the weest bit of music in her veins—is giving me orders."

"Dad!"

"Yes, yes, I'll call your mother."

"Good. Now, I'll draw you a little map to my place—you can follow me, of course, but in the dark with this weather you'll want a map."

Patricia retrieved paper and pen from her purse and started drawing.

"One whiskey, neat, and poured with a happy heart by myself, for I am delighted to meet you, Mr. Delaney. Dean O'Reilly."

Patricia looked up, startled. There was Dean, grinning happily, pulling up a chair next to her father, and there was her father, staring at him suspiciously. Patricia groaned inwardly. Dean was not as likely as Jay to take kindly to her father's brusqueness.

Joseph took a sip of his whiskey. He frowned at his glass. Oh God, thought Patricia; her dad was particular about the brand he drank, and she couldn't remember what Dean stocked.

"I take it Jay told you on his way out that my father was here?" Patricia said.

Dean nodded. "Although I'd have known it anyway. The resemblance is uncanny."

"Thanks," said Patricia dryly.

"Patricia's ever so proud of having inherited my eyes and chin. Not to mention my unwavering temper." Joseph stuck a hand out, shook Dean's hand quickly. "Nice to meet you. Decent place you've got here."

"Thanks. I'm quite pleased with it myself."

"But I have to ask—this Irish whiskey—what brand is it?"

"Jameson's," Dean said. His jaw tensed. Dean was very proud of his stock and had selected brands carefully.

"Each to his own, I guess, but I'm a Tullamore Dew man, myself. Flows more smoothly over the tongue."

"Oh, please, Dad. What difference can a brand make?"

Joseph flashed a reproachful look at Patricia. "Difference? It makes a world of difference. If you drank Irish whiskey, you'd know that." He looked back up at Dean. "And I don't know about this kara—this whatever you call it. Pretty hard to enjoy a whiskey, of any brand, and a conversation with all that screeching going on."

"Okay, now that you two have met, we'd better get on back to my place," Patricia interjected.

"What's your rush? I think I ought to get to know your friend a little better. It's not every day I get to meet a future son-in-law. Always thought Patricia would be married by now, though, settled down. Of course, following people around all day for a living makes it kind of difficult—"

"Enough. Dad, we're going now."

Joseph grinned. "Told you she has my even temper. If you'll excuse me, I'll avail myself of the facilities before we go."

Dean pointed Joseph in the right direction, then looked back at Patricia. "So that," he said flatly, "is your father."

"Yes, it is."

"I wish you'd told me he was coming for a visit. I could have restocked the bar, brought in some Irish harpists—"

"Dean, please. I didn't know my father was coming. It's a—surprise. No, a spontaneous visit. To use his words. God, I don't need this right now."

Dean sat down and put an arm around her. "Want to just come stay with me for a while?"

Patricia smiled. "I appreciate that. I really do. But I had better figure out what's going on. I can't believe he just left Mom, came here like this. . . ."

"I can."

Patricia shot Dean a disgruntled look.

"Sorry," Dean said. Then he grinned. "But he does come on a bit—strong. Look, maybe you'll just have a nice, simple visit for a few days, and then your dad will decide to go back home."

Patricia glanced up to see her father returning to their table, his face overshadowed with a profound sadness. He didn't realize right away that she was looking at him. Once he did, Joseph suddenly turned on a smile.

Simple. Oh, right, thought Patricia. Like the Carlotta

Moses case. No matter how simple the initial requests seemed—either from Carlotta or from her dad—she had a feeling that life was going to get a great deal more complex by the time the requests were fulfilled.

Chapter 6

Wayne Hackman was on the phone to room service even before the bellhop brought up his luggage.

"Scotch on the rocks—Dewar's, preferably—prime rib, and a Caesar salad," he said impatiently. As he spoke he examined his nails—neat, trim, buffed—but the sight gave him little satisfaction because the manicurist, a young woman with a full mane of curly blond hair that she flipped over her shoulders with each twittery laugh at his jokes, had turned him down cold when he put his hand, ever so gently, he thought, on her back, and asked her out for a drink. He'd stiffed her on the tip.

"Unless you use iceberg lettuce in your Caesar," Wayne added. "You use romaine don't you?" He was assured that the Omni Netherlands Hotel in Cincinnati in fact used romaine lettuce in its Caesar salad.

"Good. I've been to places in the Midwest where iceberg is used." Wayne hung up abruptly and glanced around the room. Nicely decorated. Spacious. The Omni Netherlands was one of the best hotels in downtown Cincinnati. Still, Wayne snorted in disgust. The Midwest, he thought. What did people here know about food, about living, about anything? And then he laughed aloud. There was something ironic about fate having brought him back here in an attempt to rescue his career.

Wayne kicked off his shoes, propped up the pillows on the bed, then flopped back and started flicking from channel to channel on the television. Local news, weather news, game show, shopping channel, more local news, previews of in-room movies, comedy rerun, another game show ... Wayne glanced at his watch. Another half hour and *Flash* would be on—Audrey Simmons filling in for Wayne Hackman ... Wayne Hackman on special assignment. . . .

"Don't screw this one up, old boy," Wayne muttered, settling on the comedy rerun. He needed this week's work to get back in the good graces of the Big Guy at *Flash*.

Even tabloid television news still required a kernel of truth in its reports, although it was fine—even preferred—if that kernel was enveloped with as much innuendo and speculation as the reporter could conjure. The reporter could show former household staff stating, "Oh, yes, I saw plenty of needles just lying around so-and-so-big-shot's house," without pressing, were they sewing needles, used for a nice little embroidery sample stating perhaps, BLESS THIS MESS? Pine needles left in the carpet from the Christmas tree, perhaps? Or needles for mainlining drugs?

Never mind the details, just let the viewing public draw its own nasty conclusions—and count on the viewing public never imagining needles from crafts or holidays. But a reporter could not directly state that so-

and-so-big-shot was mainlining drugs, without proof that it was so.

Wayne, however, had recently been guilty of crossing over the fine, nearly invisible line between truth gussied up with insinuation and out-and-out lying. He'd gone dry on an assignment—a rumor had surfaced about some visiting rock star from another country and his multitudes of underage lovers—but he couldn't find any maids or bellhops or anyone to say, "Oh yes, lots of people come and go from his room." Incredibly, everyone said the star was quiet, no visitors, and former employees were highly complimentary about him.

Still, Wayne got on the air and said that the star had lots of underage lovers. Perhaps it was true. But Wayne had nothing—no innuendo from others, no blurry photos that could be interpreted however one wanted—to lend even a shred of credibility to his statement.

The Big Guy, as Wayne thought of the producer of *Flash*, was really angry, ranting and raving for an hour about Wayne getting the company sued. And, it seemed, he was also angry about the number of times Wayne had been showing up lately either stoned or drunk or both. So Wayne was sent off on "special assignment" until he could get his act together—and that meant low-visibility assignments, about once a week, saying, "And now, back to you, Audrey."

And then, miraculously, there'd come the call from Lewis Switzer. Nice Mr. Lewis Switzer. With his interesting little story about the much-revered, much-beloved, but reclusive Carlotta Moses paying a woman who had worked for her to take him off her hands when he was but four years old. Of course, Mr. Switzer did

not remember Carlotta Moses. He only vaguely remembered living with his mother and another woman for a
brief time in his early childhood. But then his mother
became ill, and confessed to Lewis's sister, Alma, that
Lewis wasn't really her son, that Carlotta Moses was
his real mother. Later, as Lewis and Alma started going
through their mother's possessions, they found proof—
yes, proof, Lewis assured Wayne—that Carlotta Moses
was in fact Lewis's mother.

Wayne smiled at the memory of Lewis's next words.
Lewis was shocked, of course, he told Wayne, but what
was he to do? He was certain Carlotta would deny him.
And wasn't some retribution in order? Alma had told
him to call Wayne Hackman at *Flash*—*Flash* was one
of her favorite shows and Wayne one of her favorite
television personalities; Alma was sure Wayne would
know what to do.

Of course he would, Wayne thought. Of course. Pay
Lewis and Alma a considerable fee if the story had any
credibility at all, that's what he'd do—and that's just
what Lewis and Alma were after. That's what anyone
was after that called a show like *Flash* with a story like
theirs.

Wayne had been distant, skeptical. He asked Lewis to
send him a copy of his proof. Lewis had surprised him
by asking if he could fax it. Did Lewis have a fax machine? Wayne had asked. No, but the local copy shop
did. And an hour later the fax had come into the *Flash*
office.

The proof wasn't something that would hold up in a
court of law, Wayne was sure. But it was enough for a
tabloid television news show. It was enough to get

Lewis and Alma what they wanted—a little money; enough to get Wayne what he wanted—back into good graces at *Flash*.

The Big Guy liked the idea of the story—but he didn't directly say so to Wayne. He just said check it out. Get a reaction from Carlotta Moses. Go to Cincinnati, do some digging, meet this Lewis Switzer, see the actual proof, find some people to talk to from the Moses household. Call back in a week. Maybe, the Big Guy said, we'll send a camera crew, maybe not.

Wayne knew what that meant. If they flew out a camera crew to do the show, that meant his penance was over. If they didn't—if he didn't dig up enough to convince them—then eventually his special assignments would get more and more special—meaning further and further apart—until he'd finally be out of a job.

"But that's not the way it's going to go, is it, Wayne?" he muttered. Another commercial came on. He started flicking through the channels again.

A long time ago, Wayne thought, he'd had a nose for news, an actual, honest-to-God instinct for digging out the truth. He'd gone to Ohio State University on a football scholarship, majored in journalism and communications, really applying himself to his courses. He'd been good at journalism. Or at least he could have been good at it. He'd always planned to go into sports journalism after a nice professional football career, marry Sally, have kids, raise a family. But then the football career didn't work out; his marriage to Sally went sour almost as soon as it began, and they were divorced before they had any children. Everything went wrong quickly, so quickly that his stomach still churned when he thought of it, and he wasn't sure why it had gone wrong or when. . . .

"From the beginning," he said aloud, and flicked off the television, throwing the remote down in disgust. From the beginning, his thoughts echoed, right here in Cincinnati, where he'd grown up in Cheviot, a working-class suburb on the west side. Dad had been an unhappy plumber, Mom an unhappy seamstress, and there had been too little money, time, patience, or love to go around for Wayne or his brother, Willie.

At least Wayne had gotten out. Willie was still here, still running Hackman's Plumbing, having taken over after Dad died a few years after Wayne's graduation from high school. Mom had followed her husband to the grave a few years later.

Wayne shook his head. Enough, he thought. He checked his watch: 5:30 P.M. He called the *Flash* office to see if he had any messages. He had two. One was from a woman he vaguely remembered having met at a bar; she simply wanted him to call back. The other was from a woman he'd never heard of before, a Patricia Delaney. Wayne listened as the receptionist read her message to him, then he had her read it to him again.

Wayne smiled to himself after he hung up the phone. Get in touch with Patricia Delaney, an investigator working for Carlotta Moses? Of course he would.

Wayne Hackman placed three more phone calls.

The first was to room service, demanding to know why his order hadn't been delivered. He was assured it would be, promptly.

The second was to Patricia Delaney. He reached her answering machine and left a message: "Hello, Ms.

Delaney. This is Wayne Hackman. Of course I'd be delighted to meet with you to talk about Carlotta Moses. I just happen to be in Cincinnati. Meet me tomorrow, say, lunchtime. Noon. Omni Netherlands, Orchids Restaurant. I'll buy."

The third was to his brother, Willie. Wayne had come to Cincinnati with no intention of contacting him, but he remembered Willie and his friends; they were thugs in high school, and probably some of them still were. Maybe even Willie would want to get in on this, just for old times' sake. Wayne had a little job for them. He wanted Patricia Delaney to be followed.

It was nearly dinnertime, and Howard still had not spoken with Carlotta about Rena and the young woman who was teaching her to communicate with a computer. When he had gotten home that afternoon, Marcy, the housekeeper, had told him that Carlotta was not feeling well and had retired to her room for the day where she did not wish to be disturbed.

Howard, lingering now outside of his and Carlotta's bedroom, could not figure out why it seemed so important to him to let Carlotta know about Rena. Surely, this woman teaching Rena could only be something positive?

Yet Howard clasped his hands together, pressing the palms together nervously. Perhaps it was simply that it was a change and that right now life seemed so uncertain. Perhaps it was simply that Carlotta had been so adamant that her stepsister's existence be kept the closely guarded secret of the family; even putting her in a quiet retirement home after they received word of Violet

Powell's death had seemed risky at the time, and now an outsider was not only aware of Rena, but working with her intimately. . . .

Whatever the cause of it, his anxiety kept pushing him—tell Carlotta. Tell her now.

He rapped hesitantly on the bedroom door, and then, after a few seconds, he opened it.

Carlotta stared out the bedroom window into the darkness. "I keep dreaming of her," she said without turning. "And thinking of her."

Howard did not have to ask who—he knew very well that Carlotta meant her mother.

"She loved music so, and she taught me to love music, to really hear music. They took it away from her, though, and since then . . . since that time . . . I can't hear it. . . ."

Carlotta turned suddenly, frowning angrily, her mouth drawn up in a half snarl. She looked as though she might suddenly lunge at Howard. "You can hear it. You. You who can't sing or play a note. You can hear it. That's why you love me, of course, because you worship my power—the power I once had—of making music." Carlotta pressed her eyes closed, and suddenly all expression dropped from her face. She said placidly, "She asks me, you know. Why I can't hear it. And even in my dreams I can't tell her . . . I can't tell anyone. . . ."

Howard approached Carlotta quietly and gently led her to the edge of the bed. She moved complacently under his direction, eyes remaining closed, as if she were entranced. Howard gently helped her sit on the edge of the bed, and then sat beside her, holding her hand. The psychologist had told him not to try to break her out of these self-induced trances, that it was Carlotta's way of dealing with something that bothered her deeply, perhaps something that was at the root of her agoraphobia. But, thought Howard, sighing, the psychologist doesn't understand how everything is so uncertain now, so shaky. The problem with *Flash* seemed only to make Carlotta worse. And he needed Carlotta fully present mentally, at least for a few minutes, to help him to know what to do about Rena.

"Carlotta, I need to talk with you," he said.

Carlotta opened her eyes, stared at him, then looked around, as if she were not sure how she had gotten to their bedroom or why she was there.

She looked at Howard suddenly and said brightly, "Howard! I haven't seen you in so long. How are you, darling?"

Howard smiled. He was the only person he knew of who did not find her mood swings alarming. "I'm fine. I want to tell you about my visit with Rena today."

"Oh, yes. How is Rena doing?"

"Fine." Howard cleared his throat. "There's someone else there . . . working with her."

"Someone's with her? A roommate? I thought we'd paid for a private room."

"Yes, yes, she still has her private room. No, it's a young woman, a student from one of the colleges in the area—I'm not sure which—studying something, something to do with computers. . . ."

"Yes, Howard?"

"Kendra, the young woman's name is Kendra."

"All right, Howard, darling. And what was she doing with Rena?"

"Teaching her to communicate. On the computer. With this—this device, that Rena moved around . . ." Howard stopped, as Carlotta suddenly looked pale, as though she might faint. "Carlotta, are you all right? Carlotta?"

"Yes, no . . . it's just . . . I never . . . I didn't . . . Rena . . ." Carlotta passed a quivering hand over her brow, suddenly glistening with perspiration. She took a deep breath, her shoulders shuddering with the effort. "Howard, I have to tell you something about Rena. . . ."

Marcy Bergamore slipped into the bedroom and, kneeling by the bed, glanced at her watch. With the weather the way it was, she was going to be late getting back to the Eismann–Moses estate. Damn them—with the weather like this, couldn't they make soup and sandwiches for dinner? But then, she was lucky to have the job as their housekeeper; they paid well enough and she got two days off a week. At least, she'd kept telling herself that she was lucky, until she'd overheard Wallis, who managed household affairs, saying to Quentin that she didn't like Marcy's work, she was sorry she'd hired Marcy, and she was thinking of getting someone who'd be willing to live at the estate for just a little more money; someone who wasn't saddled with a small child. . . .

Saddled. She stroked Mark's hair to one side. She did not feel saddled by her son, just an incredible surge of love for him, and worry about his fever. Marcy's neighbor—a grandmotherly retired woman who lived in the apartment across the hall—had come to stay with Mark, since he couldn't go to his day care while he was sick. And despite the weather, and Wallis's disapproving look, Marcy had hurried home to check on him as soon as she had a break in her work.

But, she had to admit, she hadn't rushed home only to check on Mark. She had a phone call to make—one that she'd never make if she weren't always so strapped for cash and feeling certain she would soon lose her job. Still, the thought of the call made her feel a little ill. She looked down at the cordless phone she'd left on Mark's nightstand, then looked quickly away, focusing again on Mark.

He looked so peaceful when he was asleep, one arm curled around the stuffed elephant that had become his favorite toy and a required bedtime companion, even with one ear ragged from him sucking on it when he was a baby. She always thought that was funny, how he only sucked on the elephant's left ear. She remembered buying the elephant for him when she was pregnant . . . twenty-one years old, pregnant, single, the father long gone after a one-night fling, Marcy not even sure of his last name, her parents offering her temporary refuge but not without recriminations, not without judgment. But nothing in her situation had made her cry, nothing until she saw the elephant, with its floppy ears, funny turned-up trunk, and baggy knees.

And now, four years later, she had a decent enough job for making ends meet, but she knew it was only a matter of time before she lost it. The offer from *Flash* would help tide her over after she lost the job; combined with her meager savings and some loans, it might even enable her to return to college. She had just one year to go to finish her degree, which could mean a better job later on. . . .

Marcy again stroked Mark's hair. The poor boy felt so warm. He moaned restlessly at her touch. She pulled her hand back, realized she was crying for the first time since she had clutched that silly elephant so long ago.

Marcy picked up the cordless phone. She moved to a dark corner of the room and huddled down on the floor. She dialed the number she'd been given.

After a few rings he answered.

"Hello?" Marcy said. "This is Marcy Bergamore." She listened to what he said. Then she replied, "Yes, Mr. Hackman. What? Oh, okay, I'll call you Wayne. Look, I've thought about what you said, your offer. I think the answer is yes. Yes. The answer is yes. . . ."

Chapter 7

Patricia stoked the fire in her fireplace and the sparks flew up the chimney. Sammie, her beagle, gave a little sigh and settled down with his chin over her knee.

"Cozy, huh, fella," Patricia murmured, and glanced around the living room, scratching the top of Sammie's head. The glow of the fire cast a golden warmth over the tidy room's blue-and-red-striped couch, the deep red area rug, the white wicker rocker, the antique floor lamp with a fringed white shade that had been her maternal grandmother's. The small room was free of knick-knacks, but not austere; her photographs were artfully placed on the walls, and one good piece of art, an abstract white sculpture from her favorite art gallery, L'Image in the Mount Adams area of Cincinnati, sat beside the fireplace.

Patricia's home in the countryside outside of Cincinnati was actually the carriage house of an estate that had been converted to living quarters. Patricia had done her best to turn her home into a sanctuary for her and Dean after a long evening at his tavern, a warm refuge from the cold bitterness and driving snow.

Before leaving for Dean's Tavern, she had straight-

ened up the room; even the desk against the wall opposite the chimney was tidy and clear of paperwork, the
dustcover over the computer screen. She had prepared
the wood and kindling in the fireplace. Patricia had also
left two glasses to chill in the refrigerator, along with a
good Chardonnay, and a roasted chicken for reheating
in case she and Dean got hungry later. A compact disc
of Ravel's *Bolero* was on the CD player, awaiting a
touch of the play button to fill the room with the deeply
sensual, riveting music.

In the bedroom, she'd set out candles, spritzed her favorite fragrance—a warm spicy scent—on the fresh
sheets, laid out her favorite negligee.

"Sweet Saint Peter! Is there no regular bar soap in
here? What is this—this goopy green gel . . . ?"

Patricia sighed. Oh, yes, the scene had been set for
great passion, but instead her father was in her bathroom, whining about her soap. Dean was on his way to
his own condominium, never to know the plans she'd
made for them, at least not tonight. And Patricia was
sitting with her dog, in front of the fire she had gone
ahead and lit, figuring she might as well enjoy that
much. But the fire was of little comfort. The only one
who seemed to be having a nice evening was Sammie.
Even he gave a little whine of disappointment as
Patricia stood up and went to the bathroom.

Patricia knocked abruptly on the bathroom door, then
opened it and stepped in. She opened the cabinet beneath the sink, pulled out a bar of soap, unwrapped it,
and held the bar of soap in the shower.

"Patty, you startled me. What are you doing in here
anyway—me in the shower—"

"Dad, the shower curtain's closed. Just take the damned bar of soap."

Joseph took the soap. Patricia withdrew her arm from the shower and leaned against the counter.

The shower shut off. Joseph didn't say anything. Patricia didn't say anything.

Finally Joseph said, "Would you hand me a towel?"

Patricia plucked the big white fluffy bath towel off the towel bar and handed it in, then left the bathroom. She went into her bedroom, looked in the closet, found one of Dean's bathrobes and a pair of her athletic socks, and returned to the bathroom. She hung the robe and socks over the inside doorknob.

"There's a robe and some socks for you," she said, and left. She went into the kitchenette, which had just enough room for a stove, a refrigerator, a sink, a small dash of counter space, and a round table and two chairs, ice-cream-parlor style. Patricia opened the refrigerator. Might as well, she thought, have the chicken. She put a piece on a plate and warmed it in the microwave. She opted for a glass of milk to rinse it down. The wine was better kept for later; iced coffee would keep her awake too long.

Patricia was nearly done eating when her father came in the kitchen and sat down on the other chair. She smiled at his appearance. Dean's robe was a little tight on him; her socks were too small and only went a little way up his calves.

"Sorry the clothes aren't more comfortable; it was the best I could come up with."

"They're fine," Joseph said, "Although this robe doesn't strike me as your style."

"It's Dean's."

Joseph frowned, glanced away. "Oh."

Patricia stood up abruptly. "I suppose you'd like something to eat?"

"Fine."

She busied herself with preparing a second plate of chicken and another glass of milk.

"And what was that green goop anyway?" Joseph asked. "Why don't you have regular soap in the shower?"

Patricia carried the chicken over to the table and cleared her plate. "That green goop was shower gel. Feels good on the skin; nice herbal scent. I've been enjoying it ever since you and Mother gave it to me for Christmas."

A small silence followed. "Oh," said Joseph. His monosyllabic response was even smaller than the silence.

Patricia sat back down at the table. Joseph was looking at the chicken, tempted but not taking it. His arms were crossed. Somehow, even with the lines in his face that had seemed to deepen since Christmas, even with the tiredness around his eyes, her father's expression was like that of a boy afraid of being chastised.

It made Patricia feel suddenly sad and old. How quickly, she thought, she had come to the age where her own father—always so big, so powerful, in her eyes— now sat in her kitchen, in a borrowed bathrobe left from her lover's last visit. It wasn't the age in her father's face that touched her; it was that she could see beyond her father's face to the face of a man who felt tired and vulnerable.

"Let's start over," Patricia said. "Welcome to my home, Dad."

Joseph looked up, startled, then smiled slowly. "Thank you. I'm glad I can visit for a little while."

"Good. Tomorrow you can go to the Alliston Mall while I'm at work and pick up a few clothes and supplies; I'll tell you how to get there. You can sleep on the couch, or I've got an air mattress I can set up in the spare room. Which do you think you'd prefer?"

Joseph had picked up the chicken and taken a small bite while Patricia was talking. He finished the bite, then said, "Which do you think is more comfortable?"

Patricia quickly took a sip of milk, trying to hide her expression of surprise. This was the first time she could recall her father asking her opinion on anything. "Probably the air mattress, although the couch is pretty cozy for the occasional nap. I'll set up the air mattress, and you can test both."

"Thanks," Joseph said. He was devouring the chicken now. Patricia wondered if he'd eaten much of anything on the way from Maine.

"I see you have your violin with you."

Joseph nodded. It was odd, Patricia thought, that her father had his violin with him, but no clothes, no toiletries, no supplies.

"Yours still tuned up?" Joseph asked between bites.

Patricia smiled. "I get it out occasionally."

"We should try one of our famous duets while I'm here."

She nodded, keeping the smile on her face, but her stomach clenched briefly. Not famous, she thought; infamous. Their duets were known to end, most of the time, in frustration. Family members had long ago stopped requesting that Joseph and his youngest child play a tune.

"How's Mom?"

Joseph looked up at her sharply.

"No, I'm not going to pry, I'm just—I just wondered, that's all." Patricia had insisted that Joseph call Margaret as soon as they got in the door.

"She's fine, Patricia. She's fine."

"Okay, good. That's good."

"I noticed a red light flashing when I made the call."

"Oh, yes. The messages on my answering machine. I suppose I'd better check them. Just let me know when you're done in here, and—"

"Patricia?"

"Yes?"

"I can clean up after myself, you know."

Patricia nodded, went into the living room, pressed the message button, and half listened while she sorted through the day's mail. Messages were forwarded from her business answering service to her home after hours.

"Hello, Ms. Delaney. This is Wayne Hackman. . . ." Patricia looked up abruptly from her mail as the message continued. "Of course I'd be delighted to meet with you to talk about Carlotta Moses. I just happen to be in Cincinnati. Meet me tomorrow, say, lunchtime. Noon. Omni Netherlands, Orchids Restaurant. I'll buy."

Patricia calculated quickly. If she called Sonny Ridenour, her now-retired former manager from Adams Security and Investigations, perhaps he could start tailing Wayne Hackman first thing in the morning. That would free her to continue her own research. . . .

"Carlotta Moses? What about her? You're doing something with Carlotta Moses?"

Patricia startled at her father's excited voice, booming behind her. In her own excitement at hearing from Hackman, Patricia had momentarily forgotten her father.

"It's business, Dad. Don't worry about it." She was already dialing Sonny's telephone number.

"I'm not worried about it. Do I look like I'm worried about it? I'm just interested in your work, that's all. You're always saying that you wish I were more interested in your work, aren't you?" Joseph studied her for a moment, then his face lit up with sudden hope and pleasure. "Or are you doing something musical with Carlotta Moses? My God—my daughter and the great Moses—I always knew you'd do something with your talent. . . ."

Joseph's voice trailed off as Patricia turned away and began talking with Sonny, who had just answered his phone rather grumpily. After apologizing for calling so late at night, she summarized the Carlotta Moses case and explained the urgency of her need for Sonny to trail Hackman, starting early the next morning. Sonny agreed, after bargaining for a higher-than-usual fee, due, he said, to the bad weather. Patricia hung up the phone, grinning. Both she and Sonny knew she'd agreed to his high price because she hated tailing and avoided it as much as possible, given how much it cut into the time she could spend researching with her computer.

But when Patricia turned to look back at her father, she wasn't smiling. Her expression was flat. "There," she said. "I suppose you heard my half of the conversation. So, you know I am doing something with my talent. I am working as an investigative consultant for Carlotta Moses."

"Patricia, I didn't mean your talents as an investigator aren't—" Joseph stopped, then tried again. "It's just Carlotta is my favorite diva, and I thought . . ." He trailed off.

"I'm going to go set up the air mattress in the spare room."

When Patricia came back, her father was sitting on the hearth of the fireplace, poking at the burning logs. The logs crackled briefly as they settled. Sammie slept at his feet. The apartment was filled with quiet sounds: the logs; Sammie snoring; outside, the wind driving snow to earth. Patricia sat down on the couch.

"I could help, you know," Joseph said quietly. "With your case with Carlotta."

"Thanks, Dad. I think I've got it under control."

"I've followed Carlotta Moses's entire career for most of my adult life," Joseph said. "You've always felt I don't care for your line of work; now here's a chance for me to show interest."

Patricia laughed abruptly. "You're interested because it's about Carlotta Moses, not because it's my career."

"What do you care why I'm interested, if I can help you with your work for Carlotta Moses?"

"I have client confidentiality to consider. . . ."

"And you have information to find. Consider me an expert source. If anyone else were sitting here telling you he knew everything there was to know about Carlotta Moses's career, you'd tell him about this case."

Patricia sighed. "Touché. All right, all right. You'll just pester me to death anyway until I tell you." She summarized the case for her father.

Joseph didn't respond for a few minutes after she finished. He stared into space, wearing an expression like he used to years before when he was working on a particularly tough musical phrase, or concerned over a student. Patricia hadn't, she realized, seen that expression for years; since his retirement, he usually looked distant, plus a touch sad, a touch angry.

"What do you believe?" Joseph asked finally. "Do you think Carlotta could have had this son, given him up for adoption?"

"It would be easier to believe if she had supposedly given him up at birth—she could have disappeared for a few months and had the baby as a young girl, before she was well-known as a singer. But to have him, keep him four years, then give him up? That seems a little less likely."

"Because you don't think Carlotta Moses could be that heartless?"

"It's hard to believe anyone could be."

"So you think this contact is making up the story, just for money?"

Patricia considered. "I've just been on the case since this morning, so I'm not sure what I think yet. I don't have enough information." Suddenly she felt the length, the ache of her day. It seemed forever ago since she had been at the Moses estate, watching Carlotta stare, unmoving, out the window.

"I think there is probably some connection between the contact and Carlotta," Patricia said. "If the contact is the man alleging to be her son, maybe he has reason to think she is his mother. If it's someone else, maybe he or she has reason to hurt Carlotta."

"Why now?"

"I don't know. There could be any number of reasons—maybe the person hasn't been desperate enough up until now to try to cash in on this claim. Whoever has contacted *Flash*, though, has to be someone from Carlotta's past, someone who would know of the possibility of Carlotta having had a son before her debut."

"What do you know about her life before the debut?"

Patricia summarized the research she'd done that afternoon in newspaper databases.

In interviews Carlotta simply said she grew up an only child with her mother and father, in Lebanon, a town northeast of Cincinnati. When she was about twelve, her father, Samuel Moses, died in a fight with his business partner, Douglas Powell, when a gun accidently went off. Later, Carlotta's mother, Veronica, married Powell, but a few years after that killed herself. Carlotta never speculated in interviews about why her mother had committed suicide. Carlotta stated that she lived a few more years with Powell and his sister, Violet, then went to New York when she was about twenty. She studied with Bella DiSalvo, had a few minor roles, then her debut in *The Marriage of Figaro*.

"In all of her interviews," Patricia concluded, "Carlotta speaks only briefly about her past, then moves on to her musical career. And everyone from her past is dead, except Howard. Powell died in the mid-1940s. His sister Violet died a year ago. Her only music teacher died about five years ago; I remember reading about it. I will see if I can locate any other living relatives of the Powells, but I don't hold out much hope that I'll learn much from them even if I do."

"There's someone else from her past you could talk with," Joseph said. "Someone from about the time of Carlotta's debut, who probably wasn't mentioned in any of those databases you looked in."

Patricia bolted upright. "What? Who—"

"How far back do those databases of yours go?"

Patricia frowned. "I looked at interviews dating as far back as fifteen years ago."

"Well after Carlotta perfected what she says about herself. Think about this, Patricia. Bella DiSalvo was an excellent teacher. Carlotta had to have had some training before Bella took her on, right?"

"That's true," Patricia said thoughtfully. "All right, Dad. Obviously you know something I've missed."

Joseph arched an eyebrow. "Thought you didn't need my help."

Patricia clenched her teeth. Then she took a long breath and released it slowly, forcing herself to relax. After a few such breaths, she was able to smile and say, "Dad, I need your help. Please tell me what you know."

"I've been a fan of Carlotta's ever since I returned from the war. I first heard her perform when I got back, during the brief time I was in New York before I came back home to Cleveland."

Patricia nodded. She knew this, but there was no rushing her father when he wanted to tell a story. As a child, his storytelling had always delighted her.

"Since then," Joseph continued, "I've read everything I could about her, including a few unauthorized biographies."

"I can't imagine Carlotta agreeing to do a biography."

"You're right. The books go into detail about her debut, which did not go perfectly."

"I thought she sang so beautifully, she was launched to almost overnight fame."

"Oh, she did. Her debut was quite remarkable. For one thing, she was only the understudy, but the lead became quite ill, so Carlotta filled in. She was brilliant. But at the end something quite shocking happened. A man ran forward, brandishing a gun, shouting, 'I made Carlotta Moses! I am her creator!' Needless to say, he was arrested, but his ranting caused quite an uproar."

Joseph paused. He knew he had her attention now, thought Patricia, half-amused. His voice had taken on just a wee bit of the brogue he'd grown up hearing from his parents. It came out whenever he launched into a story.

"Who was he?" Patricia asked. The newspaper databases she'd searched to prepare for her initial visit with Carlotta did not archive articles back to the 1940s.

"His name was Maurice Horne. In early interviews, Carlotta explained that he had been a music teacher in Lebanon, brushed him off as unbalanced, disavowed that he had taught her much. After a few years people stopped asking her about him."

"But you think he really was important to her past?"

Joseph shrugged. "I've always been intrigued by the story. As I said, Carlotta had to have more than just raw talent to study with Bella DiSalvo. She had to have

technique as well, which she could only get with training."

Patricia stared into the fire, turning over in her mind
Maurice Horne—someone from Carlotta's past. She'd
research him tomorrow, see if she could locate him to
ask questions. Sonny would tail Hackman for her, and
later she'd meet Hackman for lunch. Patricia felt heart-
ened. She had plenty of leads, and of course she intended to ask Carlotta more questions. . . .

"I remember the first time I saw Carlotta perform,"
Joseph said quietly. Patricia looked up at him. "I fell in
love with her. Oh, no, don't look that way. What I mean
is, I fell in love with Carlotta's voice, her persona—I
and numerous other people that night. Her voice transported me, made me believe . . ."

"Believe what?" Patricia prompted gently.

Joseph smiled sadly. "Made me believe that maybe
there was a special purpose for me, maybe I'd survived
the war so I could make music, too." He stopped, shook
his head. "But the night ended, and the next morning I
left for home and my childhood sweetheart."

Her father's words hurt Patricia. She looked away.
"Mom. Your childhood sweetheart."

"Yes."

The questions flooded Patricia's mind, all at once, too
many and too personal to ask. Did you listen, then, to
Carlotta Moses, after you came home, and wonder what
other directions your life might have taken? Wondered
as you listened what your life might have been, what
dreams you might have fulfilled, if you hadn't married
your childhood sweetheart upon returning home, had so
many kids, had to work so hard to keep us all fed and

clothed and sheltered? Is that what you wondered when
you took me to all those concerts, operas, symphonies
. . . and I watched your face relax, the lines smooth and
dissolve from your face as the music transported you,
watched your face become at times more beautiful than
even the music and you so caught up in the music that
you didn't know I watched you? Is that why you're
here, because you've always wondered and now you're
tired of wondering?

Patricia could not ask any of those questions. It was
not her right to question him. It was not within his character to tell her.

There was a long silence between father and daughter
as both contemplated the dying fire.

"Patricia?"

"Yes, Dad."

"Would you like to play our duet?"

Again, silence.

"I'm kind of tired tonight, Dad. Some other night."

"All right, Patricia. All right."

Chapter 8

Six-thirty in the morning was earlier than Patricia liked to arrive at her office. But after a night of fitful sleep frequently interrupted with startled awakenings, she had decided she would no longer fight her restlessness. The little sleep she'd gotten had been riddled with dreams of her parents and siblings, of Carlotta Moses and her family, sometimes of members of both families jumbled together.

Patricia had showered and put on a touch of makeup, tweed pants, matching jacket, turquoise turtleneck, and silver loop earrings. She'd left a note for her father. Breakfast, after she got to the office, was iced coffee and a chocolate iced doughnut purchased at the Alliston Doughnut Shop—the shop's first sale of this Thursday morning.

Patricia smiled when she finally settled down in front of her computer. One of the joys of her work was that she could do much of it alone, at any hour of the day or night. Many of her fellow Cincinnatians—about one and three quarter million in the metro area—were still snugly asleep, blissfully unaware that more snow had blown in overnight. Databases don't sleep, however, and now Patricia was ready to begin her search for any living relatives to the Powells and information about Maurice Horne.

This morning's first message was *Don't quit on yourself.*

"No intention of it," Patricia muttered, and pressed the space bar to clear the screen. The saying had been her swimming coach's, used to urge her to push herself further than she thought she could go; Patricia had been on a swim team in her high-school days. She still swam and lifted weights to stay in shape.

Patricia signed on to a database that included the Social Security Master Death File, curious to review Violet Powell's records. Since the online version of the records dated back only to 1960, and Douglas Powell had died in the mid-1940s, his records would not be included in the database. Patricia guessed that Douglas would have left his benefits to Violet; what she wanted to know was to whom Violet might have left her benefits—perhaps a relative who could give Patricia insight into Carlotta's life with the Powells? She tapped the commands to enter the Social Security database and then entered a search on the name Violet Powell. That retrieved too many results to sift through. She exited briefly, entered a CD-ROM of addresses, found the zip code for Lebanon, left the CD-ROM, reentered the Social Security database, then tapped in Violet Powell and the zip code.

A message displayed stating that she had one hit on her search. Would she like to look at it?

"Of course, little gray box," she muttered, smiling. She entered a command to look at the result.

Violet's benefits had gone to a Rena Powell. Patricia exited the Social Security benefits database and entered a newspaper database. She selected a file containing local newspapers, then entered a search using Violet Powell's name. Several results appeared; there were three hits. Two referred to Violet Powells too young to be the one in whom Patricia was interested; the other was an obituary for the Violet Powell of interest. The obituary listed only one survivor: Rena Powell, niece.

Patricia reviewed the information on the screen. So, Carlotta had a stepsister that the world knew nothing about—that she had never mentioned to anyone in the media. She wondered what, if anything, the stepsister's existence meant in terms of this case. Perhaps everything. Perhaps nothing. She couldn't know until she gathered more and more facts, until she had enough to start establishing a clear picture, to know which ones to throw out, which ones she needed. Maybe knowing about the stepsister would bring her one step closer to finding out who had contacted Wayne Hackman, but she was more inclined to believe that the pictures Sonny would take for her would help her the most. Still, she made a note to ask Carlotta about Rena and to find out what had become of her.

Then Patricia turned her attention to Maurice Horne. All she had was his name, and the knowledge that he had long ago lived in the area and been a music teacher. Since she had no idea where he was living now, checking property records would not help; she'd get too many hits on his name. Checking the Social Security Master Death File would not help either; without a little more information she couldn't know if any "Maurice Hornes" who turned up included the one she was looking for, and if no hits came up on his name it might only mean he'd died before the records were computerized—or too recently for his record to appear in the database.

Patricia needed more information about Maurice Horne. Maybe he'd continued as a music teacher, just disassociating himself from Carlotta Moses after the unpleasant incident at her debut. Patricia logged into a newspaper database and entered a search of Maurice Horne's name. After several seconds a message appeared giving her the number of news stories found containing the name Maurice Horne. She quickly scanned through them—there was a Maurice Horne, real-estate maven; Maurice Horne, attorney; Maurice Horne, art-museum curator; but no mentions of a Maurice Horne who was a music teacher in the early 1940s. Patricia felt neither frustration nor anger at this fact; she had long ago learned that while most of the information she needed was available through her computer, not every bit of information in the world was computerized. And as touted as "information superhighways" and "electronic global villages" were in the media, a lot of work was still needed to make those concepts work in reality.

Patricia exited the newspaper database and logged onto the Internet. The Internet was really a super network of smaller computer networks of universities, businesses, and other groups. It had been started more than twenty years earlier by a small band of computer users, but had only recently gotten media attention as the basis of the coming information superhighway, as if the Internet had sprung up overnight. Now the number of people joining the Internet, through work, through one of the commercial electronic communication companies, or through a bulletin-board service, was growing phenomenally every day. The last numbers Patricia had read placed Internet users in the millions around the world. "Surfing the net," to use the popular phrase, struck her more as scything one's way through electronic anarchy. But with patience and persistence, useful information could be culled from the Internet.

Patricia knew of a group that "met" electronically once a week to discuss opera trivia. She herself had participated once or twice. Now she signed on and posted her query to the group: *Interested in Carlotta Moses trivia. Esp. about stepsister, Rena Powell. Also about early teacher, Maurice Horne. Thx.* Then she signed off. She'd check later that evening to see if she found any information worth using from this source. Internet/bulletin-board buffs tended to be pretty faithful about checking for messages and responding, so she would get the bulk of replies by this evening or the next day.

Patricia stood, stretched, and went to her window. It was just after 8:00 A.M. A dense fog covered Prosperity Plaza's parking lot. She could not even see her truck.

By now, she thought, her mother would be awake. Maybe she should call, see how she was doing. Patricia went back to her desk, lifted the phone, and dialed the number.

Margaret Delaney answered on the second ring with a tremulous hello.

"Oh, Mom. Are you okay?"

"Patty—I don't know. I'm worried about your father. This is so unlike him. But he hasn't been himself lately.

He usually tells me everything, but this time . . . I don't know, Patty. How does he seem to you?"

"Well, as always, he'd rather I'd live my life his way than my way."

"He just worries about you, dear. That's because you're the youngest and because you're more like him than any of the other children. Brooding."

Patricia tensed at the word, which her mother had used ever since she was a child to describe her quiet, withdrawn moods. "I don't brood—" Patricia started abruptly. Then she gave a short laugh. "Sorry. I just wanted to see how you are."

"Thanks. What have you been working on lately?" Unlike Joseph, Margaret was intrigued by her daughter's work. Patricia summarized the Carlotta Moses case.

"You know," Margaret said, "your father has always admired Carlotta Moses. Since you're working on a case for her, maybe if you could get him involved somehow—"

"I don't think that would be a good idea."

Margaret sighed. "You're probably right. I just keep hoping he'll get involved in something that would snap him out of the depression he's been in ever since he retired."

Patricia frowned. She knew her father had subtly changed since retirement—becoming a little more quiet, a little withdrawn—but she hadn't realized he'd been depressed. "I thought the two of you were having a great time in Maine."

"Oh, the excitement of moving to Maine kept your father going for a while. But now that we're kind of used to it, the newness has worn off, he's started slipping. . . . Well, I'm sure everything will be all right. Maybe he just needs a break from here, from me."

Right, thought Patricia. She couldn't imagine her father functioning apart from her mother for very long. This was partly what confused, and concerned, her about her father's actions. Not only was it uncharacteristic of him to act spontaneously, but he'd always loved Margaret, doted on her. And yet, Patricia recalled, his comments last night about returning home to marry his childhood sweetheart had been spoken with a quiet tinge of bitterness.

"Mom, I don't want to pry into your personal lives, but did anything unusual happen right before Dad left?"

"No, not really. Well, he went to give a violin lesson, but he'd been doing that for a few weeks."

"Dad's giving violin lessons?"

"Just to one boy. He and his mother go to Lady of Good Hope, and I got to talking with the mother after mass one day. She's divorced, and she's concerned about her son—he seemed restless and bored, she said; all he liked to do was play music on the stereo and tinker on their piano and with an old violin that had been his grandfather's. I thought to myself, I know someone like that—restless and bored. Joseph. So I said to her, why not have my husband come give your boy lessons? She said, oh no, she couldn't afford that, and I said, of course Joseph wouldn't charge, and then it was all arranged."

"You signed Dad up to give violin lessons without telling him about it first?"

"I know—I know. He was furious at first. No one

ever tells the man what to do. But really, it just sort of happened, and I convinced him to just give it a try. So he went three weeks ago for the first lesson, and he didn't say much, but he went again, and I thought good, he was enjoying it, maybe this would snap him out of his blues, and then day before yesterday he left for the lesson and I guess afterward instead of coming home, he just—"

Margaret stopped, her voice catching on a sob, and Patricia realized that her mother had been crying quietly all along.

"Oh, Mom. Dad will come home," she said gently. "And then, maybe he should talk to a counselor."

"You mean, a psychologist?" Margaret asked incredulously.

Patricia smiled. To her parents, only crazy people went to psychologists. Only rich, crazy people. "Someone like that. Lots of people do, Mom. Just to help him sort out what's bothering him. It's not good that he's felt down for so long."

"Well, it might be a good idea," Margaret said. "Are you going to be okay? With your father around?"

"Yes, I think so. I've given him directions to the nearest Laundromat and fast-food place."

Margaret sighed. "Always quick with the wit. You know what I mean."

"Yes, I do. And yes, I'll be fine. I'll send him on his way in no time."

"Patty, I know you're more comfortable with the idea of us together. But let your father be. He'll come back to me in time. I think he just needs to work some of his feelings out, identify what's really bothering him. Then maybe he can talk to someone about them."

"All right. Are you going to be okay?"

"Yes. Other than missing your father, I'll be fine. Love you, Patty."

"Love you, too, Mom."

After Patricia hung up, she sat at her desk, still and quiet, mentally absorbing what her mother had told her. "Back to work," she muttered to herself after a few moments. She had other projects to work on besides the Carlotta Moses case.

But before Patricia could start to organize her work on the other cases, the telephone rang, and as she answered it the front door burst open.

Sonny Ridenour was on the telephone. "Patricia, I think I have what you need. I spotted Hackman leaving with a middle-aged man, about five-foot-ten, maybe a hundred and seventy-five pounds. Couldn't tell the hair color because he was wearing a yarn cap."

Quentin Moses stood in the doorway, flushed and panicked, as if he'd just burst into the first door he could find after some grave disaster.

"Great, Sonny. Did you spot a car associated with the man, anything I can use to identify him?" Patricia motioned Quentin into the office.

"Better than that," Sonny said triumphantly. Quentin came in without shutting the door, and collapsed into a visitor's chair.

"I got a license-plate number for the guy," Sonny continued.

"Perfect!" said Patricia. She tapped in the license number in her word-processing software, then double-checked the number with Sonny. After thanking him for a job well done and assuring him his payment would be sent out that afternoon, she hung up the telephone.

Then she looked at Quentin. She smiled. "Well. I just got a good break on your mother's case. I should soon be able to identify Hackman's contact. So if you're coming here to see how my work is going, let me assure you—"

Quentin waved a hand at her. He did not seem to register Patricia's good news. "Howard," he said, "Howard is missing."

"Missing?"

"Gone. Disappeared." Quentin chewed on his lower lip. "Missing. Now what?"

Patricia studied Quentin's distressed expression. "Perhaps," she said calmly, "you could start by telling me when he was last seen."

Chapter 9

One happy result of the bad weather was that Patricia easily found a parking place in the Fountain Square parking garage; more businesses were open today, but from the scarcity of cars in the garage, many people had still chosen to stay home. Patricia pushed on her black fedora, then hurried from her Chevy S-10 pickup truck, clasping her coat collar up to her chin. The streets were fairly clear—not much more snow had fallen over-night—but it was still ten degrees below zero, made to feel more like thirty-five below with the winds whip-ping through the downtown area. More snow and ice were predicted for that night.

Once outside the garage, Patricia was assailed by a blast of arctic air that momentarily stopped her breath-ing. She bowed her head into the wind and started toward the Omni Netherlands Plaza.

Patricia cut through Fountain Square. The fountain it-self was shut off, the water in its base frozen. All those coins tossed in on warmer, kinder days, frozen at the bottom of the fountain, Patricia thought; did that mean the wishes tossed with them were temporarily frozen, too?

Patricia's wish was that her meeting with Wayne Hackman would yield more information about Lewis Switzer—the man associated with the license number Sonny had reported. Patricia had called her contact at the license bureau to get Switzer's name, and with that used property records, tapped into via her computer, to find his address. He jointly owned the house with an Alma Switzer, presumably his wife.

Patricia had waited to get this information after Quentin left her office. He had finally calmed down enough to tell her that Howard had left the previous afternoon and not returned. He had not called either. This was completely unlike Howard, Quentin said. His mother was nearly hysterical. He'd gotten her to take some tranquilizers; then he'd contacted the police, who noted his concerns but did not seem concerned themselves. Patricia explained that since Howard was a fully functional adult, they would not immediately expend much time or resources looking for him. Sometimes, adults simply take off, even adults who don't seem likely to do so.

Perhaps, she reflected as she neared the Omni Netherlands Hotel, she'd have been more sympathetic if her own father hadn't suddenly left his home. He'd shown up at her place. Howard would show up somewhere—probably at the Eismann–Moses estate, contrite, and with an explanation that he'd needed to get away from the stresses of the household. This explanation had not suited Quentin, though, and Patricia had ended up agreeing to come to the Eismann–Moses estate tonight to bring Carlotta up-to-date on her progress with the case. Quentin thought that might distract her from her worry over Howard.

At last Patricia reached the Omni Netherlands Hotel and entered its lobby. The Omni had been restored to 1930s Art Deco style, the decor a subtle but elegant mixture of black, mauve, green, and gold designs on walls and flooring. This afternoon, Patricia appreciated the hotel's splendor as well as its welcome warmth. She started to take off her gloves and hat.

"Are you Patricia Delaney?"

Patricia started at the sound of the deep male voice behind her, then turned to face a man dressed in a finely tailored double-breasted gray suit.

"Yes, I am," she said.

The man's amused smile crooked to one side as he extended his hand. "Wayne Hackman."

Wayne looked his role of slick anchorman, Patricia thought. It didn't surprise her that he had not given her a few moments to collect herself before approaching— here he stood offering her his hand, while she was still gloved and dealing with her hat. His job, of course, was to find and capture quarry—and the easiest way to do that was to catch the quarry unaware. And his one-sided smile made her wary. Patricia had an instinctive distrust of people who couldn't smile evenly.

Patricia took her time removing her gloves, tucking them into her coat pocket. Then she extended her hand. "Yes, I'm Patricia Delaney. Thank you for agreeing to meet with me."

"The pleasure is all mine, Ms. Delaney," Wayne said, taking her hand. Rather than shaking it, he gave it a brief kiss across the top. Patricia felt her ire rising. At the rate this meeting was going, she'd have hopelessly condemned the man as an idiot before they were even seated in the Omni's Orchids Restaurant.

The restaurant, situated off the lobby, continued the hotel's Art Deco decor. The next few minutes were taken up with the maître d' taking Patricia's coat and fedora, with Patricia and Wayne being seated, and with the waiter bringing them water and menus. After a few minutes they ordered lunch and drinks. The drinks were brought quickly.

Patricia studied Wayne as he sipped at his Scotch. He was handsome, at least by media standards, but she was put off by the self-congratulatory, self-aware expression that indicated he was all too conscious of his good looks, all too convinced of his charm and sense of power. His dark hair was gelled back from his evenly tan face, a look that was currently popular but that Patricia did not find particularly appealing. She preferred Dean's sort of look—face tanned and lined from outdoor activity, rather than from a tanning salon; hair shampooed and towel-dried; and somewhat asymmetrical, but rugged features.

Before leaving her office, Patricia had done a little research on Wayne, who, she discovered, was originally from Cheviot, a town on the west side of Cincinnati and about as far removed in wealth and status from eastside Indian Hills as it was in location. Was that part of his motivation in taking on the assignment to pursue Carlotta Moses as his latest quarry? Had he asked for the assignment or been given it? In either case, Patricia sincerely doubted that he had shared much about his humble beginnings with his colleagues in Los Angeles.

In fact, reports about him stated simply that he was from the East, and of course, Cincinnati *was* east of Los Angeles. She guessed he would be irritated if she brought up his true background. She decided to test her theory, maybe give herself a bit of an advantage.

"So have you had a chance to visit your old friends and family since you've been back?"

Wayne looked at her, startled. "What?"

Patricia smiled innocently. "In Cheviot. You're from there, right?"

Wayne hesitated. "Yes. How did you find that out? My PR material states I'm from the eastern United States. . . ."

Patricia nodded. "Yes, I saw that in some articles about you on-line. I also ran across a brief article in an entertainment rag referring to your first divorce, from a woman named Sally Ivanoffa—rather unusual name, don't you think? So tracking down a Sally Ivanoffa Hackman was not difficult, with a quick search of property records, and lo and behold, I found several such people. But a quick check of census records revealed that only one of these Sallys was of the age to have been your wife. So I gave her a call, told her I was trying to locate a Wayne Hackman for an upcoming who's who directory of people in and from Cincinnati and that I thought she was your ex-wife and I hoped she could tell me where you were, something about you. She admitted—rather reluctantly, I must say—that she had been married to you but didn't have any information on you she cared to share. I asked if your former high school might, and she told me you had gone to Cheviot High School. I called and asked about you, and the nice secretary there did a quick check and told me you'd graduated class of 1977, and wasn't it great you are such a star now?"

Patricia noted with some amusement that Wayne couldn't resist a brief smile at the secretary's comment. She took a sip of water, then continued. "I realized that if you graduated in 1977, your twenty-year reunion is coming up, and so I asked who was organizing the class reunion. A Shelly Smith Silverston. Do you remember Shelly?"

Wayne stared at Patricia, stunned. If it were possible, he'd have gone pale beneath his tan. Patricia suppressed a smile.

"Shelly? Um, yes. Cheerleader . . ."

"And you were a football player. But you never dated Shelly, she told me with a sigh, after I found her phone number—which was quite easy, that just took a phone call to directory assistance—but she was so delighted to hear you were going to be in this who's who directory. I told her I was interviewing people about you for the directory, and she told me all about what a hero you were. She told me about your brother, Willie, and that your dad, who had a small plumbing business now operated by Willie, had died a while back. She'd contacted Willie to find out where you were for the reunion, but he said you didn't keep in touch, and she'd thought about trying the show, but she wasn't sure if she should. So I gave her your home phone number."

"You *what*!"

"Oh, yes. You should be expecting a phone call anytime now from dear old Shelly."

"You're kidding. Oh my God . . ." Wayne trailed off in a string of curse words.

Patricia waited until he was done, then said. "Okay, I'm kidding. About giving Shelly your home phone number, at least. I didn't bother to find out what your home phone number is. I did encourage her to call your office, though, so I wouldn't be surprised, if I were you, to find a message from Shelly back at your office."

Wayne stared at Patricia a long moment, then started laughing, at the same time that the waiter came over with her shrimp scampi and his fettuccine.

The waiter left, then Wayne said, "All right, Patricia, I'm impressed. You're good at what you do."

Patricia simply nodded.

"But," he continued, "you can't honestly expect me to believe that you're meeting with me because you want to go in with me on the story I'm working up on Carlotta Moses."

Patricia arched her eyebrows. "Why not?"

"Partly because you showed just a little too much glee in telling me how much you could find out about me with so little effort. And partly because I had my own private investigator check you out after I got your message. You're scrupulous."

"I made up the story about the who's who directory," Patricia said defensively.

Wayne shook his head. "You know what I mean. You've been in the business long enough to get your own reputation with your fellow investigators. The word is the lady is scrupulous. Tell a little lie to get a bit of information—yes. Sell out your client to me—no.

As happy as I'd be to go in with you on such a deal, I don't believe it."

"Then why did you meet me today?"

"Because I said I would."

"You are not known as that scrupulous."

Wayne grinned. "You're right. Okay, I met you because you're also known as good. Very, very good at what you do. So I wanted to see for myself the kind of help Ms. Carlotta Moses hired. And to pass on a simple message." He leaned across the table, his face close to hers. "We're not backing down. I've got this story now by the balls. It's hot. Carlotta's son—and yes, I've seen solid proof he is her son—isn't going to back down. Even if you find him, and try to buy him off, it won't work."

So the contact, probably this Lewis Switzer, believed he was Carlotta's son. Even though she was pleased to learn that the contact was the alleged son, and not someone else, Patricia kept her expression unchanged. She didn't want Hackman to realize he'd tipped his hand.

"Why not? Flash Productions isn't exactly *60 Minutes*, Wayne," she said placidly. "It's not like you've got a huge budget. Moses can up the price on anything your producers would be willing to offer."

Wayne shook his head, clucked his tongue. "You're not thinking. You're right; we can't outbid whatever Moses would offer. But our subjects get far more than the few thousand we throw them. They get exposure. Fame. A moment of national attention. For some of these people, it's the most exciting thing that's ever happened in their pitiful little lives, or ever will happen.

You can't put a price on that. And not only that, but if it's a hot story, like this one, it means movie deals. Who knows what kind of deals. More money, more fame than Moses can ever offer. It's huge, Patricia, huge. It's something Moses can't touch. It's something you can't touch. It's what the American public wants, can't get enough of, sucking it off the tube night after night. And you know what, I'm going to give it to them. Because you know what that makes me?"

"Yes. I know exactly what it makes you."

Wayne leaned back, laughed. "Oh my, along with the scrupulousness we also have self-righteousness. No, you don't understand what it makes me. But I'll tell you. It makes me a hero."

Patricia stared at Wayne for a long minute. "A hero? Last time I checked, a hero was the firefighter pulling the baby out of the burning building."

Wayne shook his head, clucked his tongue. "Wrongo, again. The people filming the firefighter, the people like me there interviewing the hysterical mother of the baby—we're the heroes now. Because we're giving the viewing public what they want." He grinned. "I make you sick, don't I?"

Patricia pushed her untouched plate aside. "I was hoping we could come to an understanding," she said flatly. "Are you sure this man's claim is true? Because I doubt that it is. If I could prove to you that it is not true, then you'd have to back off. Even a show like yours needs to have a shred of truth in what you're reporting. So why don't you give me a week? Possibly save yourself some embarrassment. Of course, you'd have to let me know what you've learned so far, who this man is. . . ."

Wayne laughed. "You don't think I'm going for that, do you? And yes, I do know there is truth in what this man has told me. I've seen the evidence. Nothing, nothing is going to kill this story for me. Like it or not, Moses is about to become the latest bit of big news. Beloved star with a dark secret in her past . . . ah, just imagining the media feeding frenzy I'll create with this one nearly gives me a hard-on."

Wayne leaned back in his chair, then took a bite of his fettuccine. He finished the bite, wiped his mouth, then said, "I'll tell you what. I'll make a different deal with you. You tell me everything you know about the Moses–Eismann household, every juicy tidbit. For each bit, I'll give you, say, a thousand dollars. You can play undercover detective for me. But I'm not telling you squat, until you've earned, let's say, five thousand dollars. Then I'll think maybe you're really starting to see things my way."

Patricia was now so angry that she wanted to throw her plate of scampi into Wayne's pretty-boy face. She forced herself to take several deep breaths, then said, "No thanks. I don't sell out my clients. And I don't believe that this shred of evidence—if it really exists— gives you the right to invade the privacy of others' lives. The public doesn't need this kind of information."

"Oh, come now, Patricia, the public wants it. That's the game we're playing here. We've moved past need and right-to-know. Information has become a commodity and people want to consume it. So that makes a few people nervous about privacy. So what? It's the price most people are willing to pay. You just used me to demonstrate how easy it is to get the information you want. Was that supposed to bother me, that you could, as some would put it, invade my privacy so easily? But even you didn't see it as an invasion of my privacy. Look, we have a lot in common. We're both just seeking out the truth."

"No. No. I'm after facts. Knowing the truth, to me, is understanding every aspect of a situation—not just what people have done but why they've done it. I don't presume to know the truth, certainly not about other people's lives. I simply find facts for people who have a legitimate reason to need them, while you—"

"Who gets to decide what's legitimate?"

"Don't try to bait me, Wayne. I find complete facts, solid facts, for people. You know what you are? You're the medicine man of the information age. Instead of going from town to town each month hawking some medicinal that's ninety-nine percent water and one percent potential healing, you're on a screen, in every town, hawking your illusions of truth. That's all you are."

Wayne studied Patricia a long moment, his eyes momentarily narrowing with anger. Then he laughed and shrugged. "Maybe. But it pays well. And it impresses most of the women I meet. Sorry it's wasted on you. . . ."

Patricia reached in her purse, pulled out some money, and threw it on the table. "Thanks for meeting with me." She stood up.

"You're leaving so soon? You haven't even touched your scampi. And the desserts here are supposed to be superb."

"No thanks," Patricia said. "I'll leave you to enjoy your feeding frenzy by yourself."

Wayne's boisterous laughter followed her out of the restaurant. She retrieved her coat, hat, and gloves, put them on quickly, then headed for her truck. The cruel coldness mercifully distracted her from dwelling on the scene she'd just left. Patricia didn't think of it again until she got to her truck, got in, and tried to start it.

Damn, she thought. She'd made a mess out of that meeting. She'd learned the contact was the man claiming to be Carlotta's son, and that Wayne thought he had proof of the claim. But she hadn't been able to make a deal with Wayne to hold off on his media persecution of Carlotta—and why had she been so naive to think she could? And she had totally lost her professional demeanor, letting his attitudes throw her. . . .

The truck wasn't starting. Patricia turned the key in the ignition again. All she got was a weak, grinding sound.

Patricia sat very still for a minute. Then suddenly she began pounding her fists against the steering wheel, yelling every curse word she could think of.

Chapter 10

Patricia stood in the lobby of the PanAm Building, watching through the large glass windows for Dean's red Corvette. Fortunately, with her car phone—a recent acquisition after a few cases during which she'd regretted not having one—she'd reached Dean at the tavern and he said he'd pick her up. She'd chosen this building to wait in because she did not like the idea of returning to the Omni Netherlands and possibly again seeing Hackman.

Since her mind was set on seeing Dean's car, it didn't quite register when her father's Buick Skylark pulled up. In fact, it wasn't until Joseph got out of the car and started for the lobby door that she realized it was her father and not Dean who had come to pick her up.

Patricia got to the door just as her father came in.

"And what are you doing here?"

"Oh, that's a fine greeting," Joseph said. "No, why thank you, dear father, for leaving a nice warm lunch and a good draw of ale to come for me ..."

"Sorry—it's just, I was expecting Dean, and ..." Patricia began. Then she paused and frowned. "What *are* you doing here? How did you know ...?"

"Did the tow truck come for your truck yet?"

"No. They're so busy it will probably be tomorrow morning before they get to it. Now, how did you—"

"Let's get back to my car while it still has a wisp of warmth in it," Joseph said, turned, and went back outside.

"Dad . . ." Patricia started, but Joseph did not pause. Knowing him, he'd take off without her if she didn't keep up. "Right," she mumbled, then pushed her hat down on her head and followed him out to his car.

When they got in, Patricia said, "You can drop me off at the car rental place. It's about a mile from here."

"Car rental place? What do you mean? We have my car."

"Ooo-kay," Patricia said with exaggerated patience. "We can go back to my place then, drop you off, I'll take your car—"

"Wait a minute, I didn't say anything about you driving my car. I know how you drive. I had to put up with teaching you how."

"My driving is just fine—" Patricia began. Then she pressed her fingertips to her temples. How was it that her father could make her act like an outraged seventeen-year-old? He's my father; I won't kill him, she thought to herself. She repeated the words a few more times. Then she looked up at her father and made herself smile brightly. "What are you suggesting, Father?"

Joseph grinned. "I'll drive you. Where to?"

Patricia started to protest and insist on going to a car rental place. Then she remembered her conversation that morning with her mother. "Your father needs to feel useful," her mother had said.

Patricia sighed. "Lebanon." She gave directions to the highway.

"That's Carlotta Moses's hometown. Why are we going there?" Joseph asked after they were on their way.

"I'll tell you that in a minute. First, you tell me why you came to pick me up, and not Dean. Obviously, you were at the tavern when he got my call. What did you do, insist upon rescuing me?"

"No. I wasn't going to come get you. If you didn't think of calling me—"

"I thought you were at the mall! What was I supposed to do, have you paged? Besides, I was doing what I'd have done if you weren't here for a brief visit."

"Fine. And no, I didn't insist on coming to get you. Dean asked me if I would."

Patricia looked at her father. "What?"

Joseph shrugged. "It was lunchtime. He was busy. So he asked me. So I left my nice warm lunch and my pint of ale to come get you."

"Busy! Oh, right. In this weather, he was busy. Lots of people out for lunch, weather like this."

"You were out for lunch. I was out for lunch."

"All right, all right. What were you doing at lunch at Dean's anyway?"

Joseph frowned, giving the look of confusion that he always feigned when he didn't want to answer a question directly. "It's not a private club, is it? Why shouldn't I have lunch there?"

"Dad—" Patricia started, her voice going up sharply.

Her hands and teeth were clenched. Her forehead felt knotted into a lump with a sharp stabbing pain. "Look. I'm having a crummy day. So don't test me any further, okay? Just tell me why, of all the places available for lunch, did you go to Dean's Tavern?"

Joseph shrugged. "Seemed like a nice place, the other night. And you rushed me out of there so fast—almost as though you didn't want me there. So today, after I finished shopping, I thought I might give it another try. And I have to say, Dean does accommodate special orders like my sandwich nicely. Roast beef on pumpernickel with Russian dressing and—"

"You're checking him out, aren't you?"

"Who?"

"Dean, of course, Dean, you know very well who!"

Joseph looked offended. "I just wanted a roast beef on pumpernickel with—"

"Right!" Patricia banged her fist against the glove compartment. "Right. Whatever you say."

They drove on for a few minutes in silence when Joseph said, "So what are we going to do in Lebanon?"

"I am going to talk with Lewis Switzer, hopefully. You are simply going to drive me to his house."

"Who is Lewis Switzer?"

Patricia explained that Sonny had called with a license number, and she had in turn called the Bureau of Motor Vehicles, where, to her relief, she found that Marlena was in. Patricia had made a friend of Marlena, who was willing to quietly give her information over the phone. Anyone could contact the Ohio Bureau of Motor Vehicles and request the name associated with a license-plate number, and in a few days get a written report. But

Patricia didn't want to wait; she'd gotten the information and promised to send the nominal payment required by the bureau as soon as possible. And the rest of the information from property records was Lewis Alvin Switzer, 2910 Ridgeline Road, Lebanon, Ohio.

"Lebanon. That has to be more than coincidence," Joseph said. "Did you find out anything else about him?"

"Not much. I checked on the property records, found that he and an Alma Switzer own a house with three bedrooms, one bath, on forty acres. The house and land were assessed at a modest value; the house was about sixty years old. The Switzers have been in the house a long time; the 'last sold' date was for fifty years before."

"You found that with your computer?"

"Yes. It's in tax assessor records."

"You mean someone could look that up on me?"

Patricia smiled. Many people became upset when they discovered what could be learned about them with a computer, even though the information was no different from what had been legally available before the electronic information age. It was just that the computer made the information so accessible, so quickly, to so many people; that's what made people nervous.

"Yes. Someone could look that up on you. Or they could check the census records for you, as I did on Lewis. Alma, interestingly enough, was not listed as spouse. She's only six years younger than Lewis, who was born in 1941, so I assume she must be his sister. . . ."

Patricia's voice trailed off.

"What is it, Patty? Is something wrong?"

"No—no—I'm just thinking." Something about the information—something about the dates of when the Switzers had moved into their house, and about the date of Lewis's birth bothered her, now that she had said them aloud. If Lewis was fifty-four and had lived in the Ridgeline house for fifty years, he had moved in when he was four years old. Obviously, the deed to the house had been transferred to him and his sister, probably by a parent. Patricia could check the deed transfer records later to confirm that. But something else about the date was niggling at her.

Finally it hit her. Four years after Lewis was born was also the year that Douglas Powell, Carlotta's step-father died. It was also the age that Lewis supposedly was given up for adoption by Carlotta—and now the age, Patricia knew, that he had moved into a house in Lebanon, where Carlotta and her stepfamily had lived, where her stepsister still lived. All these connections . . .

She sighed. One day before, she'd only known Carlotta Moses as a grand operatic diva. Now she had all of this information about Carlotta's stepfamily, and about a man who alleged that he was her son. It was somewhat overwhelming, even to Patricia. That was the trouble with the computer age. One could get vast amounts of information at lightning speed. But that ability had not changed the time a human psyche needed to absorb the information, to sift through it for actual meaning and value.

"Patricia!"

"Oh, I'm sorry. What?"

"I just asked you how are we going to find this house once we get to Lebanon?"

"Oh, that's easy enough." She lifted up her briefcase and pulled out a book of Ohio county maps. She thumbed through them, located the appropriate county, and found Ridgeline Road.

"Are you always this prepared?" Joseph asked.

Patricia grinned. "Just like my daddy taught me."

Chapter 11

The Switzer place was as secluded as the Moses estate, but there the similarity ended. The one-and-a-half-story house was set close to Ridgeline Road, a few miles beyond the town limits of Lebanon. No other houses were within sight of it. Acres of corn-stubbled, snow-covered fields surrounded the property; a few bare-limbed trees dotted the fields. Stuck in the cornfield was a sign—40 ACRES FOR SALE, ZONED RESIDENTIAL. Patricia and Joseph parked on the edge of the road near the sign. The narrow drive was occupied by an old Dodge Duster, which had a license-plate number matching the one Sonny Ridenour had given Patricia.

"This is it?" said Joseph.

"This is it," replied Patricia.

"Where Carlotta's supposed son lives?"

"Where a man lives, claiming to be her son. Yes."

Joseph inhaled sharply. "Wouldn't look too good on that show, would it? Carlotta, all her wealth and fame, and the son she gave up for her career living here . . ."

Patricia understood what her father was trying to say. The house had deteriorated from modest simplicity into dilapidation. The porch roof sagged at one end. Of the six porch columns only three were intact. Two columns were broken from the bottom of the porch, one from the top, like snaggled teeth. Inside the maw of the porch was a washing machine and piles of wood. Paint, faded to a shade of bile green, peeled from the wooden siding. The house looked abandoned, but smoke curled from a brick chimney, so presumably someone was home.

"Let's go," said Patricia.

"You want me to go in there?"

Patricia looked at her father sharply. "You're the one who insisted on driving me. If you want to stay out here and freeze to death ..."

"I'm coming."

"Fine. Just let me do the talking."

Such a deteriorated house—and yet, as they got closer, Patricia noted that on either side of the porch steps sat clay flower pots in which yellow plastic daisies had been stuck. White lace curtains hung inside clean windows. Various wood-carved animals, painted bright carnival colors, were lined up inside the windows. Someone was trying to keep the house a home.

Patricia knocked on the door. After a few seconds it creaked open. A tall, stout, older woman peered out.

"Good afternoon, ma'am," Patricia said. "I'm here because of your interest in the *Flash* television show."

The door opened suddenly, widely.

"Come in, come in," said the woman. "I'm Alma Switzer."

Patricia and Joseph stepped in the house. Alma, salt-and-pepper hair swept up in a bun, wore a navy sweater and gray corduroy slacks. She grinned widely at them, her hands shaking a little as she swept a stray strand of hair back from her face. "Please, let me take your coats and then we can go into the living room." Alma hung their coats on a rack, on which hung two other coats, both brown wool and indistinguishable.

Joseph and Patricia stepped into the living room and settled into the couch. The furniture was old and worn; even when it was new, it was obvious that it was basic, solid furniture, but nothing fancy. It was a sure bet, thought Patricia, that it had not been purchased at Eismann Furniture Stores.

The room was spartan and neat—a marked contrast to the front porch. A braid rug lay on the hardwood floor in front of the brown couch. Two chairs, both with pink-flowered throws over them, and two end tables, both with ceramic brown lamps with lamp shades still in their cellophane wrappers, completed the room's furnishings.

There were no knickknacks, no books, no ashtrays, no photos on any of the tables—just a cluster of the gaily painted, carved animals gathered in a little menagerie on the coffee table. The room's only other decoration was a dimestore rendition of the Last Supper hung over the couch.

A freestanding stove in the corner provided warmth. On the wall behind it was a rack of twelve guns of various kinds. One gun per disciple, Patricia thought— surely the gun rack had been unintentionally juxtaposed to the Last Supper.

The dominant feature of the room was a large-screen television. It was the only new item in the room. A game show was on, its volume turned down to a low buzz.

Suddenly the sound was overwhelmed by a man's a cappella rendition of an old hymn Patricia vaguely recognized.

Alma watched her closely, and for a moment the only sound was the man's husky, slightly wavering voice singing, "Rock of Ages cleft for me, let me hide myself in thee . . ." Lewis, Patricia guessed.

Alma, she realized, was waiting for her or Joseph to make the next move. Amazing, she thought. Alma knew nothing of them, other than Patricia's true but misleading claim that they were here because of the *Flash* show. And she had eagerly let them into her house.

Patricia smiled at Alma. "I'm Patricia Delaney. This is my father, Joseph. He doesn't usually accompany me on these visits, but my truck broke down, and with this weather . . ."

"Yes, I understand. What do you do on *Flash*? Are you a producer?"

Patricia smiled again. "I'm here to see Lewis, your brother, right?"

Alma nodded.

"Is he home?"

"Yes."

"I'd like to see him."

"Oh, yes, I'll get him." Alma started from the room, then hesitated and turned. "I'm sorry, how rude of me. Would you like something to drink? Coffee? Cocoa?"

"No, thank you," Patricia said.

Alma left the room.

"You lied to her," Joseph hissed, leaning close to Patricia.

She looked at her father and whispered back, "I most certainly did not! I do not lie."

"She thinks we're from that show."

"No, she thinks *I'm* from that show. She probably just thinks you're overprotective, which you are."

In the other room, the music stopped. Alma was saying something.

Joseph shook his head. "I can't believe my own daughter—"

"Shh!" Patricia hissed. Alma was entering the room again, followed by a man who walked with a slight limp. Slightly taller than Alma and with a trimmer build, he wore a white shirt, overalls, a John Deere cap, and wire-framed glasses. He had a florid face and gray hair cut into a burr. The man stared at Patricia evenly, but with none of the joy Alma had shown when she thought Patricia was with *Flash*. He simply looked weary.

Patricia stood up. "Lewis Switzer?"

"Yes."

"I'm glad to meet you. I'm Patricia Delaney."

Lewis did not respond. Alma gave him a little prod. Lewis cleared his throat. "Likewise," he said finally.

He sat down in the chair nearest the potbelly stove. Alma took the other chair, and Patricia sat back down.

"What can I do for you, Ms. Delaney?"

"Please, just call me Patricia."

"All right, Patricia. Why are you here, and not Wayne?"

"I'm not with *Flash*," Patricia said.

"But you—" Alma started from her chair, her face reddening.

Patricia looked at her pointedly. "I said I was here because of Lewis's interest in *Flash*. And that I wanted to talk with Lewis." Alma settled back in her chair.

Patricia looked again at Lewis, but gently. "I work for Carlotta Moses, Mr. Switzer."

"Call me Lewis, if I'm going to call you Patricia."

Patricia smiled. She hadn't expected to like this man, but she found that she did. She liked his quiet, simple, unassuming manner. "All right, Lewis. I work for Carlotta. I know you claim she is your mother—"

"Claim! She is! Why, we found the proof, right here in this house, after Mama died. After *my* mama died, that is . . ."

"Quiet, Alma," Lewis said. "Let Patricia finish."

"Thank you. I know you claim, or believe, she is your mother, but Carlotta was incapable of bearing children. She adopted a son. I don't know what kind of proof you have, or believe you have, but it would be very embarrassing to her and her family for you to go onto national television and claim her as your mother—"

"Do you think we care about embarrassing those people? Why, we . . ."

Lewis quieted his sister this time with a glance.

"I'm here, on behalf of Ms. Moses, to ask you to stop working with *Flash*," Patricia continued. "I believe my client would be willing to make arrangements that would make it worth your while. You have distressed her greatly, and she's eager for you to drop your claims."

Lewis looked at Patricia a few seconds longer. Then

he closed his eyes and bowed his head. After a few minutes Patricia said, "Are you all right?"

Lewis didn't answer.

Patricia looked at Alma. "Is he all right?"

Alma glared at her angrily. "He's praying. That's what he does. Prays. Carves. Sings. And if you think we can be conned by your client's arrangements—" She said the last word nastily, as if it were vulgar. "We can get a lot more in the long run from *Flash*—and we need all the money we can get. Why do you think we're selling off the land? We can't work it ourselves, it's not worth it to try to farm it out anymore. But selling the land won't be enough. Why do you think we called *Flash*?"

"What happened that made you think you had a story hot enough for *Flash*?" Patricia asked quietly.

"Mama, God rest her soul, told me a year ago when she was dying that Lewis wasn't really my brother. He was adopted, she said. And she told me the name of the one who'd given him to her. She'd been hired to take care of this woman's child, in New York, she said. And then she was given money to come back here and claim him as her own. Can you imagine, a woman giving away her own son? Mama married and I was born after that. Never knew my father; he died when I was little. But Mama still had this farm.

"And when Lewis was old enough, he worked it," Alma continued. "Maybe that's why Mama always favored him. That always made me mad. Out of guilt she told me the truth. She told me the name of his real mama. Carlotta Moses. I'd never heard of her. Until a month ago. On the television. There was a show about opera singers. I watched it—I watch a lot of television; I like to learn things—and there wasn't anything else on but sports anyway, and so I watched it. This Carlotta Moses was talked about, and I realized she was a big star. Why, I thought, why abandoning her son to a poor woman like that, she should be made to pay. It's only fair and right. So I did a little research about this Carlotta Moses. And later I had Lewis call *Flash*."

Alma looked triumphant.

"A deathbed story," Patricia said flatly, "does not constitute proof that Lewis is Carlotta's son."

Alma narrowed her eyes. "I know that. But Mama was a pack rat. You should have seen what we had to clear out from here after she died. And while I was clearing out, I kept my eyes open looking for something to prove what Mama had said. And I found it."

"And what would that be?"

"I'm not telling you. The only thing I'm telling you is to tell that Carlotta Moses we can't be bought off by her. We don't want her money."

"You want *Flash*'s money, though. And she can pay far more than *Flash* can."

Alma's eyes narrowed again. "But she can't do movie rights. And all them other rights that pays big money, lots of money."

Just as Hackman had said, Patricia thought. And Alma was, Patricia was sure, going to keep pushing her brother into this. But of course, she believed that Lewis was not her brother . . . what a triumph after a lifetime of sibling rivalry, Patricia thought. She imagined Alma's thoughts: Mama loved you better, but you're not even her son! You're not my brother! Now I'm going to get something out of it—and you're going to pay with your privacy.

And, Patricia thought, looking back at Lewis, his privacy was important to him. Carving. Singing. Praying. The three things he loved—not television, money, or publicity. That was the key, she thought, to getting him to back down. Without him, even with Alma's claims, the show would lose its appeal. *Flash* needed him to claim to be Carlotta's son himself.

Patricia started to say Lewis's name, then decided she would wait until he finished his prayer. She looked over at her father. Joseph was staring at his hands. He was embarrassed, she thought, at witnessing this. Her family's problems were ordinary, simple ones that could be expected in any family. A miffed feeling here. A thoughtless comment there. The problems only seemed big, Patricia thought, because at times they forgot to keep them in perspective. And yet the family always moved on past the tense times to gather on holidays, in times of loss, in times of rejoicing. The Switzer family, she guessed, had little of such sharing.

Finally Lewis held up his head, opened his eyes. He looked at Patricia. "I don't know what to say—to do—" He looked at Alma, then sighed. "Tell Carlotta—Ms. Moses—"

"Your mama," Alma interrupted tauntingly.

"Tell her I'm doing the show."

He stood slowly and left the room. A door opened, then shut. His voice came through the small house, though, singing, again "Rock of Ages cleft for me, let me hide myself in thee . . ."

The volume went up on the television. Patricia looked at Alma.

"Get out," Alma said, her voice low. "Get out. I've got plenty to do around here without being bothered by you—wood to chop, clothes to clean . . . God knows he does nothing since Mama died and left us with nothing much but this death trap of a farm and her confession. So get out."

Patricia and Joseph stood, went to the entryway, and started slipping on their coats.

"And if you come back," Alma's voice called over the sounds of the game show and of Lewis's singing, "I'll get down one of them guns and blast your hides to hell."

Patricia and Joseph left, walking to the car as quickly as they could over the frozen earth. They sat in the car, shivering, waiting for the engine to warm up.

"You do," Joseph said finally, "meet some interesting people in your line of work."

Patricia sighed. "I guess I do." She glanced at her watch. Now it was time to go to the Moses–Eismann estate and bring them up-to-date on what she had learned.

She sighed again. "I certainly do."

Chapter 12

The headlights cut a swath of light that ended abruptly in darkness filled with snow. The snow swirled so furiously that it was impossible to tell if it was falling or being blown up by the heavy gusts of wind from drifts along the side of the road. According to the weatherman on the car radio, no one should be out on such a night.

Patricia snapped the radio off. "We're half an hour late. I hate being late."

"You said that before," Joseph said. "Several times."

Patricia glanced over at her father, who was hunching over the steering wheel, as if doing so would enable him to see a few inches farther. He was tense.

"I said I'd drive," Patricia said. "If you'd like to pull over . . ."

"I know how you drive," Joseph said.

The car skidded and Joseph deftly straightened it. Immediately, they were going down another hill on the narrow road. Joseph jerked the car into low gear, and through gritted teeth uttered a string of oaths—not a single of his usual Sweet Saint Peters among them.

Patricia decided this was not the time to debate her perfectly fine driving skills. She looked back out the

136

window, watching for the graystone gateposts that would signify the narrow lane to the Eismann–Moses estate. Even as slowly as they were going, they could easily miss them. Patricia had done so the first time she visited and had to drive several miles before finding wide enough berm on which to turn around. On this miserable night, she didn't want to be out any longer than necessary.

Indian Hills was beautiful in the daytime, Patricia thought, with the snow and ice covering the trees along the roads. Unless one was privileged enough to turn into one of the long drives to the estate homes, or into the upscale but small developments, trees were about all one saw in Indian Hills from the roadways. The town did not have a proper town center, although there were shopping areas in the bordering towns. Composed of homes, the Carmago Country Club, schools, and churches, Indian Hills was where seriously moneyed people lived, including well-known people. Pete Rose, of Cincinnati Reds baseball fame, had once lived there; Marge Schott, the owner of the Reds team, still did.

And, of course, so did Carlotta Moses, renowned, retired, reticent diva.

Patricia and Joseph had returned to Patricia's office after leaving the Switzer place. Patricia had called Carlotta, offering to come by in the morning with information regarding Lewis Switzer, but Carlotta had insisted that she come tonight, so Patricia had written up a report about her visit with Lewis and Alma, then gone to dinner with her father. By the time they left the restaurant, the roads were covered with snow and ice, and more snow was falling.

Carlotta, of course, would only observe the perilous, frozen world from behind glass, never venture out into it, and think nothing of summoning those she needed from the outside world, even on such a night.

Still, it was foolish to obey her summons. But Patricia took client satisfaction quite seriously and it was obvious that Carlotta was anxious for the information Patricia had and wished to discuss it in person. And Patricia was already eager to be done with the case. Quentin's desperate visit earlier in the day had made her feel as though the Moses family was drawing her too deeply into their personal problems. Tonight's meeting would, she hoped, speed progress on the case.

Patricia's plan was to share the information she had with Carlotta, then ask her about Maurice Horne and Rena Powell. Then she simply wanted to go home, take a long, hot shower, and collapse her aching body into her own bed. The next day she'd have a long talk with her father. Hopefully he'd come to his senses and go home. Then maybe the following night she'd collapse her body into Dean's bed. She missed Dean, missed talking with him, missed touching him.

"Wait—that was it," Patricia said suddenly.

"What?" Joseph let the car slow down nearly to a stop.

"The turn-in. Can you back up?"

"Back up? In the middle of the road?"

"No. I was thinking more of you staying on the right side of the road, where you are now, and backing up."

"Patricia, I'm in the dip of one of these blasted hills. I'd be backing uphill, not to mention traffic—"

"Traffic? You're worried about traffic on a night like

this? If you don't back up, you're going to have to drive about three more miles before you can find a decent turnaround, assuming it isn't covered with snow by now. And I don't think that's a safe assumption."

"All right, all right. I'll try."

Joseph put the car in reverse and started to ease back up the road. The car lost traction on the first two tries before he was able to back up far enough. Then he quickly put the engine in low gear and turned, nearly plowing the car into the snow drifted up around the gatepost.

The dark lane, lined by pine trees, was straight and long and narrow. Then it curved sharply to the left, away from the pines, revealing a sudden view of the estate. Floodlights were on outside, as were lights inside.

Joseph gasped. Patricia smiled to herself—she, too, was stunned the first time she saw the estate. The pines seemed to have been set purposefully to shield the manor from view, until at the final second it was revealed, suddenly and completely, momentarily filling eyes and mind with itself only, blotting all thoughts one might have had on the drive up to the manor.

The manor-sized house was a simple enough design—all graystone, two stories tall, eight shutterless windows on the facade of the first story, and twelve on the facade of the second story. Three stone chimneys topped the house. A wide expanse of steps led up to the only color of the facade—a huge red door.

Instead of a lawn, various plantings and beds, now covered in snow, were placed around the front of the house. To the sides and back of the house were woods.

In the middle of the circular drive was a fountain, currently not operating, and around the fountain a large flower bed.

"I'm not sure where—"

"Just park behind those cars," Patricia said.

Two older cars were parked between the fountain and the front door. Patricia wondered who they belonged to—not to anyone in the Eismann–Moses household, of course; those cars were garaged behind the house.

Joseph parked. As Patricia started to get out he said, "Just a minute, Patricia—I—"

"Dad, we're late as it is—" she began, then stopped when she glanced over at her father. He was staring in the rearview mirror, his hat removed, patting his hair carefully with a gloved hand.

Her father was nervous, she realized. For the first time he was about to see his operatic idol in person— and not only that, but to be in her home.

Joseph put his hat on again carefully and looked at Patricia. "Well, are you ready or not?" he said a bit gruffly.

Patricia grinned. "Sure, Dad. I'm ready."

They stepped out into the bitter cold and worked their way to the front door.

The housekeeper greeted them. As she took their coats Patricia mentally sifted through the list of names Howard had given her at their first meeting. Marcy Bergamore, she remembered. She was supposed to be a daytime employee. Perhaps Carlotta had asked her to stay for a special reason. Marcy, a younger woman than Patricia expected, looked tired. Then Patricia recalled

Howard saying that she was the single mother of a young child. That was not, Patricia thought, an easy role to fill.

Marcy escorted Patricia and Joseph into the music room. Four faces looked toward them expectantly as they entered; four faces fell in disappointment upon seeing them.

Patricia quickly assessed the room. A young woman, in a long white dress, stood beside a grand piano at which a young man sat. Quentin and Wallis sat together on a couch. Everyone looked tense. Quentin stood up and approached Patricia and Joseph.

"Patricia! So glad you could make it," he said, as if she and Joseph had been invited to attend and were merely late for whatever was going on in this room. His earlier desperateness had either disappeared or was now well hidden.

"I came because Carlotta insisted—"

"Oh yes, we'll go over all that later, but Carlotta will want you to stay for Ashley's first practice recital. And our housekeeper agreed to stay late to prepare a little reception in the dining room afterward."

"That's very kind of you, but given the weather, pretty soon it will be difficult to get back home. So, if we could just go over—"

"I understand Patricia, but the recital is set to begin as soon as Carlotta joins us," Quentin interrupted again. He looked at Joseph. "I'm afraid I don't know you, sir. . . ."

Patricia introduced her father, explaining briefly about her truck trouble. Then Quentin introduced the others in the room—Ashley, standing at the piano; her accompanist, Eli Goldstein; Wallis Moses. Quentin sat back down by his wife while Patricia and Joseph moved to the couch situated perpendicular to Quentin's and Wallis's.

The tableau struck Patricia as surreal: Ashley Moses standing by the baby grand piano, her family gathered about her as she was about to sing, nervously waiting for Carlotta to make her entry—never mind the crisis of tabloid media's intrusion into Carlotta's privacy; never mind the crisis of Howard's disappearance. Wallis stared ahead stonily while Quentin stared down at the floor. Eli was the only one who seemed to concentrate on Ashley. He was young, with dark, unkempt hair and a pale complexion. He wore a tweed jacket and jeans and gazed raptly at Ashley. Patricia knew Eli's expression—young love. Was Ashley even aware of it? she wondered.

Ashley, who stared off in space as if her spirit had long ago left her body, wore a white floor-length dress—almost ridiculous in its elaborate Victorian style on a modern woman who was more likely used to jeans and sweatshirts. Patricia was surprised that Ashley would choose such a dress and then realized she probably hadn't. Undoubtedly, it had been Carlotta's choice. Carlotta, of course, was engineering all of this—the museum, the debut of her granddaughter, her legacy carried on ... no wonder she wouldn't want Hackman's interference, not at any time, but least of all now.

Finally, the door opened, and Carlotta entered. No one said anything as she took the remaining chair, between the two couches.

For a few more seconds Ashley stared off at some point above their heads. Her parents looked at her, wearing forced smiles, as if instead of expecting to hear a beautiful song, they were waiting to hear their only child make a terrible announcement. Carlotta looked at Ashley but seemed distracted. Eli, meanwhile, continued to stare raptly at Ashley. Joseph glanced briefly at Carlotta, then looked politely at Ashley and Eli. Patricia watched the whole tableau and wished she could disappear from the room.

At last, Ashley gave a slight nod. Eli immediately began the piece. Patricia felt a sinking in her heart; she could tell from Ashley's nod, from the slight quiver of her head, from the sudden skittishness of her gaze, from her weak attack on the first note, that she was too nervous. And the nervousness, inevitably, would find its way into her voice.

A chill came over Patricia as she realized Ashley was singing *Voi che sapete*, an aria about love sung by the character of Cherubino in Mozart's *The Marriage of Figaro*. The song was perfectly suitable for a young soprano voice student, but that Carlotta had picked for her granddaughter a piece from the opera with which she'd made her debut struck Patricia as controlling, even frightening. Carlotta so wanted to make Ashley into a rendition of herself, a continuation of her life and talent. But, it was painfully clear, Ashley did not have the talent. It was not simply that her gifts were masked by nervousness. While Ashley's voice was probably pleasant enough when she sang along to a tune on the radio, she had no potential for professional singing. That her parents and grandmother pushed her into playing this role angered Patricia.

At last Ashley finished, and everyone but Carlotta applauded.

"Beautiful! Beautiful," said Quentin after they finished applauding. He stood up. "Come here and give me a hug, Ashley."

Ashley was still staring at Carlotta. "Grandmother? What do you think?"

Carlotta did not say anything for a moment. Then suddenly she looked at Ashley. "You still are not controlling the upper register of your range," she began.

When Carlotta was done, no one spoke for a long moment. Ashley looked evenly at her grandmother, as she had during the entire critique, while everyone else looked at Ashley. Ashley looked stricken, but said quietly, evenly, "Thank you. I'll be sure to work on that." Her voice was even until the last word, on which it gave a little squeak, betraying the emotion beneath her poised facade. Suddenly she lurched from the room. After a few seconds Eli followed her.

Another long silence ensued, and Patricia wondered what Ashley's parents would say. Surely, they had to be stunned by Carlotta's thorough criticism, none of it couched in kind terms, and in front of strangers.

Quentin shook his head in disappointment. "She's going to have to learn to take criticism better than that."

Wallis sighed. "I know. She is young, though—"

Carlotta looked at Wallis sternly. "She needs to know

the truth if she is to become any good at all. And she is hardly a child. By the time I was her age I had already studied long and hard, preparing."

"I know, I know," Wallis said. "I guess I'd best go calm her, though." She left the room.

Quentin looked at Patricia, smiled evenly. "Well, I suppose the rest of us can go enjoy the light buffet in the dining room."

Patricia was stunned at what she had just witnessed, at Wallis and Quentin's total acceptance of Carlotta's cruel treatment of their only child. She glanced at her father. He was looking at Carlotta. He had not, she realized, been introduced yet.

"Carlotta, I'd like you to meet my father, Joseph Delaney. He accompanied me here tonight because my truck has broken down in this weather."

Joseph moved over to her and Carlotta lifted her hand to him. He took it and pressed his other hand over it gently. Patricia smiled to herself. That was her father. No brush kisses across the top of the hand from him, not even for his most admired diva.

"I am so delighted to meet you, Ms. Moses. I have admired your music for so long—"

"Have you?" Carlotta cut him off, withdrawing her hand. She spoke blandly, as if she were suddenly bored. "How nice for you." She turned to look at Patricia. "Now, if we could get the report about this awful man . . ." She pressed her eyes shut.

Quentin grabbed her elbow. "Steady mother," he said. "Are you sure you're up to this?"

Carlotta nodded. Quentin looked at the rest of the

group, his forehead furrowed in worry. "Let's go on to the library. I suppose the buffet will wait."

Joseph and Patricia followed Carlotta and Quentin into the library. Patricia was fuming with anger. First she'd been cajoled into coming out here on this dreadful night, then she'd had to witness the humiliation of a young girl, all in the name of immortalizing the great Carlotta Moses, and now she'd seen her own father treated rudely by this woman. She wanted to glance at her father, but dared not. If any pain was showing on his face, it would only hurt him more to know she'd witnessed it.

In the study, they settled into chairs, Carlotta and Quentin together on a love seat, Patricia seated across from them, Joseph in a chair beside Patricia.

"First, I'd like to express my concern about Howard," Patricia said. "Have you heard anything?"

"Not yet," Carlotta said, her face twisting with sudden anguish. She looked away, and after a moment her face cleared and her eyes blanked, as if her mind could not cope with the anguish, at least publicly, and so mercifully drifted off into some hazy other world.

Quentin frowned at Patricia. "Mother is easily upset by mentions of Howard. We're hoping to hear something—soon."

So that was why no mention had been made of him so far. "I see," Patricia stated flatly.

"Mother, Patricia is about to tell us what she's learned."

Carlotta's focus snapped back to Patricia. "Yes. Do tell us."

"A man named Lewis Switzer is the one claiming to be your son. He even claims to have proof. Interestingly enough, he lives in Lebanon. Does the name Switzer sound familiar to you at all?"

"Yes, Darlene Switzer worked for me as a housekeeper when I first went to New York. I was kind enough to let her bring her little boy, a baby when she first started for me, with her. They stayed with me for four years," Carlotta said. "Up until just before my debut. Perhaps the boy's name was Lewis. I don't recall."

"Carlotta, how did you manage to afford an apartment in New York and a housekeeper with a baby before your debut?"

"Actually, my stepfather covered my expenses."

"Even your choice of a housekeeper with a baby?" Patricia was pressing, she knew, but a housekeeper for a single young woman seemed an extravagance, even for the well-off Powells. And a housekeeper with a baby seemed an even unlikelier choice, unless there was a compelling reason to want to help them.

"All right, Patricia. You've found me out. I didn't ask for a housekeeper. My stepfather insisted he'd pay my way only if the housekeeper and baby came with me."

"Now why," Patricia asked, "would your stepfather want to do that? If he really thought you needed a housekeeper, wouldn't one without a baby have been a better choice?"

"Undoubtedly. But my stepfather was not one to offer explanations with his demands. If I took the girl and her baby, he'd pay my way. If I didn't, he wouldn't. I don't know his reasons—except the girl began working for us as a housekeeper in Lebanon, not long after my mother's death." Carlotta smiled thinly, contemptuously. "I'm sure my stepfather had reasons for wanting to protect the girl, to get her out of Lebanon."

Carlotta was speaking in half-truths and insinuations, Patricia thought. If Douglas Powell had impregnated Darlene Switzer, he might want to help her and get her out of town. But surely he would not want to maintain a connection to her through Carlotta. Wouldn't he have been likelier simply to send the girl far away from anyone in his family?

Patricia studied Carlotta, who now stared off distractedly, her expression inscrutable. She realized she was not going to get much more out of Carlotta and chose not to press further about Lewis Switzer. Patricia still wanted to ask about two other people from Carlotta's past.

"Carlotta, I want to ask you about some other people from your past. Carlotta?"

"I think my mother has had enough for now," Quentin said, standing up.

"No, no, it's all right," Carlotta said. "People from my past, Patricia? There are plenty of those."

"These two knew you well before your debut, at the time when you allegedly had Lewis Switzer."

"My mother is not this Switzer's—"

"Quentin, please!" Patricia snapped. "I'm not saying she is his mother. I'm saying I've discovered two people who knew her from the time period when Lewis is alleging she gave birth to him. Perhaps they could give us information to back up what we already know—that she's not Lewis's mother."

"Like witnesses."

Patricia sighed. "Yes, Quentin. Something like that." That seemed to satisfy Quentin. He sat back down. "Now, Carlotta . . ." Carlotta had drifted again. Patricia leaned forward and placed a hand gently on her arm. "Carlotta."

"Hmm?" Carlotta regarded Patricia, as if from behind a veil that rendered all things pleasantly dim, edgeless. Then, suddenly, she snapped into focus. "Yes. People from my past. You have questions." She moved her arm from Patricia's. Patricia briefly wondered what, in Carlotta's mind, had rent the veil this time.

Patricia leaned back in her chair. "I'm curious about two people from your life before your debut. One is Maurice Horne. The other is your stepsister, Rena Powell."

"I don't think either will be of much help to you," Carlotta said. She was fully herself again: sharp, regal, imperturbable. "Maurice Horne was a music teacher in Lebanon. I took a few singing lessons from him, and unfortunately he tried to claim credit for my success."

"Have you stayed in touch with him at all?"

"Of course not. He's occasionally contacted me, and I've always made it clear I wish to have no contact with him. Politely, of course."

"Of course. When's the last time you heard from him?"

"A Christmas card, I think."

"That recently? Do you still have the card?"

"I am not sentimental about Christmas cards. Particularly not about one from a teacher who was mediocre at best, and who embarrassed me."

Half-truths again, Patricia thought. Horne could not have been so awful a teacher if Carlotta learned enough from him to prepare her to study with Bella DiSalvo.

"And Rena Powell?"

"I have not spoken of Rena to anyone over the years because she is not well, and I did not want her bothered by the media attention she would inevitably get as my stepsister. My stepaunt took care of her up until her death about a year ago, at which time both the old family house and the care of my stepsister were left to me. Rena cannot help us with this case."

"I'm going to speak with her," Patricia said quietly. "It will save me time in locating her if you simply tell me where she is now."

Carlotta stared at Patricia for a moment. "Very well. She's at the Heartland Retirement Home in Lebanon." Carlotta smiled knowingly—Patricia would have thought playfully, if it weren't so uncharacteristic. "But I don't think she'll have much to say to you."

"Isn't the best thing, anyway, to pay off this Lewis Switzer, get him out of our lives, now that we know he's the one who contacted *Flash*?" Quentin said.

Patricia shook her head. "I don't think it will be that simple. Money isn't going to be enough."

"What, then?" Quentin asked.

"You can't really offer money, directly. That just looks like you think he has a case, and you're trying to buy him off. He could take the money and still go on *Flash*." Patricia paused, considering. "You'd better consult your attorney, but I think a carefully worded letter threatening lawsuits that would tie up any money Lewis would get from *Flash* would help. He may still contact you demanding money, but that combined with vague threats might be enough to put him off."

"And if that doesn't work?" Quentin was standing again. He started to pace.

"Then you have your attorney look at frightening off *Flash* with the fear of a lawsuit."

Quentin frowned. "But all of this—lawsuits, payoffs— could still bring Switzer's claim out to the public. And some people would believe it."

"Probably," Patricia said. "But I'm not sure what else you can do."

"If I got a letter from our attorney tomorrow morning, would you deliver it to Lewis tomorrow afternoon?"

"Yes," Patricia said.

Quentin nodded. "Very well. I'm calling him in a few minutes."

"This Lewis Switzer," Carlotta said, looking at Patricia. "Describe him."

"Mother, really, you don't need to put yourself through this." Quentin moved over by her and put a hand on her shoulder.

Carlotta thrust his hand aside. "Describe him."

Patricia stared at her for a long moment. She had all along, of course, realized it was possible that Lewis was Carlotta's son. And Lewis, while not stating that he was her son during their afternoon visit, or confirming Alma's claim of evidence, had not denied it either. He had struck Patricia as a simple man of integrity. Even Wayne, although not a man of integrity, had to have something, however thin, connecting Carlotta and Lewis. Patricia was convinced there was a connection there deeper than Lewis simply being the son of a long-ago housekeeper, as Carlotta was claiming.

Was Lewis Carlotta's son? Patricia didn't know. She didn't care at this point—except that if he was, it was possible, it was just faintly possible that even one so self-absorbed as Carlotta had lain awake all those nights wondering what had become of the son she had paid someone to take off her hands. In that case, it would hurt her to hear about him. And after witnessing her treatment of Ashley and of Joseph, hurting Carlotta was something that Patricia felt the woman deserved.

And so Patricia described in full detail everything she had learned about Lewis: his clothes, his looks, his hobbies, his home. And his singing.

Throughout the description, not once did Patricia's eyes waver from Carlotta's. And not once did Carlotta's waver from Patricia's.

When Patricia finished, a long silence filled the room. Carlotta shut her eyes briefly, and when she opened them again to look at Patricia, they were cold and hard with an emotion Patricia did not identify at once. And then she realized it was hatred. And the hatred was toward her.

Patricia took the opportunity then to reach down for her briefcase and look away, a sense of shame suddenly sweeping over her. She picked up the briefcase, took

out a report, and put it on the coffee table between
them, keeping her eyes on the pages.

"It's all summarized here," she said. She had to clear
her throat. Her voice was rougher than she liked. "A detailed report of my visit with Lewis Switzer this afternoon. Your attorney will want to see it before writing
the letter."

The library door opened. "I'm sorry to interrupt, but
we've got a problem," Wallis's breathy voice said.

Patricia looked up toward the library door.

"Ashley will be fine, Wallis," Quentin said abruptly.

"I know, I know, but it's not that. Marcy's car is
stuck, and with this weather there is no way she can get
out. The snow has stopped, but our lane has become im-
passable." Wallis paused to catch her breath, then added
derisively, "Of course, Marcy's in a snit about it, but
I'm afraid she's stuck here for the night, and so is Eli."
She looked at Patricia and Joseph. "I'm afraid you are,
too."

"Have Marcy make up the spare rooms. There's
plenty of room here," Carlotta said blandly. She stood,
started to leave the library, then turned and looked at
Patricia.

Patricia looked her directly in the eyes again, but
now there was no expression of hate. Carlotta's expression was as flat and empty as if no emotions at all had
ever brushed her conscious or wrinkled her brow.
Again, the veil was drawn.

"Thank you for your report," Carlotta said.

Patricia was not sure what emotions her own expression might be revealing. She was not sure, even, what

she was feeling at this point, beyond a sense of over-whelming exhaustion.

"You're welcome," Patricia replied evenly.

Carlotta nodded, stood slowly as if her own weight were almost too much for her, then left the library.

Chapter 13

Lewis could not sleep.

He got up from bed, turned on the light in his small bedroom, looked at his bedside clock: 10:00 P.M.

He glanced around his tidy bedroom. Lewis liked things to be tidy, neat, spare. Mama had been neat and tidy, too, but not spare. She had kept everything.

Lewis missed his mama. He missed even the final days of feeding her like a baby, of helping her out of bed to the bathroom, of singing to her all the dear hymns she had taught him by taking him to Lebanon Baptist Church, where he'd first heard them, the hymns she couldn't sing because she was tone-deaf and had no ear for music, the hymns she'd loved to hear him sing, even unto her death. Your voice is beautiful, son, Mama would say. Sing to me "When I Survey the Wondrous Cross," "Amazing Grace," "Precious Memories. . . ." Sing them to me again, son, Mama would say.

But not son. Not Mama. Not Mama.

The shock of learning that she was not Mama was worse, far worse than her subsequent death. But he'd kept singing, in the three days of her life that remained after her confession to Alma, a confession that she never made to him, and that he never mentioned to her. He'd kept on calling her Mama, and she'd kept on calling him son, and he'd kept on singing to her. Mama had died holding his hand while he sang to her.

A hymn came to his lips now, a low moanful humming, as Lewis got out of bed. He put on his robe and slippers, and words joined the humming. He went down to the basement, to his scroll saw, singing softly, "Just as I am, with but one plea . . ."

Giraffes. He had cut out three giraffes that day, after the Delaney woman and her father left. A giraffe family. One big giraffe, two smaller giraffes. He thumbed the biggest one, brought sandpaper to its edge. After he smoothed it to a silky finish, he'd start painting this mama giraffe, bright orange and yellow. . . .

Not Mama. He'd seen Alma's proof. But he'd known it was true even before this, as soon as Alma told him. There were the memories . . . so vague, so distant, he'd thought them just memories of childhood dreams, but now he knew they were real memories, of the small place with big noises outside where he lived when he was very small with two mamas . . . one who sang often, who had a special flowery smell, who never enfolded him in her arms as the nameless other one did, the one who had taken care of him, the one who could not sing, the one who later took him from the small place with big noises outside. The memories came to him throughout his life, when he plowed the fields, when he went to church and sang the hymns . . . but he had thought them memories of dreams, until Alma told him. . . .

He heard a sound, startled, turned. It was Alma.

"What are you doing up?" she asked.

"Couldn't sleep. You?"

"Same. You know how I am before a trip." Alma was leaving early the next morning, at 4:00 A.M., to drive over to Indianapolis to a cousin's house, to help with the children while the cousin had minor surgery in the morning.

"You gonna be fine while I'm gone?" Alma asked. She pulled her robe tighter around her. The unheated basement was freezing cold. She shivered, but Lewis did not seem to notice the cold.

"Yep."

After a few minutes of silence Alma asked, "What are you going to do?"

"I'm working on these giraffes. Are you going to watch TV?"

"No—I mean about that woman."

Lewis frowned, uncomprehending.

"The woman your mama sent," Alma said with a little smile.

Lewis looked away. "Nothing." He sighed. "Nothing."

"You're still going on *Flash*, right? Because we need the money, Lewis. We need the money, or we're going to be hurting, Lewis, really hurting."

Lewis nodded. Mama's illness had taken nearly everything they had. "I know. I'll go on the show, Alma."

"I wouldn't want you to change your mind, Lewis. I'd hate to think what would happen if you changed your mind."

Lewis sighed again. "I know, Alma. Now go watch your TV."

Alma watched him a few seconds more, then trudged heavily back up the stairs.

Lewis gently massaged the bigger giraffe with the fine-grained sandpaper. He began singing, "Rock of Ages cleft for me . . ."

Patricia could not sleep.

She turned on the bedside light. For a few moments she looked around the small bedroom, filled with antiques. Just tell yourself you're in a nice bed-and-breakfast, she thought. Then she shook her head. It wasn't going to work. She'd been tossing and turning for an hour.

She picked up her watch from the nightstand: 11:30 P.M. It wasn't too late to call Dean, she thought, at least let him know where she was, why he hadn't heard from her today. She looked around the room again—no phone. She got out of bed, drew on her robe and slippers, borrowed from Wallis. Then she quietly slipped out of the room. Maybe, she thought, there would be a phone in the library; she thought she'd seen one there earlier.

She worked her way through the quiet, dark house, going by memory and feel down the staircase toward the library.

The library door was ajar and a light was on. Patricia started in, then stopped.

In the love seat were Ashley and Eli. Ashley was weeping. Eli watched her, touching her only to stroke her hair. His desire to pull her into his arms was obvious from the tension of his body, by how he leaned toward her.

Patricia stepped quietly away from the door, and started working her way back to the bedroom.

Patricia thought Ashley seemed dependent on Eli, yet she sensed that any passion Eli felt for Ashley was unrequited—perhaps Ashley was not even aware of his obvious passion for her. That, Patricia thought, sometimes made the passion all the more compelling, even obsessive.

Joseph could not sleep.

He turned on the light, picked up his watch: 3:00 A.M.

He sat up on the edge of the bed. He'd been dreaming of Margaret, then woke from the dream, and had lain awake, trying to remember it. But he could not recall the details. It seemed to him it had been a pleasant dream up to a point . . . he'd had the sense of her, the warmth of her, and then there came something, something distressing, and suddenly Margaret was Carlotta. . . .

Joseph shook his head. Enough. Dreams were just dreams. He'd never believed they were anything more than the subconscious processing the stuff of the day to clear the mind. And Margaret, as always, even in this time of trouble, was never far from his thoughts. As for Carlotta . . .

He didn't know what to think of her.

Joseph put on a robe, one of Quentin's. It was a little small on him. Maybe a snack, he thought. Maybe that would help him sleep.

He left the bedroom, worked his way by memory and

feel to the kitchen, turned on the light, then stopped. Carlotta was sitting at the table.

"Oh, I'm sorry, I didn't think . . ." Joseph began.

Carlotta looked up at him. She smiled. "It's all right. I sometimes like to sit in the dark here, that's all. I'm having a cup of tea. Would you like some?"

Joseph stared at her. Was this the same Carlotta as before? This soft-spoken, gentle-mannered woman offering him a cup of tea? Maybe she was in some sort of half-sleep trance.

But she tilted her head, smiled, and said quite clearly, "Or warm milk, if you can't sleep."

"Tea—tea would be fine," he said.

He went to the table after she'd already moved from it, busy with making tea.

"I like the night better than the day," she said. "It's easier somehow, to be in the dark. . . . I can relax. And the fog. I love fog, especially in the morning. It's supposed to be warmer this morning, very foggy . . . on a bright day, so much is expected of you. . . ."

Carlotta brought Joseph the tea. He watched her as she sat down. Then he took a sip from the cup she gave him.

"The tea's good. Thank you," he said quietly.

Carlotta nodded. "I'm sorry about earlier. Brushing you off about your being a fan."

"It's—it's quite all right."

Carlotta smiled. "I don't think your daughter would forgive me so easily. I don't think she likes me."

Joseph looked into his teacup. "Patricia—Patricia is just a little protective of me, that's all."

"That's nice. I can understand how she felt at my reaction . . . but it seems so long since I performed, almost as if it never happened, and with all that's going on . . ."

Carlotta smiled at him again and put her hands over his. Her hands were cold.

Joseph realized with a growing sense of unease that he didn't trust her.

"It occurred to me, as I sat here in the dark, that you could tell me . . . you could describe to me . . . you, a fan . . . could tell me how it was to hear me, when I could sing. . . . I haven't sung in years," Carlotta said. "For you to be here and then to come down to the kitchen as I was thinking, maybe you could tell me. . . ."

And then Joseph understood his sense of unease with her. Without her voice, she was hollow. There was nothing at the core. She had stopped living, really living, when she stopped singing. That's why she'd eventually stopped leaving her home. It was as if he were speaking with a dead person, who somehow kept living on and on, in a strange half state . . . he'd heard of spirits with unresolved business that would not move on from this world. It was as if for Carlotta the opposite were true. Her spirit had moved on, but her body was still here. And the only way she could regain any of that spirit was to hear how once her music, her voice, had touched someone.

Undoubtedly this was a vulnerability that Carlotta did not want her family to see and that was why she was being so kind to Joseph now. Alone with him, she wanted something from him—his memories of her.

Joseph paused and then thought, Why not? Whatever

Carlotta was now, she had given thousands and thousands of fans untold pleasure with her music, and he was but one of the people she had touched, had lifted with her voice from soul-weariness. Surely he could give this back to her, this little bit of his memory, of his time.

He smiled. "I was a young man the first time I heard you, just home from the war. . . ." he started.

Carlotta closed her eyes and listened.

Chapter 14

Patricia awoke twice Friday morning.

The first time was with a pleasant drifting to consciousness, then the unsettling awareness of being in a strange room. She jolted upright in bed, clasping the blanket and inhaling sharply. After a second, Patricia realized where she was. She exhaled slowly, and relaxed.

Patricia picked up her watch from the nightstand: 5:50 A.M. She sat on the edge of the bed and held back the drapery to look out the window. The earth was thick with fog. It would be a while before it lifted, and she didn't want to risk driving in it. She'd rather deal with the icy roads when they were visible. Patricia curled up under the blanket and closed her eyes.

The second time Patricia awoke with a panicked jolt that had nothing to do with being in a strange room. The essence of a dream lingered: images—a white room, a box in the room, something in the box, ghastly and horrifying but important; sounds—a baby crying, a cruel laugh, singing.

Patricia pressed her fingers to her temples and forced herself to breathe evenly. There was something in the dream she had known, had put together . . . and now—

163

nothing. She got out of bed, admonishing herself for being startled by a simple dream, which was surely the result of too much excitement over the past few days.

She dressed, checking the time as she strapped on her watch. It was 8:45 A.M., a late hour for her to awaken, yet she did not feel rested.

Patricia went down to the kitchen for a bite to eat; there she walked in on Wallis berating a red-faced and humiliated Marcy. Quentin was pouring himself a cup of coffee, ignoring the scene between his wife and the housekeeper.

"It's your duty to stay here for the day! What do you mean you need to—"

"But my son—he's sick and he's been all night with a baby-sitter and—" Marcy's words tumbled out.

"I don't care if—" Wallis stopped in midsentence when she saw Patricia. "Oh. Good morning."

Marcy took the opportunity afforded by Patricia's unexpected entrance to retreat hastily from the kitchen. Wallis followed her quickly.

Quentin turned and gave Patricia an embarrassed smile. "Good morning. Sorry about that scene. We've been having trouble with the housekeeper—"

"Don't worry. I'm sure she'll find someone to care for her son," Patricia said sharply.

Quentin's expression hardened with displeasure. Patricia smiled slightly, glad that he understood her opinion of his wife's treatment of the housekeeper.

"I've just come from our attorney," Quentin said coolly. "Marcy has set out a light breakfast in the dining room; we can go there and review what you are to do next. Coffee's here if you'd like it—"

"No, thank you."

In the dining room, Patricia helped herself to orange juice and a croissant while Quentin explained how he had met very early that morning with the family attorney to draw up a letter for Lewis Switzer, which Quentin asked her to read. In essence, the letter stated that if the Switzers took their story on the air with *Flash*, Carlotta's attorney would sue them on several grounds and make sure they'd never enjoy a penny they got from the show. Of course, the letter was more subtly worded than this, couching the threat in enough legalese to make it appear a reasonable and civilized response— with the merest hint of outrage—to an intolerable situation.

"I want you to deliver the letter as soon as possible," Quentin said. He pulled an envelope from a pocket inside his jacket. "And then this is for you."

Patricia took the envelope, but did not open it.

"Your payment for tracking down the Switzers," Quentin said. "With a considerable bonus for working so quickly."

Patricia frowned. "I don't consider my work done. I would like to talk with Rena Powell and Maurice Horne. Since they knew your mother as a young woman, they might be able to provide testimony to discredit Lewis's claim, should things not go as well as you hope—"

"No." Quentin cut Patricia off sharply. He smiled smoothly, but without warmth. "You contracted to find the person who'd contacted *Flash*. You did so. You've already disturbed Mother greatly with your questions about Rena and this Mr. Horne. There is no need to disturb them as well. Our attorney will handle the case from here."

She was being dismissed, Patricia realized. Not simply thanked and paid for an assignment completed, but dismissed, and the reason was that she had pressed Carlotta Moses to talk about people she'd sooner forget.

Patricia took both the letter and the payment. "Fine. I will deliver the letter to Lewis. Later this week I will send you a statement to formally conclude our business agreement and settle our account."

"You have been paid fairly, plus given a bonus. If you'd like to open the envelope and verify now . . ."

Patricia stood. "I follow certain procedures to conduct my business professionally."

Quentin's mouth straightened into a harsh, cruel line. "The bank has instructions not to clear your check until I know you delivered that letter. . . ."

"I will verify it in my statement to you." Patricia allowed herself a brief, amused smile. "But by then, I'm sure the Switzers' attorney will have already responded to your attorney. The Switzers will not back down so easily. I wish your mother the peace of mind she'll need for the days ahead."

Both Quentin and Patricia knew that Carlotta would find no such peace, had in fact lost any capacity for peacefulness long ago, and Quentin's face twisted with anger at Patricia's statement. But then something like fear softened his angry expression, a look that reminded Patricia of his panicked visit to her office the previous day.

Suddenly she understood that Quentin had no idea why his mother lived without peace. Perhaps no one knew except Howard, and now Howard was missing. Carlotta had always relied upon someone to do her bidding, to be her emotional buffer, and now undoubtedly she would turn to Quentin. The realization shook him.

But, Patricia thought, she had been dismissed. She had one last duty to perform for the Moses family, and then all obligations to them were over. She left the room.

Chapter 15

By 11:00 A.M., Joseph had driven Patricia to Sparky's Auto Shop, where her truck was repaired—the pickup had had a faulty spark plug—then returned to her home, where he intended to take a long nap. After a quick stop by her office and an even quicker lunch, Patricia headed for Lebanon.

Around 2:45, Patricia pulled into the small town of Lebanon. All she had to do was deliver the letter to Lewis Switzer. Then she could go back home and, following her father's example, take a long nap. She was very much looking forward to some additional sleep.

Yet, at the last intersection, by the Lebanon First Baptist Church, she lingered at the stop sign. If she went straight, then turned right at the bridge, she'd be on Ridgeline Road, the country road where the Switzers lived. If she turned right at the church onto Elm Street, eventually she'd come to the Heartland Retirement Home, where Rena Powell, Carlotta's stepsister, lived. She had looked up the address when she stopped by her office.

Patricia was curious about Rena Powell, even though Carlotta and Quentin had ordered her to stay away from

Rena. And being curious was one of Patricia's motivations for becoming an investigator in the first place. Once this case was wrapped up, she'd have no reason to come back to Lebanon to visit Carlotta's stepsister, a woman no one else outside of Carlotta's family seemed to know existed.

Patricia turned right onto Elm Street.

After driving past a sign for the Heartland Retirement Home, she drove up a long, winding, tree-lined road, past clusters of small but nicely kept duplexes, before coming to the parking lot of a large, two-story building, which was, according to the sign in front, the nursing center.

In the parking lot of the Heartland Retirement Home, Patricia hesitated. She sat for a few minutes in her truck, leaving her engine and heat still running while she considered the best way to approach Rena Powell. Carlotta, of course, did not visit Rena; Carlotta had not left her home in recent years. But what kind of contact did Carlotta have with Rena? Probably none other than paying the fees for the home.

Patricia shut off her truck, got out, locked and shut the door. She hurried to the entrance of the nursing center; temperatures were still hovering around the zero mark. Patricia would present herself as being here in an official capacity, on behalf of Carlotta Moses, she decided. That way, she hoped, she would find out from someone inside where Rena lived in the complex, and perhaps learn a little bit more about Carlotta's arrangement with the Heartland Retirement Home.

At the reception area, Patricia found a smiling young woman in a white uniform who was eager to help her.

"I'm Patricia Delaney. I'm here on behalf of Carlotta Moses, to visit Rena Powell," Patricia said.

"Are you a relative?"

Patricia glanced at the badge on the young woman's uniform. "As I said, Ms. Tolsen, I'm an associate of the family." Using the more familiar phrase *friend of the family* would have been stretching the truth a bit thinly.

"Have you visited before?"

"No. I'm here as—"

"Then you're not registered as a regular visitor here."

"No. I am here on behalf of Carlotta Moses. However—"

"You'd better talk with Betty." The young woman turned and entered an office behind the reception area. Minutes later she came out and gestured for Patricia to enter.

Betty Hanlon, an older, attractive black woman, greeted her with a careful smile and a wary expression. Patricia took off her red gloves and red-and-black coat and sat down in a visitor's chair.

"I understand you're here on behalf of Carlotta Moses," Betty said. "So of course you may visit Ms. Powell, if she is up to it and will see you. But as director here, I would like to know exactly in what way you represent Ms. Moses."

"I am an investigative consultant." Patricia pulled a business card out of her purse and handed it to Betty. "And I'm working for Carlotta Moses on a personal matter. In doing so, I learned of Rena Powell. I thought it might be helpful to my work if I visited with her."

Betty arched her eyebrows as she looked at the card. Then she put it down on her desk with a little snap and looked up at Patricia. "An investigator. I'm hoping Ms. Moses is not displeased with the facilities and services here. We have given Rena the best care we possibly could."

Betty stopped, waited. Patricia said nothing. It was amazing how often people assumed silence was disagreement—especially if they felt defensive—and were intimidated by the silence into saying more than they otherwise might.

Betty sighed. "Is this about Kendra Allen? Mr. Eismann did express some concern the other day—"

"Howard Eismann came here?" Patricia blurted before she could stop herself, then damned herself for her lack of control. She had assumed, from Carlotta's reaction to her mere mention of Rena, that no one from the household ever visited Rena.

"Why yes," Betty said, eyeing Patricia suspiciously. "He visits faithfully, every week."

Patricia smiled smoothly. "Of course. I just meant with the weather—"

"Of course," Betty said. But she still looked at Patricia dubiously.

"Ms. Hanlon, I want to be honest with you. I'm here because I know little about Rena Powell. As I mentioned at the start, I'm investigating a matter for Ms. Moses."

Betty frowned. "I don't see how Ms. Powell could have anything to do with your investigation. She's been here a year, and before that—" She stopped herself, unsure about whether or not to continue.

"I'm not sure she does have anything to do with it."

"I'm confused. Perhaps if I knew more . . ."

"It's a private matter, and I'm sure you can appreciate someone of Carlotta Moses's renown wanting to protect her privacy. All I can say is that it's a matter stemming from Carlotta's past—her distant past—and since Rena knew Carlotta back then, I thought perhaps she would be willing to talk with me about Carlotta's past, maybe tell me something that would help."

Betty stared incredulously, then said, "I don't know if I should call the police or throw you out myself. If you were really working for Carlotta Moses—"

"Wait a minute. I *am* working for Carlotta Moses. I am investigating something which concerns her distant past. But she has told me little about Rena; I learned of her on my own. If you don't want to tell me about Rena, that's fine. But I can find out anyway. I'm sure a lot of your staff works here in town."

"Are you threatening me?"

"Ms. Hanlon, I never threaten. I'm a reasonable person. I simply have all sorts of ways of finding out what I need to know. And I'd like to know a little about Rena. The simplest, most reasonable way for everyone would seem to be for you to tell me about her and let me visit her." Patricia spoke evenly, leaning forward. "Maybe we could start with your telling me why my desire to talk with Rena provoked a threat—your threat—to call the police?"

Betty Hanlon looked sternly, unwaveringly, at Patricia. "Because if you knew anything at all about Carlotta's stepsister, you'd know she can't talk with you about anything in the past—not hers, not Carlotta's, not anyone's. In fact, she quite literally can't tell you anything at all. She's mute. And she cannot do sign language."

Patricia fell back in her chair as if struck. She recalled Carlotta's knowing smile when she had said she wanted to talk with Rena. What were Carlotta's words then? *I don't think she'll have much to say to you.* Carlotta knew Rena was mute, of course. She had withheld that knowledge; her smile had been mocking as well as knowing. Patricia supposed Carlotta had a reason not to want her to meet Rena. But if Rena could tell her nothing, why did Carlotta care if Patricia visited her? Why hadn't she simply told her that her stepsister could not communicate?

Betty looked at Patricia with a mixture of pity and bemusement. "You look stunned. I take it Ms. Moses did not tell you of her stepsister's condition—assuming you really are working for her."

"No, she didn't," Patricia said. Her voice was coarse. "And yes, I really am working for her." At least for a few more hours, she thought. She leaned forward again. "Please. I really would like to know about Rena."

Betty sighed. "All right. You're a very determined woman. And since I don't want you hassling my staff, and since what I know isn't exactly a secret in this town, I'll tell you. Ms. Moses—or rather her attorney—contacted us a year ago. It seemed her stepsister, Rena Powell, had long been under the care of her maiden aunt, Violet Powell, who had just died of old age, but had not arranged care for Rena. Violet had contacted her own attorney, with instructions for him to contact Carlotta in the event of Violet's death. Carlotta's attorney in turn contacted us, and we agreed to care for

Rena, who was brought here a year ago by Howard Eismann, Carlotta's husband. He's the only member of that household who has ever visited or contacted Rena.

"Rena, you see," Betty continued, "could not possibly take care of herself. She cannot speak. I don't know the details, but she was injured long ago, and her voice box was destroyed. And Rena also does not have use of her hands. They are congenitally deformed. So you see, learning sign language is impossible for her as well. And her aunt, from what we've been able to piece together, kept Rena in the Powell home and cared for her. Rena was never seen by neighbors to leave the house. Violet went out only occasionally, for groceries, and after a while even those were delivered. It was when the groceries were left on the front steps for two days that a neighbor thought to investigate. Violet was found dead in her bed. And Rena was wandering around the house, dazed, confused, dirty, hungry. You see, she is fully capable of moving about, but she has no knowledge of how to care for herself.

"I learned all this, you understand, by talking with the neighbor who found Violet and Rena," Betty continued. "Actually, it was the neighbor's visiting daughter who found them. The neighbor herself could no doubt tell us much about the Powells; she's lived next to them since she was a little girl—even raised her own family in the house where she was raised. Unfortunately, she's ill. I learned what I could from the daughter, and I've been intending since to go back and catch the neighbor on a good day. This was my only choice if I wanted to learn as much as I could about Rena's background, and I felt it was important that I did if we're to help Rena at all. Of course Howard could tell me little. I've never met or talked with Carlotta. She has shown no interest in direct contact with Rena or anyone here, working only through her attorney or Howard."

Betty regarded Patricia then, as if checking to see if Patricia understood the full horror of what she'd described: Rena, incapable of expression, kept in the Powell house from the outside world and the help it might offer by an overly protective aunt, whose motives and reasons for that protection had gone with her to her grave; Carlotta, beloved of the world, doing nothing to intercede on her stepsister's behalf, even now acknowledging Rena's existence only so far as she must, now turning the house into a museum devoted to herself.

Patricia shivered involuntarily; she understood the horror, and it made her client seem contemptible. Still, Carlotta could be pitied for being as withdrawn as Rena had been. Was her withdrawal some self-punishment after all these years, triggered by her return to Cincinnati? Patricia knew that during her career Carlotta had declined all requests for performances in the area.

And she wondered about something else Carlotta had said the evening before, that she wanted to protect Rena from media attention; perhaps she really wanted to protect herself from the world learning about her neglect of Rena while she pursued her own career. Did Carlotta fear that *Flash* would learn of Rena? Her neglect of her stepsister, who surely could have benefited from her help, certainly would serve as proof of her total self-absorption. Had Carlotta's neglect been simply an act of selfishness, Patricia wondered, or was there some other reason for it? Some reason why neither Violet nor

Carlotta wanted Rena to connect with the world, to learn, in some fashion, to communicate?

"I'm not sure what to say, Ms. Hanlon," Patricia said. "I'm—I'm stunned by what you've told me. I had no idea—"

"You said you're investigating something from Carlotta's past, something that might be connected in some way with Rena."

"Possibly."

"Would figuring this something out help Rena?"

Patricia shook her head. "I don't know."

"That means it possibly could."

Patricia shrugged. "I've learned, as an investigator, that until you're sure you've pursued every possibility, tied up every loose end, anything is possible."

Betty tapped a pencil several times against her desk. "I know I shouldn't say this to you. But I don't like Carlotta. I don't have to meet her to know that. I don't like someone who simply uses money and other people's time to take care of a relative. But I care about Rena. So if helping you with this investigation could possibly help Rena, I'll try to help."

"You mentioned that Howard visits every week."

Betty arched an eyebrow. "Yes, and you seemed surprised at that."

Patricia smiled dryly. "You don't miss much. Can you tell me anything about his visits?"

"Only that he's faithfully come at the same time every week. He's always kind and jovial with the staff. I've been grateful for his involvement. Our staff psychologist and physical therapists have helped Rena progress considerably over the year; she can now do some things for herself, and she is much stronger physically. In fact, Dr. Sara Lamont, our psychologist, will be here tomorrow if you'd like to talk with her further about Rena."

Patricia nodded. "Is two o'clock all right?" By then, she'd be officially off the case, but she still wanted to learn what she could about Rena. It was possible that Rena was somehow connected with Lewis Switzer's belief that he was Carlotta's son; Rena's father's death, and her aunt's subsequent sheltering of Rena from the world, was timed too closely with Carlotta's dismissal of her housekeeper and Lewis from her life for the events to be coincidence. And those events were timed too closely for mere coincidence with Carlotta's debut. Somehow, Patricia believed, all those events were connected.

Patricia intended to find out how. She was not satisfied with having merely hunted down Lewis Switzer for Carlotta. She had meant it when she told Wayne Hackman that she did not consider it her place to find truth for her clients, only facts. But in this case, she did not believe she'd found all the facts pertinent to Lewis Switzer's allegation that he was Carlotta's son, and until she did, she would feel she had been, in some way, used by Carlotta. She did not like that feeling.

"I can't speak for Dr. Lamont's schedule," Betty was saying, "but I'll let her know that that's when you intend to come. You might want to call in the morning and see if the time's okay. And I can't say how much more Dr. Lamont can tell you about Rena—no one has seemed to be able to connect with her."

"What do you mean?"

"Rena has always been expressionless. Vacant. I'm not sure how much intelligence she possesses, and of course we don't have a way of asking. But recently we've had a student come visit who has seemed to make progress with her. I'm starting to see expressiveness—barely perceptible—where there was none before."

"This is the Kendra Allen you mentioned before?"

Betty nodded. "Yes. She's a computer engineering student who is interested in developing computer systems to help the handicapped. Kendra herself is disabled, paralyzed from the waist down, so she has a personal as well as academic interest in this. She's been working on developing some kind of interface—forgive me if I'm not too detailed, but I don't know much about computers myself—an interface, she calls it, that will enable Rena to communicate with the computer—put letters up on the computer screen—"

Patricia leaned forward excitedly. "And in this way Rena could communicate?"

Betty nodded. "Yes. Eventually. Using an artificial voice box requires some manual dexterity, which of course is a problem for Rena, plus major surgery and months of therapy to learn how to use, and we're not sure Rena is up to either. What Kendra's doing is Rena's best chance, right now, for possibly communicating with others."

Patricia recalled that Betty had mentioned at the start of their interview that Howard had been concerned about Kendra's work with Rena. If Carlotta had some purpose for keeping Rena away from the world, other than simple neglect, the potential that Rena could learn to communicate would be upsetting to her. Patricia smiled ruefully at the irony; at the end of their lives, Carlotta withdrew, while Rena learned to communicate.

"What kind of progress is she making?"

Betty smiled. "Why don't we go see Rena now? Kendra is with her."

Patricia followed Betty from her office into the residential wing on the west side of the central administrative building.

"Most of our residents are able to live independently. They live in the units you probably noticed on your drive up here. They can be as independent or involved as they want. We schedule regular trips to the shopping mall, or to the symphony, or the occasional Reds game."

Betty stopped in front of one of the doors and knocked. "Other residents, like Rena, need almost constant supervision."

The door opened, and a young woman in a wheelchair greeted them. "Hi, Betty. I was just about to wrap up my session with Rena."

"Kendra, this is Patricia Delaney. She is an associate of Carlotta Moses's." Betty spoke quietly, as if she didn't want Rena to hear.

Kendra's eyebrows lifted in surprise.

Patricia smiled. "Betty told me about your work with Rena, and I'm fascinated."

Kendra wheeled back into the room. "You're welcome to come see. So far, though, I haven't made as much progress as I'd like."

Patricia and Betty entered the room. It was small but adequate for one person, really a large studio apartment

minus the kitchen. A neatly made bed was in one corner, partially hidden by a decorative screen. A couch
and chair occupied the center of the room. A small tape
player sat on a coffee table. An opera—Patricia recognized *Carmen*—was playing. Beneath the window was
a desk, and at the desk sat a slightly built, dark-haired
woman. She did not turn, as if she had not heard them
enter.

Patricia stepped a little closer. The woman was sitting
before a computer, maneuvering a mouse with a hand
on which the fingers were developed only partially beyond the knuckles.

"Rena," Kendra said softly. "This is Patricia Delaney.
She's an associate of Carlotta's."

Rena looked up suddenly, moving toward the computer as if she were suddenly trying to protect it. She
stared at Patricia, her eyes not at all vacant as Betty had
described. There was fierceness, a deeply burning wrath
as she stared up at Patricia. There was intelligence in
her eyes.

Somehow, Patricia thought, since she associates me
with Carlotta, she thinks I'm going to take the computer
away from her. Why? she wondered.

Patricia smiled and knelt down. "I like computers,
Rena." She hesitated. She couldn't be entirely sure how
much Rena understood; yet she didn't want to sound
patronizing. She decided to speak to her as she would to
anyone else. "I think that it's great that you're using a
computer to learn to communicate."

Rena's eyebrows quivered only slightly, as if she
were surprised. It's been so long, Patricia thought, since

Rena's communicated with people other than her aunt that she's forgotten facial expressions.

Patricia smiled kindly. "It's cold outside. Very snowy. Have you looked out?"

Rena stared a moment longer, then gave a slight nod.

"Could you describe what you see on your computer?"

Suddenly the expressiveness, as fragile as it was on Rena's face, went dim. She shrank back, withdrawing.

Patricia looked at Kendra and Betty.

Kendra sighed. "I'm afraid there's only one thing she'll put on the computer screen. And she won't do that unless music is playing—we're just lucky the psychologist here decided to see how she'd respond to music, and noticed she perks up most when singing is playing. But she still only writes one thing on the computer screen. I'm going to install some very basic music composition software before I leave today, see if that inspires any more interaction with the computer. It's all I can think of, given her reaction to music and the message she keeps writing."

Patricia stood up and looked over Rena's shoulder to see the message. And when she did, she had to fight back a stunned gasp, had to clutch the back of Rena's chair to steady herself.

Rena's message, put on the screen over and over and over, was simple: *i sing i sing i sing i sing i sing. . . .*

The two simple words took on cadence and rhythm and melody as Patricia drove down Ridgeline Road toward the Switzers.

i sing i sing. . . .

Did Rena really want to sing? But how? Why? She had not spoken for a long time, so how could it be that she now wanted to sing? Or were her words simply a reaction to the operatic music played for her?

i sing i sing. . . .

The words had become a haunting chant in Patricia's mind by the time she pulled to a stop in front of the Switzers' home.

The car was gone, but dark smoke still chugged out of the chimney. Patricia got the letter out of her briefcase, went up to the front door, and rang the bell. No answer. She could hear the television on inside. Maybe they couldn't hear the bell over its sound? Patricia glanced at her watch. It was getting close to dinnertime. Maybe they were back in the kitchen, and had the television turned up loudly so they could hear it there. Patricia decided to go around to the back of the house to see if there was a door.

The rhythmic sound of her boots crunching in the snow brought to mind again the refrain: *i sing, i sing, i sing*.

As she rounded the side of the house Patricia nearly laughed out loud at herself—stuck on two words that were simple enough yet made little sense in the situation she'd just seen them. She wished she could laugh, not out of any real sense of humor, but to try to knock the singsong words out of her mind.

Then she came to the backyard and to Lewis Switzer.

Patricia almost tripped over Lewis before she saw him; his body had sunk down into the half foot of snow. The top of his head had been shot away; blood and brain matter were spattered over his face. His uncovered hands were above his head, as if he'd thrown his hands up in surrender or appeal just before being shot.

Patricia sank to her knees in shock, then forced herself to assess the scene. A handgun lay near his body; she recalled the gun case by the *Last Supper* print inside the house. There were numerous boot prints; it would be impossible, she thought, to sort them out.

Patricia's stomach started churning, but she forced herself to look at Lewis and observe as much as she could. He was not dressed for the weather. No gloves. No coat over his flannel shirt. No hat. He did wear boots. And there was something near his hand.

Patricia shuffled closer.

A giraffe. A wooden, carved giraffe. The orange-and-yellow paint on it was smeared. Orange-and-yellow specks of paint were on Lewis's hands. He had been working on his menagerie when someone or something had called him outside, and then someone had shot him at fairly close range.

Patricia stood, started stumbling toward the house, then stopped. No. The murderer could be in there. Perhaps even Alma . . .

Patricia turned and ran back toward her truck. But her running seemed the slow, impossible kind of nightmares, the snowy ground gripping her boots, the image of Lewis shimmering before her on the snow, the awful refrain—*i sing, i sing, i sing. . . .*

Chapter 16

Detective John Tate, of the Lebanon Police Department, leaned back in his chair, pressed his fingertips together, and looked thoughtfully at Patricia.

"What you've told me," he said, "is incredible."

Patricia nodded. Two hours had passed since she'd gotten back to her pickup and telephoned 911. Her initial statement had been taken at the Switzers' house, and then she'd been given instructions to appear at the small police department. Lewis's murder was the first homicide in Lebanon since a bar fight had gone too far three years before, Detective Tate had told her. He had spoken with irritation, as if he blamed her for breaking the usual string of car-stereo thefts and bad checks with which he usually dealt. His reaction had not eased the ordeal of describing why she had been the one to find Lewis, of explaining Lewis's connection to Carlotta Moses.

"I've known Lewis and Alma for a long time," John Tate continued. "Knew their mama, Darlene, too. Quiet folks. Never had trouble from them—I know them mainly through the Baptist church in town. I know they had a hard time when their mama was so ill. Probably wiped them out financially. But I can't believe they'd make something up like this—a different mama for Lewis. And an opera singer at that." He shook his head in disbelief.

Patricia looked at the detective. She guessed him to be in his late fifties. His hair was a burr cut of silver and black; he had a thick waist, leathery skin, dark brown eyes, and many wrinkles, most of them, it appeared, worn into his face from laughter and smiles. His desk was crowded with numerous photos of family gatherings of his wife, children, children-in-law, grandchildren.

Yes, she thought, the bitterness of the Switzers' lives—no doubt duly covered over in church with carefully managed smiles—would shock him. Patricia was too tired to feel any more shock at the Switzers, at Carlotta and her family, even at the image of Lewis lying dead in the snow, an image that kept flashing in her mind with thought-obliterating brightness. She rubbed her eyes.

John looked at her sympathetically for the first time. "I understand what a strain this must be for you. But I appreciate your telling me all you know. It at least helps me understand why Lewis might do something like this."

Patricia found her capacity to be shocked, after all. She stared at Detective John Tate a long moment before saying, "You mean you believe Lewis Switzer committed suicide?"

Irritation again furrowed John's brow, whether at her or at revealing his theory, Patricia was not sure. "I didn't say I believe he killed himself," John said, signs of sympathy erased from his voice and expression. "I'm simply considering it as a possibility. That was his gun by his body."

"That doesn't mean it was the gun used to kill him. Someone could have planted it. And why go outside to commit suicide—" Patricia started.

"Obviously I won't know what kind of gun was used to kill him until I get the coroner's report." John's voice was brusque with increasing irritation. He glared at Patricia. After a long silence he sighed. "All right, Ms. Delaney, what's your theory?"

The question surprised Patricia. She wondered if he really was interested in her thoughts, or if he was hoping by encouraging her to keep talking, she'd reveal something more of use to him.

Patricia spoke carefully, knowing how passionately protective small townspeople can be of their own, especially if seemingly under attack by an outsider. "I find it curious that Alma was away from home this morning. And I know she was much more adamant than Lewis about going on *Flash*. If Lewis had decided to back out—"

"Alma was visiting her relatives in—" John began, then stopped himself, scowling again. "All right, Ms. Delaney. First of all, from what you've said, Lewis had no intention of backing out of the show. And even if he did, how would murdering him profit Alma? With Lewis dead, there'd be no show, and so no payoff. Alma would stand a better chance of trying to change his mind."

"It's possible she killed him out of anger. Or maybe she killed him, and tried to make it look like suicide,"

Patricia said. "Alma can still go on the show with this evidence she supposedly has. His suicide only makes his story all the more melodramatic for prime-time television."

John tapped his forefinger on his desk. "She wouldn't have to stage his suicide for that."

"True, but how do you count on someone conveniently committing suicide? For that matter, if Lewis refused to go on television, Wayne Hackman would lose a good show, which I suspect he needs. Lewis possibly backing out gives each of them a good motive for murder."

John leaned forward suddenly, grinning. "I know, Ms. Delaney! Alma and Wayne Hackman planned Lewis's murder together!" His voice rose sarcastically. "It's a conspiracy! Don't you think that makes sense?"

Patricia folded her arms and gave John a fixed look. She said nothing.

John's grin curled into a sneer. "I see you don't like my theory, Ms. Delaney, which surprises me. Just like your theory, it conveniently lets your client and her family off the hook."

"I'm sorry I've made such a poor impression," Patricia said quietly. "But I'm not trying to manipulate you into believing that my client is innocent. If you'd like, I can tell you why and how someone in my client's family could have killed Lewis."

John studied Patricia for a minute. His face relaxed into its customary pleasant expression. "All right."

"The motivation is obvious. No one in my client's family wanted Lewis to do the show. Last night, I gave Carlotta a report which summarized my meeting with

Lewis and Alma, and also included their address. Anyone in the family could have seen it. We all went to bed fairly early. I got up around eleven-thirty that night, and saw only Ashley and Eli awake as well. After that I was in my room until nine this morning, and then I saw Marcy, Quentin, and Wallis. It's possible anyone in the house could have left in the night, driven out here, killed Lewis, and returned home."

"And who do you think would be most likely to do this?"

Patricia considered, then said, "I can't understand why any of them would kill Lewis, not without first trying to use their attorneys to keep him off the show. And then, of course, there is the matter of Alma and the evidence—she could still cause problems. So I'd think someone from my client's family would wait. Unless, of course, someone is really terrified and desperate to silence Lewis, and is panicking." She paused, rubbing her temples. She felt the beginning of a headache. "And the person with the most to lose, the most likely to panic, is Carlotta. There are two people from her past, from about the time she allegedly would have given birth to Lewis, who she does not want to talk about. Perhaps there is something she fears Lewis might have recalled or figured out about them, something even more damning than her having a son and giving him away."

"Do you really believe that?"

"I don't know. It's possible. I don't know why else she would refuse to talk about them." Patricia filled John in about Rena Powell and Maurice Horne.

"All right," John said, "let's say Carlotta had some

reason, something compelling her to want Lewis out of the way quickly. But you told me in the beginning of our interview that she's agoraphobic."

Patricia nodded. "Yes. But she could have sent someone to murder Lewis for her."

John grimaced with distaste. "Someone in her family would do that for her?"

Patricia smiled ruefully. "I think so—yes. Carlotta—has an encompassing control over her family members."

"Who's most likely?"

"I'd say Howard. But he's missing."

John drew in a deep breath. "Oh. How convenient."

Patricia frowned. "What do you mean?"

"If he's missing, he can't be a suspect, right? But what if he's not missing? What if he's just been hiding somewhere, waiting to get the word from Carlotta once she learned from you the name of the contact?"

"But at the time Howard disappeared, we didn't know that the contact was the supposed son . . . and Quentin came to my office quite distraught that Howard was missing . . . unless of course he just wanted me to think—" Patricia stopped, rubbed her temples harder. The headache was worsening. "I thought you didn't like conspiracy theories."

But what John was suggesting—that Howard had killed Lewis, then disappeared, with his family's knowledge—was possible, just possible. It would mean that Patricia had been used as a pawn by the Moses family in the worst way.

"I don't," John said. "But I have to consider every angle. Was Howard reported missing?"

"I don't know. I suggested that Quentin contact the

police, although I did say the police usually don't take a missing person's report about an adult too seriously, at first."

"Hmm. Well, now it becomes more pressing to do so." John was making notes. "Another question. If someone from the household killed Lewis, why send you out here this morning?"

"Only Quentin talked with me this morning about delivering the letter to Lewis. I assumed that he had told the others of his plan to send me out, but that wasn't necessarily so."

"So someone else from the household could have come out here and murdered Lewis, early in the morning before he or she realized Quentin was sending you out. . . ."

Patricia arched an eyebrow. "You know Lewis's time of death?"

John smiled ruefully. "The county coroner has to do an autopsy, but is estimating roughly in the early morning, sometime between five and eight A.M. Poor Lewis having been in the extreme cold makes it harder to tell. I doubt the coroner will be able to narrow the time much further."

"And during that time Alma—"

"Had already arrived at her relative's house. I've talked to them on the phone, and I have someone out there now getting details." John paused, regarded Patricia with a kind of sympathy. "And you say you were at the Moses house until after nine A.M.?"

"Yes, but—" Patricia stopped. Of course. She had found the body. She worked for the Moses family. She had no alibi other than that provided by the Moses family and her father for her whereabouts when Lewis was murdered. She was a suspect, too, and would remain so until Lewis's actual murderer was discovered.

"How long a drive is it from the Moses–Eismann place to Lebanon?"

Patricia paused, considered. "Maybe forty minutes. In bad weather—with the ice and fog wc've been getting—maybe an hour."

John jotted more notes on a pad, then looked back up at Patricia. "I'll want to talk with you again. And with your client and her family. Assuming the coroner doesn't rule Lewis's death a suicide." He smiled with a mixture of kindness and sadness.

Patricia looked over at John's window, out at the snow again swirling outside. She should want to believe that Lewis had simply, out of anguishing guilt, killed himself.

Yet she couldn't believe that when she thought of the little giraffe she had seen near his corpse, and of the paint spatters on his hand. He'd apparently been working on the giraffe when he'd gone outside. Working on a hobby was not usually part of the mind-set of someone who would commit suicide.

And even more strongly compelling to Patricia was the memory of Lewis's singing. His singing had shown her that he was a deeply religious man. For some, religion could be so guilt inducing that perhaps suicide would seem a way to escape the anguish. But she could not believe that of Lewis, not after hearing the sincerity of his singing. She could not believe he'd killed himself, and she didn't want to believe it.

Detective Tate would interview the Moses family

members, find out all the details of their whereabouts when Lewis was murdered. He'd focus on the present. Patricia determined that she would keep looking to Carlotta's past, to the time when she allegedly had Lewis. She was convinced that Carlotta was hiding something that related to Lewis; why else so completely discourage Patricia from meeting Rena or Maurice Horne? It would be a while before Rena could tell her anything, but if she could find Maurice, talk with the neighbor who'd lived next door to the Powells all of her life, if she could find out what kind of evidence Alma and Lewis had ...

"This evidence Alma and Lewis have," Patricia said. "I'm sure you're going to want to get it from Alma, keep it safely under lock and key, in case someone from the Moses family tries to return for it?"

John arched an eyebrow. "Yes."

"I'd like to see it when you get it."

"That's a bold request. Why should I honor it?"

"Because I'm going to be learning everything I can about Carlotta's past to see if she'd hiding something that would make her or someone in her family so desperate that they'd have killed Lewis."

John pulled his mouth into a half smile. "That's *my* job."

"I won't get in the way of your investigation. I just have some leads that came up in the course of my work for Carlotta. I intend to follow them."

John tapped his forefinger, considering. "You didn't have to call emergency after you found the body. You didn't have to tell me all you have about the Moses family. So I'll consider letting you know about the evidence Alma and Lewis have—if I think you can tell me something about it that will help me with this case. But—" He leaned forward suddenly. His brow puckered in severe lines. The set of his mouth became harsh, the gleam in his eye intensely serious. "But, Ms. Delaney. Anything—anything at all—that you learn that pertains to this case—that might even in your wildest imagination pertain to this case—I want you to let me know. Because I always liked listening to Lewis sing in church, and I want to hear Lewis's voice again, if only in my memory. And I don't think I'll be able to until I figure out what happened to him out there this morning. Do you understand?"

"I do," Patricia said. She stood up. "I very much do."

Patricia stared at her computer screen, trying to concentrate on her work. She had come back to her office after leaving Detective Tate and tried to catch up on the work she'd ignored in the past two days while working on the Moses case and dealing with her father's sudden appearance.

The assignment she was working on now was simple, she reminded herself. All this particular client wanted her to do was research the financial backgrounds of three companies she was considering for a business partnership. Standard work. Bread-and-butter work. She'd done this kind of research innumerable times before.

And now she couldn't concentrate. The headache that had started in Tate's office was now a vise grip. A dose of aspirin an hour before had not alleviated the pain. And Patricia could not stop thinking of Lewis, who sang and created little wooden animals, blasted away on a frigid day ... of Rena, who could not speak or sing or use her hands, and her constant message, *i sing i sing* ... of Carlotta, once a world-renowned singer but now self-imprisoned in her home ... of Wayne and his show. ...

Patricia saved her work and turned off the computer. Perhaps meditation would both ease her headache and clarify her thoughts.

She rummaged in the side drawer of her desk. She got out the incense, selecting a vanilla stick. She lit the incense, put it in an incense holder. Then she got out a scentless candle, put it in a candle holder, and lit it. Finally, she turned off her desk lamp.

For a few moments Patricia focused on just the candle's tiny flame. She relaxed, letting the tension dissipate from her head, neck, and shoulders, holding her hands palm-up in her lap. Then she closed her eyes, and breathed slowly in and out, in and out, focusing on her slow, even breaths, until finally her mind was clear of thought.

Start at the beginning, she told herself, and let your mind guide you. Carlotta Moses wanted her to find out who had contacted Wayne Hackman of Flash Productions, claiming that she was his mother, even though Carlotta could not bear children, and had in fact adopted a son, Quentin, later in life.

And Patricia had found the person, a Lewis Switzer. A simple man. A man who seemed kind. He was being pushed into appearing on the show by his sister, Alma, who claimed their mother had told her Lewis was

Carlotta's son, and that she herself had then found evidence of this statement. And Wayne had claimed to have seen the evidence. To Wayne, it would not have to be concrete, absolute proof that Lewis was Carlotta's son. It would have to be enough to show a link between Lewis and Carlotta, a possibility that she could possibly have been his mother.

And while learning this, Patricia thought, she had also learned of Rena, Carlotta's stepsister, one of two living links to the time when Lewis claimed Carlotta gave him up to the woman who raised him like her own son. When Lewis was four. Just after Douglas, Rena's father and Carlotta's stepfather, died. Just before Carlotta made her debut. A debut at which a Maurice Horne, the other living link, claimed to have been Carlotta's teacher a few years before, before her stepfather agreed to send her to New York. But a few years before, Carlotta had still been in Lebanon . . . living with Douglas, living with Violet, living with Rena. . . .

Patricia's eyes opened suddenly as she sat bolt upright in her chair. She stared into the candle's flame. Of course. Of course. What if Rena were actually Lewis's mother? And Carlotta had been in charge of raising him, perhaps in exchange for having her living expenses in New York covered by her stepfather? And then her stepfather died just as she had a chance for a debut? So she gave the boy to Darlene Switzer, who, Alma claimed, had worked for Carlotta in New York. Douglas couldn't protest because he was dead. Rena couldn't protest because she couldn't communicate. And Violet—perhaps Violet was glad to have the boy out of their lives. A child born out of wedlock at that time was considered an embarrassment.

Patricia snuffed out the candle, switched back on her desk lamp and her computer, started up her word-processing software, pulled up the file of her notes about the Moses case, and began tapping in this theory, along with an update of her activities. There were a lot of unanswered questions in this theory—like why would Darlene Switzer have agreed to take the boy? What evidence did Alma supposedly have? And who was the father? Maurice Horne? Possibly; he was strongly connected to Carlotta in her past, so he could have known Rena as well.

Patricia started to reread what she entered and then she saw the final bit of the last entry she'd made. She paged up and read over the previous entry. Her last remark was that she'd posted an opera-trivia inquiry on the Internet bulletin board about Maurice Horne.

Patricia saved her work in the word-processing file and exited the software, then logged onto the Internet.

There were four responses to her inquiry. Three stated that they knew nothing about Maurice Horne, but they were interested in trivia about Carlotta Moses, and could p.delaney (Patricia's user ID) post a response back to them if she found out anything?

The fourth reply, however, was from a local musical history buff who knew of a Maurice Horne who had taught choir in several local high schools and privately to voice students, using innovative breathing techniques, during the late 1930s. His choirs and students had been among the best in the state. In fact, the buff's father had been in one of the choirs, in Cincinnati. But

Horne had quit abruptly to fight in World War II, then returned to the area, trying again to teach his breathing techniques, but this time was unsuccessful. He'd turned to piano tuning as his livelihood, at least until the late 1950s. The last newspaper article the poster had about Maurice was from 1958, when he was still trying to promote his techniques. Patricia sent a reply of thanks to the poster, then logged off the Internet. She was smiling and excited, the remnants of her headache forgotten.

It was possible, Patricia thought, that Maurice had been a member of one of the associations for musicians. Maybe an association could help her track him down. She logged into a news-and-business database that included the *Encyclopedia of Associations* in its offerings. A search in the encyclopedia yielded several possibilities, the most promising of which was the Association of Music Technicians, which included piano tuners. Patricia printed the information about the association, then logged off the database. Then she dialed the number listed for the association.

A young man answered after the second ring.

She introduced herself, then stated that she was trying to locate a Maurice Horne who may have been a member of the association at some point.

"We don't routinely give information about our members over the telephone," the young man said skeptically.

"Oh, I can understand that. But I'm an investigator with a client who knew him long ago, and would be very—interested in meeting him again. I'm sure he'd be interested as well." That was stretching the truth rather thinly, Patricia knew.

But the hint of intrigue seemed to work; indeed, Patricia had learned that few people could resist helping with matchmaking, especially of the long-lost-love sort. She could hear the grin in the young man's voice. "Well, let me see what we can do, then. Your telephone number?"

Patricia gave him both work and home numbers, thanking him profusely. Then she telephoned Lebanon High School and asked to speak to the yearbook adviser, who luckily was on break. Patricia gave her a similar story, saying she was trying to track down a Maurice Horne who, she believed, had directed the choir at Lebanon. Were there any yearbook pictures of the choirs from then that might include Maurice Horne? The teacher wasn't sure, and didn't have time to look just then, but assured Patricia she would as soon as she could. Again, Patricia gave her both her home and work numbers.

After she got off the telephone, Patricia went back to her word-processing program and started a list of what to do next. Find out what "evidence" Alma supposedly had. Visit the neighbor next door to the old Powell house—now being turned into the Carlotta Moses museum—whom Betty, the director of the Heartland Retirement Home, had described, and find out what the neighbor remembered about Carlotta or Rena, or even Maurice. He could have taught Carlotta at the Powell home. Talk with Kendra and Dr. Lamont, the Heartland psychologist—find out from them if somehow she could encourage Rena to "talk" about her past on the computer.

Patricia smiled to herself as she worked, feeling almost lighthearted. She was in pursuit of facts, information again. And there was nothing she loved better.

Chapter 17

Despite the weather, Dean's Tavern had a fairly good turnout; it was, after all, Friday night. Patricia, who sat at the bar surveying the patrons scattered at the booths and tables around the room, recognized a few regulars who came several nights a week, including Tuesdays when the Queen River Band played. Friday nights usually featured a different band every week, but the Queen River Band was playing an additional gig tonight, since the scheduled band had canceled, with the same reason that everyone gave these days—bad weather. In this case, it had left Friday's band leader stranded on the East Coast.

Patricia was the drummer of the Queen River Band. She glanced over at the small stage. She was eager to start playing. Her lighthearted mood earlier in the afternoon had faded and now she needed a session at the drums to relieve the tension—the sense of foreboding, even—that grew in her mind. The Moses case and her father's unplanned visit had taken over her life, stretching time unrealistically, breaking all the rhythms of her life, giving her life a sense of unreality. She was used to a certain pattern to her days—a calm, easygoing pattern.

It was hard to believe that only two nights before, she had sat in this bar, having just started work on the Moses case, when her father had unexpectedly walked in.

"One iced coffee with bourbon," Dean said. Patricia swiveled to look at him and smiled. She took a long drink. She'd told him about her day and he had, as always, offered what she needed—an ability to listen with few comments.

"Are you sure you don't want something warm on a cold night like this?" Dean asked. He looked amused as she sat the glass down; it was half-empty.

"Yeah, I do," Patricia said. "But not to drink."

"Ooh-la-la," Dean said. "I like that. After we close up here tonight, I could come over to your place. . . ."

"Mmmm. Only one small problem."

"What's that."

"Dad."

"Oh, yes. Well, come to my place, then."

"Don't you have your son for Christmas break?"

"Patricia, Christmas break was over last week. He's back in Texas." Dean was divorced and had a son Patricia had yet to meet—one small boy she was actually terrified of meeting. She had been in Maine for the week of Christmas and had found plenty of work reasons not to meet him after she was back.

"Oh," she said.

"In fact, he's not going to be back up until Easter break, although I'll probably fly down to see him before that." Dean sounded, and looked, forlorn.

"Oh." Patricia said.

"And then of course he'll be here all next summer. I'm sure you'll want to meet him then."

"Oh. Oh, yes," Patricia said. Her mind started racing. But what if she liked him? What if he liked her? Would he then have a relationship with her? What would he call her? What if he hated her? Or she hated him? Would that be worse?

Dean laughed. "Get the panicked look off your face. Right now we're just talking about tonight."

"Right," Patricia said. She smiled weakly.

Tonight. She had yet to spend the night at Dean's condominium, and she wasn't sure why. Somehow, they always ended up at her home, and she was more comfortable with that. Maybe because she felt more in control at her place? She still had a hard time letting go with Dean; only recently had she put to rest old loyalties and emotional ties to a man who had died long ago, a man she had loved dearly, been engaged to, and lived with. But maybe it was time to let go a little more. She knew she missed Dean. Did she really need to know any more than that?

Patricia smiled up at Dean, and this time her smile was warm and strong. "Tonight sounds wonderful. I'll just go by my place for a few minutes after we leave here, and get some clothes, then come back over to your place."

"That sounds great," Dean said, then suddenly his face fell. "What will we tell your dad?"

"Tell Dad? How about hello, good-bye."

"But he'll figure out—"

"That I'm at your place? Yes. So? That doesn't bother me."

"Oh," said Dean.

"Look, I'm a grown-up woman."

"Oh."

"What I do is really none of Dad's business."

"Oh."

Patricia rolled her eyes and laughed. "Oh, for pity's sake. Would you listen to us? We're just talking about me spending a night at your place, right?"

"Right. You're right. Of course you're right, but—"

"But what?"

"But I like your dad and I want to get along with him."

"Since when did you become buddies with my dad?"

"We're not buddies, we just—"

"And come to think of it, why did you send him over to pick me up yesterday afternoon when my truck broke down? Why didn't you come?"

"He was here, we got to talking, it was kind of slow—"

"Dad said you sent him because it was busy."

"I know. That's what I told him, but—well, the truth is, Patricia, you mean a lot to him, and I thought if you spent a little more time around each other—"

"Oh, great, so now you're family counselor to the Delaney clan!"

Dean sighed. "Patricia, I wish you wouldn't get mad so easily. Your dad and I talked, that's all."

"About what?" Patricia practically spat the words out. All she needed was her lover and her father talking with each other—and she could guess about what. About her. About her alleged stubbornness. Her alleged quick temper. They both commented to her about those alleged traits. Often. Too often.

"About you, okay?" Dean said.

"I knew it!"

"Look, your father just said how important you are to him, and he knows you've been hurt in the past, and he doesn't want to see you hurt again. And I assured him that I care a great deal about you."

"Oh, so now the two big men in my life have everything all worked out for me so my fragile little female feelings won't get hurt. Oh, please. What did you do then? Invent fire? Or the wheel? Ooga shocka, ooga shocka—"

Dean laughed.

"What's so funny?"

"You. You're taking it all out of proportion. And you sound just like your dad when you're angry."

"Ooh, you're winning points now, Dean. 'Scuse me. I have to go play with the band." She jumped off the stool and headed for the stage.

"Hey, does that mean we're on for tonight, or not?"

Patricia shrugged and said, without turning around, "Ask me later."

The other band members—Jay, Ken, and Jasmine—were assembled and ready for her. As they started into their first number Patricia slowly felt herself relax. All right, maybe she'd reacted too quickly, maybe she shouldn't be so hard on her father and on Dean, they both loved her, after all. . . .

At the end of the set, she was completely relaxed. After the smattering of applause died down, she headed back to the bar, intending to let Dean know that of course she would come over tonight. Partway there, someone stepped in her way. She nearly ran into him before she stopped abruptly, stepped back, and realized it was Wayne Hackman.

He had the bleary-eyed, unfocused expression of someone who has drunk too much. His hair was unkempt, his shirt partly untucked, his tie missing. Wayne held up a glass in her face.

"A toast, Patricia," he said, slurring her name.

"Wayne, go home. No, better yet, I'll call you a cab." Patricia started to step around him, but he blocked her.

"No, a toast, I said! A toast to your dear client. For killing my new TV phenom. Or having him killed."

"Wayne, I'm getting you a cab."

Wayne shook the glass in her face, sloshing alcohol onto her blouse. "No, a toast! A toast! You Irish are supposed to be good at that. A toast!"

Patricia tightened her jaw. "May you be in heaven an hour afore the devil knows you're dead."

Wayne looked puzzled for a second, then laughed, stumbling back, sloshing more drink out of his glass. Patricia took the opportunity to maneuver around him, but he grabbed her arm, twisting it behind her. She winced.

"I think you'd better let go of me now," Patricia said.

"Your clients had Lewis killed, didn't they?" Wayne's voice was no longer out of control. He was deadly serious.

"You can't prove that."

"Oh, but it figures. It figures. That kind always has the money, the power, to think they can get away with things like that. But the power of the media—the power of the media is stronger than they know. . . ."

"Give it up, Hackman."

He twisted her arm harder. "This isn't over, Delaney. I'm not through with you. I'm not through with the story. If anything, they've done me a favor. You just stay out of my way, understand? You just leave this case alone, understand? I'm going to be watching you—"

Suddenly Dean was before them. "Let her go, I'm warning you—let her go."

"What's going on—" Joseph's voice. Suddenly he was beside Dean. Patricia hadn't even known he was there.

Oh great, she thought. Great. All this testosterone was going to get her killed. Hackman, drunk, holding her painfully hard, and Dean and Dad coming to the rescue. She'd hoped to put up with Hackman a little longer, to find out all she could from him about what he was planning to do now that the star of his show was dead. But both Dean and her father were closing in, looking as though they were going to physically rip her away from Wayne.

She lifted her free arm and rammed her elbow as hard as she could into Hackman's ribs. He yelped and loosened his grip. She pulled away, then turned to face him. He grinned nastily and started toward her. She brought her knee up, hard, into his groin. Moaning in agony, he immediately fell to the floor.

Patricia looked up at her father and Dean, who were in turns staring at her and at Hackman. "Thank you," she said, "for coming to my rescue. Dean, call this man a cab and send him back to the Omni."

She looked down at Hackman, who had stopped moaning but whose face was pale. He looked like he might throw up. She walked away, moving through the cluster of people that had gathered. There was nothing more to say to Hackman.

She sat down at a table. After a few minutes her father sat down with her. He had a beer for himself, an iced coffee with bourbon for her.

"Are you okay?" he asked.

She sipped the coffee. "Fine."

"Pretty impressive moves you had there."

"I learned them in junior-high gym class during self-defense week. And I knew Hackman was not thinking clearly, because he was drunk, and he's not a very large man, and I wasn't alone. Pretty easy to look tough under those circumstances. But if I'm ever trapped in a dark alley with an attacker, I hope there's a good cop around."

A silence stretched between them. They watched as Dean half shoved a moaning Hackman toward a back room.

Patricia looked at her father. "Didn't know you were going to be here."

Joseph shrugged. "Dean told me yesterday your band was filling in tonight. I didn't think I'd want to see you playing in a rock-and-roll band. Not after the hopes I'd had for you . . ."

Patricia sighed. "I know, I know. You always—"

Joseph put his hand over hers. "You don't know. I was saying I had hopes for you to have a musical career. It didn't work out for me like I wanted, so I hoped it would work out for you. I felt hurt when you gave up."

Patricia nodded.

"So I thought I wouldn't want to see you with music as a hobby. But Dean told me I should come tonight."

"Dean did? He did?"

"Yes. So I came." Joseph took a deep breath. "You looked—happy. Like you were having fun."

Patricia nodded. "I was."

"And—you're pretty good, too."

"Thanks."

"Now, about this investigative business of yours," Joseph said.

"Yes?" Patricia braced herself to hear, again, all of her father's usual concerns that the work was risky, both financially and physically, and that it wasn't exactly what he'd always dreamed of for his youngest child. While he was at it he'd probably point out again that she was the only child who hadn't gotten married and had children.

"You know, I worry about you."

"I know, Dad."

"I worry too much about all my kids ever since we lost Joe Jr."

Patricia looked up at her father. This was the first time she'd heard him refer to her oldest brother, killed in the Vietnam War, since Joe Jr.'s death. His voice had shaken while saying his name. Patricia squeezed her father's hand.

"But that's my problem," Joseph said. "And I can see your business is important to you."

"I love it, Dad."

"Are you good at it?"

"Yes."

Joseph nodded. "That's good. That's good. Being

good at something you love—that's the best thing in life."

Behind them, Patricia could hear Jay and the others going up on stage.

"Sounds like the band's about ready to start again," she said.

"Do you mind if I stay and listen?"

Patricia smiled and shook her head. "No. That's fine." She started to stand up, then paused. "You know, I talked to Mom yesterday."

Joseph lifted his eyebrows. "You did? How—" He paused, took a drink of beer. "How is she?"

"She's fine. Misses you."

Joseph was silent. He stared away from Patricia.

"You know," Patricia said, "I always thought you and Mom were good at being parents. Okay, not always, not when you told me I couldn't do something I thought I had to do or I'd just die. But as I've gotten older I've come to realize you're good at being parents. And I always felt you loved being parents."

"We did. We do."

"You know why I think that's true?"

"No, Patricia, why?" Joseph sounded a little impatient now. He looked at her, a frown creasing his brow.

But Patricia just smiled at him. "Because I think you were good at being together. And I think you loved being together."

Then she stood up and headed for the stage, ready to play another set of rock and roll.

Chapter 18

Wayne Hackman cursed as he searched in his pockets for the key to his hotel room. He hated winter and the bulkiness of coats and gloves and all that was required just to keep from freezing.

He cursed again as he tried the key in the lock, getting it wrong the first time. He hated all the little extra things one had to keep track of while traveling—keys, traveler's checks, phone cards, airline tickets.

And Wayne cursed yet again when he entered the room and fell back unsteadily on the bed, making the pain in his side surge. Right then, he hated Patricia Delaney most of all. After the bar owner had taken him to a small office in the back to call a cab, he'd had to throw up in a trash can from the pain in his groin, from the sharp ache in his side where she'd elbowed him.

Wayne hated to throw up. And the bitter taste of it was still in his mouth.

After a few moments of lying on the bed, groaning, he pulled himself up. He stumbled to the bathroom, winced at the suddenness of the bright light as he turned it on, rinsed his mouth out with water. Then he took a great gulp of water and immediately started gagging.

He'd taken too much too fast. He threw up again in the toilet.

Too much liquor, he thought.

Too much Delaney.

He rinsed out his mouth again, but this time he did not so much as sip any water.

Wayne stumbled back out to the bed and this time eased himself down on its edge. He lifted the phone. With trembling hands, he dialed a number.

After a few minutes his brother answered.

"I've got a job for you. Your favorite kind."

Even though his eyes were closed tightly, even though he was talking on the phone, Wayne could see little brother grin at that, a sudden greedy slash of teeth and gums and tongue and lips. Little brother already understood what Wayne wanted done.

Joseph gazed into the fire, which he'd started just after Patricia had left. That had been about half an hour ago. Now he sat alone in her apartment, the only light in the room coming from the fireplace. Sammie, who was sleeping with his chin hooked over Joseph's leg, stirred and sighed. Joseph scratched the beagle lightly between the ears. Not strictly alone, Joseph thought as Sammie settled back down to sleep. He had, after all, his youngest daughter's dog for company.

Patricia had always wanted a dog, he remembered. He and Margaret had always meant to get her one, but they never quite seemed to get around to it, never quite found the time. But Patricia, eventually, had gotten her own dog. And she'd turned out just fine. Joseph had never seen that before, he reflected. Patricia had been the youngest and the wildest, and had caused them the most worry.

And he always would worry about her. Tonight, he'd been terrified when he saw that man grab her—and yet she'd handled it almost easily. And now he worried about her out on the icy roads. She had left without saying where she was going, just quietly said she'd be gone overnight and left with her overnight bag. To Dean's, of course.

That didn't bother Joseph—although he'd never admit that to his daughter. What bothered him was being alone on this night.

He missed Margaret. For the first time since leaving, he completely, thoroughly missed Margaret. For the first time in years, come to think of it, he missed Margaret. In over forty years they'd never been apart this long.

He'd thought about calling her the night before, and he thought of it now. The night before, he'd only sensed his loneliness for her. And after all, he'd had an excuse not to call—he'd been in a stranger's house.

No, not a stranger's house. Carlotta Moses's house. Hadn't he known her from afar all these years—charmed by the wonder of her musical talents? She had been brilliant.

And the boy he began teaching back in Maine . . . he showed signs of brilliance as well. What, thought Joseph, could he possibly teach the boy? The boy reminded him so much of himself at that age—the eagerness, the desire to play music shining through the awkwardness, the fear.

But Joseph's fears of failure kept him from trying as hard as he needed to achieve his own boyhood dreams.

Perhaps even if he had tried, he would not have succeeded. The simple truth was that he had not chosen to find out; he had chosen a path that had taken him away from his boyhood dream of playing in a symphonic orchestra. And now this other little boy, who wanted Joseph to teach him the violin, had reminded him. He could try all he wanted to blame his life's responsibilities for the fact that he had relinquished his boyhood dreams, but no one had pushed him away from them—not his wife, not his children.

Joseph waited until the fire had nearly died down. Then he moved to the desk, picked up the phone, and dialed home.

Margaret answered on the third ring.

"Hello," he said.

There was a silence.

"You old idiot," she said finally, softly. "Are you okay?"

Joseph closed his eyes, smiled, and began to cry as he started talking.

Ashley wavered in the doorway of Carlotta's bedroom.

"Come in, Ashley," Carlotta said softly, but her eyes glinted sharply.

Ashley looked away, not wanting her grandmother to see that she did not want to come in, that she had responded grudgingly to her summons. She leaned wearily against the door frame. "Those policemen here today—it's so tiring, having them stomp about the house, asking questions of us about that man, like we're just anyone. They're not coming back tomorrow, are they?"

Carlotta drew her mouth down in a mix of contempt and pleasure. At least in some ways, she thought, Ashley was like her. "I don't know, dear. Possibly. Your father will handle it. We need to speak of other things."

Ashley moved slowly into the room. Now, she thought, now what would grandmother ask of her?

Chapter 19

Patricia awoke slowly, drowsing in and out, lingering in a half-sleep state. It was a pleasant feeling.

After a while the awake state took over. Patricia was only momentarily disoriented as she realized that she was lying next to Dean, who snored lightly as he continued sleeping.

She grinned, stretched, ran her fingers lightly through Dean's tousled dark hair. Normally she awoke suddenly to the shrill of her alarm clock. Patricia usually was up by 6:00 A.M. on a weekday, so sleeping in on a Saturday morning was a treat. She leaned over Dean to look at the alarm clock: 8:20 A.M.

"Mmph . . ." Dean mumbling beneath her. Patricia got quietly out of bed. After showering and putting on the clothes she'd packed the night before, she went into Dean's kitchen and started making coffee.

Patricia knew she was welcome to make herself at home anytime in Dean's condominium, but she moved through the kitchen carefully, quietly, trying to ward off a sense of invading. Maybe it was the knowledge that Dean's ex-wife and son used to live here, too. Maybe it was the son's photo and his grade-school art that covered the refrigerator—the only excess of decoration that could be found in the house.

But Patricia made coffee, and then peered in the refrigerator. Dean didn't keep the kitchen overly stocked, but there seemed to be enough for a decent omelette. And Dean loved omelettes for breakfast. Why not, she thought, surprise him with his favorite breakfast? They hadn't spent much time together lately. She just needed to call Betty at the Heartland Retirement Home and confirm her two o'clock appointment with Dr. Sara Lamont. Then she'd start on breakfast.

Betty, who sounded as though she'd come down with a nasty cold, answered after several rings and confirmed Patricia's appointment. Patricia also asked for the names of the Powells' neighbor who had found Violet and Rena; Nadine Bender was the neighbor, and her daughter was Janet Moyers, Betty said. Patricia did not explain that she intended to visit them while she was in Lebanon.

After talking with Betty, Patricia decided to check that no pressing calls had come in yesterday afternoon, since she'd left her office to take a long nap before going to Dean's Tavern.

She picked up the wall phone, dialed in to her voicemail service. There were two messages. One was from an insurance company she'd worked for before, helping the claims adjustors investigate some suspicious claims. That was good. Patricia liked working for them; she punched the number "7," to save her message; she'd listen to the message again on Monday and return the call.

The second message was from Detective John Tate.

Under pressure from the police, and the realization that she was a suspect in her brother's murder and would help herself by cooperating, Alma had given Tate her "evidence," which supposedly proved Carlotta was Lewis Switzer's mother. Tate wanted Patricia to come in, this morning if possible, hear what Alma had to say, and see how it fit with what Patricia knew of Carlotta Moses's past.

Patricia started to call Detective Tate's office. Then she stopped and shook her head. Yes, she'd go this morning. But first, she was going to make that omelette.

Alma Switzer looked neither mournful nor frightened, as one might expect given the circumstances of her brother's death. She wore green stretch pants, a pink-and-yellow-striped sweater, and high-top sneakers that ended just before her pants began, revealing a slice of pale flesh. Her hair had yet to make that morning's acquaintance with a brush. She looked tired and angry, and turned her rage onto Detective John Tate as soon as she entered the interview room where he and Patricia waited for her.

A young woman officer had escorted her, lightly holding Alma's elbow.

"Let go of me! I can walk just fine!" Alma said, her voice nearly a shout. The officer released Alma's elbow.

John smiled calmly. "Good morning, Alma."

"Good morning? You send an officer over to my cousin Lou Mae's to bring me in for more questions, like I'm some kind of, some kind of common chicken thief, waking up the whole household, getting everyone all riled up, and you say good morning like I'm here on a social call?"

John lifted his eyebrows in mild surprise and looked at the young officer. "Mary Beth, did you explain to Alma that I just want to ask her a few questions, that her presence here is still"—he paused to underscore the words—"entirely voluntary?"

The young woman nodded. "Yes, sir."

John looked back at Alma. "You understood that?"

"Yes, but—"

"And of course you want whoever did this caught, don't you? You'll talk to us if it will help, right?"

John smiled thinly. Alma looked suddenly contrite.

"Well, since you're here voluntarily, and we're all feeling friendly, why don't you pull up a chair and talk with me and Ms. Delaney here. I want her to hear what you have to say so she can then tell me how it fits with what she knows about the Moses family."

Alma turned her gaze on Patricia as her presence suddenly registered. Her eyes narrowed.

"What's she doing here? She's the one got Lewis so riled up he killed himself." Her voice was rising hysterically. "That Carlotta woman sent her out to our place, oh, my poor brother . . ."

"Alma, sit down." John's voice was a command.

Alma stopped moaning, scuffed over to a chair, and lowered herself into it. She tried to run her fingers through her hair, but it was too tangled for her to do so. She let her hand fall to the table with a thump, as if the mere act of trying to smooth her hair tired her. Her brother's death, Patricia realized, was wearing on her.

John glanced up at the officer and said, "Thank you, Mary Beth." The officer left.

Alma eyed Patricia suspiciously. Patricia looked back at her evenly, refusing to look away. She studied Alma frankly. Could Alma have killed her brother? she wondered. Certainly, she would have had opportunity, and motive. Would she have had the presence of mind to plan and carry out such an act? Not this Alma, Patricia thought. This Alma was rattled, a little confused. But the Alma of a few days ago would have. So was Alma now shaken simply because she'd lost her brother, a brother she'd long resented, or because she'd killed him and was afraid of being found out?

"I'm going to show Patricia now what you gave us," John said. "I'd appreciate it if you tell her what you told us. And I'm sure she'll have a few questions for you. You don't mind answering a few questions, do you, Alma?"

Alma looked away from Patricia. "No."

John picked up a box and a manila envelope off the table and pushed them toward Patricia.

Patricia opened the box first. All that it contained were envelopes, yellow with age. They all had dates and times written on the front, along with an amount for the day, usually "$5.00," sometimes a little more, with a note, *reimbursement, talcum powder*, for example; most totaled thirty-five dollars. On a few, additional notes—*please pick up bleach, canned milk*, for example—had been added. The envelopes were empty; no names or addresses were written on them. They appeared to have been used long ago—shortly after Lewis's birth and ending four years later—to make payments. They were neatly in order.

The manila envelope contained three black-and-white photos, now faded and dull. One was of a young baby, an older man, a younger woman, and an older woman. The baby smiled, but none of the adults looked happy. The younger woman gazed lovingly at the baby, while the older man and woman stared stonily into the camera.

In another photo, the young woman held the baby, her arms wrapped tenderly around him. Patricia looked more closely at the younger woman. It was hard to be sure, since the picture was so old, but the woman looked more like a younger version of Rena than of Carlotta. In the third photo, there was a toddler, about three years old, with the young woman, and the older man behind her.

Patricia examined the backs of the photos carefully. No names, no dates. She put them back down on the table. "This is your mother's evidence that Carlotta Moses is Lewis's mother?" she asked.

Alma glared at her. "Yes." She spat out the word.

"What did she tell you about it?"

"That she knew Carlotta was Lewis's mother."

"Look, I don't have all day to go around in circles with you," Patricia said. "Start with the envelopes."

"You don't have the right to bark at me like that—"

"Alma, she asked you to tell her about the envelopes. Do it," John said.

"They're the envelopes Carlotta Moses used to pay Mama."

"When? For what?"

"For watching little Lewis," Alma said. "When Carlotta and him was in New York, after he was born. Up until Carlotta got tired of him and paid Mama to take him." She couldn't keep the gloating out of her voice.

"Alma, what did your mother say about her work for Carlotta?"

"Oh, it wasn't Carlotta that hired her. It was Douglas Powell, Carlotta's stepdaddy. That's what Mama said; she was working for him already, cleaning house, when that stepsister got attacked, and Carlotta got pregnant. So then—"

"Wait, what did your mother say about the attack on the stepsister?"

Alma looked irritated; she did not like having the flow of her story broken. She shrugged. "Just that. The stepsister was attacked. Stabbed, I think. Sent off for a long time to recuperate. Not long after that, Carlotta was sent off, too. Then she came back. With a baby."

"Well," Alma continued, warming up again, "the Powells couldn't just keep her at their house. They were proud folks. Her unwed, baby a bastard." She laughed. "Poor little Lewis, it was. Mr. Powell asked Mama if she'd go to New York with Carlotta and the baby, Lewis. Mama was just barely eighteen herself, but she figured if she said no, she'd be out of a job, and if she said yes, she'd still have a job, and she'd be in a big city that she'd likely never get the chance of seeing again in her life. So she said yes, she would.

"So she stayed in New York with Carlotta and baby Lewis in an apartment. Mama took care of that baby like it was her own—said Carlotta barely had a thing to do with it. Then about four years later Carlotta said she didn't want the baby no more. She'd given Mama a lot of money to keep it, and to stay away from her, and keep her mouth shut. Well, by then Mama was pretty attached to that baby. And she was afraid to ask what would happen to that baby if she didn't take him— Carlotta acted like she hated him, Mama said. So she took him. She came back here, 'cause she didn't know where else to go, and everyone just thought Lewis was hers, and she didn't tell no one any different. And a few years after that Herbert Switzer, that's my papa"—Alma put an emphasis on the word *my*—"Herbert Switzer married Mama and they used that money to buy our farm and then I was born a few years after that." She paused to smile. "I was legitimate."

"And your mother told you this on her deathbed?"

"Yes."

"You found the photos and envelopes after this. She didn't tell you about them?"

"That's right."

"How do you know they are connected to your mother's story?"

Alma snorted in disgust. "The dates on the envelopes line up with when Mama said she was in New York. And the pictures were in the box."

"You think the baby was Lewis."

"Yes. There are some pictures at the house after Mama came back with him, when he was five or so." Alma tapped the edge of the photo with the toddler. "It's the same child."

"And the others in the photos?"

"The stepsister, and her father and aunt, I reckon. Mama said they came to visit every now and then."

"Carlotta isn't with Lewis in any of the pictures."

"So?"

"Don't you think a mother would want to be in a picture with her baby?"

"I told you, Mama said Carlotta 'bout hated little Lewis."

"How do you think she got the pictures?"

"What? I don't know. Maybe Carlotta sent her to get them developed, and she kept a few."

"Now, why would she do that?" Patricia asked.

"What? I don't know." Alma started to stir uncomfortably.

"Have you noticed that Carlotta's name is nowhere on the envelopes?"

"Well . . . yes. But it's her handwriting."

"How do you know that?"

"The dates. And it could be matched with her autographs to prove it." Alma was looking at John desperately now. "Why is she asking me these questions like I am on trial?"

John pressed his fingertips together. "Well, now, Alma, I'd say Ms. Delaney here doesn't think your evidence is worth too much."

"But the dates—the handwriting—an autograph could match and prove—them celebrities are always doing autographs—and the photos—"

Patricia shook her head. "Ah, Ms. Switzer, you know, those photographs could have been taken anywhere. Even if you could prove they were taken in Carlotta's apartment in New York—so what? Why shouldn't her stepfamily visit her? And who's to say that baby wasn't Darlene's after all? As for the envelopes—well, let's say you'd gotten ahold of Carlotta's autograph. Practiced writing like her. Faked the writing on some old envelopes you found lying around in your basement. I'd say as evidence, this isn't much." Patricia leaned back, crossed her arms, shook her head.

Alma's mouth was gaping now. "It's enough—it was enough for Wayne—he said—"

"Oh, I'm sure he did. I'm sure he did, Alma," Patricia said. "But *Flash* is just a show. This is real life."

"And this is real evidence! It is! I didn't make this up. . . ." Alma pounded her fists on the table.

"Alma Switzer, you're going to have to calm down, or I'm going to have to lock you up." John pressed a buzzer. The officer came back in. "Mary Beth, take Alma back to her cousin's. Alma, now, you stick close around. I'm sure I'll have more questions for you."

"Actually, I have one more question for Alma," Patricia said.

"Go ahead," John instructed.

Patricia looked sharply at Alma. "Did Lewis say, or indicate in any way, that he intended to back out of the show?"

Alma frowned, not comprehending the importance of her answer to the question. "Of course not. I talked to him about it the night before—before he died. He said he was going on the show. We needed the money." Her lips suddenly curled into an ugly curve, more snarl than smile. "I still need the money. So you can tell your fancy clients I'm still going on that show, I'm telling the world about—"

"Enough, Alma!" John barked. He waved a hand to indicate he wanted her out. Mary Beth escorted Alma away.

After the door was shut, John looked at Patricia. "You really think she faked this evidence?"

"No."

John stared at her a long moment. "Well, why'd you get her all riled up like that?"

"I don't like her attitude about Lewis."

"You got a mean streak in you, lady," John said. He shook his head, but was unable to fully suppress a smile.

"You think she didn't deserve that?"

"No, she probably did. But why do you believe her? Do you think Carlotta is Lewis's mother?"

Patricia shook her head. "No. But I think Darlene Switzer thought so. And I think when she first was there, taking care of the baby, she did snitch a few photos, thinking she could blackmail Carlotta and her family later. But then she probably did develop a real affection for Lewis. And later changed her mind."

John nodded. "They were always very close, Lewis and his mama. I can see why Alma became so bitter, why'd she be gloating now if she thinks Lewis wasn't really their mama's son." He paused, then frowned. "But wait, why don't you think Carlotta was Lewis's mother? And if she wasn't, and Darlene Switzer wasn't, then who was?"

"I don't think a mother could give up a child like that. Not after four years. Not even Carlotta. And she later adopted a child, with her first husband, and obviously loved him very much. I don't think she'd fake being unable to have children if she actually could. Plus the timing of her giving Lewis up corresponds with her stepfather's death. I think that Rena is Lewis's mother. I think Douglas Powell didn't want anyone to know his daughter was pregnant, and made a deal with Carlotta for her to go to New York with the child and later with Darlene Switzer, just as Alma described."

"What would Carlotta get out of it?"

"A chance to be in New York. Probably a chance to study with some fine teachers. I'm guessing that Douglas couldn't resist visiting his only grandson, and of course Rena, although she couldn't express it, would want to see him, too. It was a way for Douglas to stay in contact with his grandson, but save face in this town."

John nodded thoughtfully. "An out-of-wedlock child back then would have been a disgrace. And the Powells were a powerful, respected family in this town."

"I'm also guessing, from Violet's expressions in the photos and what I've heard of her protectiveness of Rena, that she didn't approve at all of the setup," Patricia said. "So after Douglas died, she was all too glad to cut off the visits. Rena, of course, couldn't protest. And Carlotta was free then to rid herself of Lewis. So she made the deal with Darlene as Alma described."

John shook his head. "And Lewis grew up, just a few miles away, in the same town as Rena and Violet. No wonder Violet and Rena stayed in that house all the time; probably Violet kept Rena there out of fear Rena would see the boy and know who he was."

"Someone else mentioned to me that Violet and Rena were recluses."

John nodded. "I was at the scene after Violet was found dead, and Rena found disoriented and alone. Thank God the neighbor's daughter, who's over at her mother's house next door pretty often, thought to check when she saw the groceries piling up at the front door. Everyone in town just thought of Violet and Rena as eccentric recluses. But if you're right, and Carlotta's known all along, why wouldn't she just tell the truth?"

"I don't know. Only two people can tell us."

"Rena, who can't talk, and Carlotta, who won't talk?"

"That's right." Patricia studied the photos for a few minutes longer, then asked, "What do you know about the attack on Rena?"

"Not much, I'm afraid. I remember hearing about it when I was a boy, years after it happened. No one talks about it now, but people did talk about it for years, partly because it was the Powell family. And partly because it was around here, and nothing ever happens around here much worse than some of the good ol' boys getting a bit too much beer in their belly and shooting up the streetlights. At least nothing much worse ever happened here, except then." His eyebrows went up. "And now, with Lewis."

"Do you have the records of what happened to Rena available?"

John shook his head. "I don't know. Not easily, I know that—that's been so many years, and the police department has moved twice since then. I'll check around for you. Meanwhile you might want to check at the *Lebanon Weekly News*. They've put all their issues on microfiche—dating back a hundred years." He grinned. "My nephew Lenny is the editor. I'll call ahead and tell him you're coming and what you want."

Patricia laughed. "God, I love small towns. All right, I'll check there. But I have a favor to ask of you."

"What's that?"

"May I borrow the photos for today?"

John looked at her for a long moment. "You got a way of finding out things I can't?"

Patricia laughed again. "I'd say yes, but most law officers hate it when investigators say things like that."

John shook his head. "You've been helpful, so I'll say yes. And God knows I need the help on this one. But I want those photos back before you leave town today. And I want to know what you find out."

Patricia nodded as she gathered up the photos. "I wonder—have you found out about the time of Lewis's death? Or about the gun used to kill him?"

John gazed at her levelly, saying nothing.

Of course, thought Patricia. He'd share information about Lewis's death only when he thought it might cause her to give him information in turn. She was still associated with suspects in Lewis's death, was still, at least tangentially, a suspect herself.

Patricia gave a thin smile along with another nod, then left.

Chapter 20

Nothing at the old Powell house indicated that it now belonged to Carlotta Moses, that it was going to become the Carlotta Moses Opera Museum. It was a two-story lemon-yellow, large Victorian gingerbread house.

Patricia got out of her truck and walked carefully up the icy walk and steps, slipping once but catching herself on the rail. No one answered her ring of the doorbell or her knock at the door. She walked around to a side window and peered inside. There were no furnishings, only ladders and tools and wallpaper stripped from the walls and piled on the floor. She checked her watch; it was nearly 1:00 P.M. The workers had gone for lunch. Patricia wouldn't mind lunch herself, but she wanted to keep working while she was onto something.

Onto something, she thought as she walked around the house. Something, what was the something? She couldn't define it. She thought that if she knew why Carlotta had not spoken up about Rena being Lewis's mother, she'd understand Carlotta, or at least understand why Carlotta had not spoken up, instead putting her and everyone else through this damned investigation. She couldn't really believe that Carlotta was simply trying to protect her stepsister, not when she'd been willing to let Rena languish all those years in this house.

Patricia came around the back of the house. The garden house described in the article at the newspaper was still there. She approached it slowly, thinking of the articles she had just read at the local newspaper.

Lenny, just as John had promised, had been at the newspaper. He was waiting for her, even had the articles from the year Patricia was interested in loaded in the microfiche reader. It didn't take her long to peruse them. The attack on Rena had been two months' worth of front-page local news.

This was where, according to the paper, Rena had been found—inside the garden shed. She had been found by the neighbor's child, who liked to come into the garden shed and play. The child, Nadine, started screaming upon seeing Rena covered in blood and ran for help. Rena's throat had been cut. She was taken to the hospital, not expected to live. But she had lived, then been removed to a place left unnamed in the newspaper. It was reported—in terms so delicately phrased that they seemed quaint by today's journalistic standards, thought Patricia—that Rena's voice box was so damaged that she couldn't speak. And of course, with her hands as they were, she couldn't sketch the person. She'd been shown numerous photos of men from the area—investigators assumed the attacker was a man—and had given no indication that it was any of them. There were few clues to go on. The attacker was never found.

The garden shed had been painted the same cheery

lemon yellow as the house. Patricia checked the door. It
was unlocked. She opened it and stepped in.

The inside was freshly painted white and was totally
empty, except for empty glass shelving on the walls and
an L-shaped counter with cabinets below it and shelving
behind it. Heat was running in the small building, but it
was still cold. Gift shop, Patricia thought. Of course,
how perfect. She nearly laughed out loud. Wallis's expertise as a museum coordinator showed.

Certainly any traces of the attack on Rena were now
long gone, scrubbed away, painted over. Patricia closed
her eyes, inhaled deeply, and in spite of the smell of
new paint forced herself to focus on exhaling. Then she
tried to imagine this place filled with gardening
implements—the rakes and hoes and shovels—any of
which might have been used as a weapon; she tried to
imagine a young Rena in this building. . . . Had the attacker come up behind her? And what was she doing in
here—she couldn't garden, what with her hands. Had a
young lover come to meet her? And an argument ensued? Had Carlotta herself attacked her years ago? But
why? It was just possible to imagine, Rena in here . . .
taken by surprise—

Something touched Patricia's back, and she jumped,
and whirled, briefcase drawn back ready to hit.

A young man drew back, saying, "Whoa, lady, watch
it."

Patricia let out a long sigh. "You scared me."

The young man grinned. "You gave me a pretty good
fright, too. Who are you?"

"I'm Patricia Delaney. Investigative consultant." She

gave him a business card. "I'm working for Carlotta Moses."

The young man studied the card, put it in his wallet, and handed her a card, too. "I'm working for Wallis Moses." His card identified him as Don Crutchfield, Crutchfield Painting and Wallpapering, Inc.

"Your own business?" Patricia asked.

Don nodded proudly. "This is one of the biggest jobs I've gotten. The other guys are back to work in the main building. But I saw a truck, footprints leading back here, and thought I'd better find out what was up."

"I understand. Do you mind if I take a walk through the house?"

Don studied her, obviously not sure whether to trust her.

Patricia held up her hands. "I won't touch anything, honest. You can walk through with me if you like."

Don nodded slowly. "All right. Of course, you don't mind me mentioning that you stopped in when I talk to Ms. Moses next, do you?"

He would anyway, Patricia thought. She smiled. "Of course not."

She followed him out of the small garden shed, to the main house. They started in a back door. Don worked on the doorknob with his key, jiggling it a few times. He looked around at her and said, "Sorry to make you stand out here in the cold. That door needs to be replaced—let's go around front." Patricia could have shown him a trick of using a credit card to slip down between the door and frame, but she followed him around front. No use alarming him.

In the front room of the house, two men were work-

ing on stripping wallpaper. The walls in about half of
the house were already stripped, spackled, and sanded,
ready for fresh paint or wallpaper. There was no furniture in the house. Still, even in its empty, half-refinished
state, Patricia could easily envision its former grandeur,
the grandeur it would again enjoy, as a museum for
Carlotta.

A chandelier and a floating staircase dominated the
foyer of the house. Stained glass filled the top half of
the front door and two small windows on either side of
the door. Large rooms were on either side of the staircase, and the kitchen at the back. Patricia realized that
it was the kitchen door they had tried to open earlier. A
bathroom had been added by the kitchen.

On the second floor were five bedrooms, the smallest
of which had been converted to a bathroom as well.
There was a third floor, which was all one room, a
finished attic. It was the only room with any furnishings—a desk, a chair, a phone, some books, lots of
boxes. Wallis's work area, Patricia supposed.

All of the rooms had high ceilings and ornately
carved wood moldings. This was a grand home for its
day, and Patricia could no more imagine the place filled
with furnishings, with Rena wandering alone and disoriented and helpless and Violet dead in one of the bedrooms, than she had been able to conjure the image of
Rena in the garden shed. All indications of past life,
both tragic and mundane, had been stripped away.

At the end of the tour, Patricia said to Don, "Thanks.
You do nice work."

Don smiled. "Thanks."

Patricia left through the front door, backed her truck

out of the driveway, then parked in the street. She went
to the neighbor's house and rang a bell. An older man
came to the door, opened it a crack, and eyed her.

"I'm looking for Nadine Bender," Patricia said.

"You've got the wrong house. On the other side of
the Powells'," he said, and shut the door abruptly. He
wasn't being rude; the temperature had dipped again to
nearly zero. It wasn't expected to get warmer for a few
more days.

Patricia drew her scarf back up around her face and
trudged past the Powell house—how long, she wondered, would people in Lebanon still think of it as the
Powell house, even after it became the Carlotta Moses
Museum—and then walked up to the door of the other
neighbor. This time a woman in her thirties answered.

"I'm looking for Nadine Bender."

"What do you want with her?"

"I'm Patricia Delaney. I'm an investigative consultant, and I work for Carlotta Moses. I want to ask her
a few questions about Rena Powell."

The woman stared at her for a moment, then sighed.
"Come on in."

Patricia entered, wiping her boots off on a mat by the
front door. The Bender house was similar to the Powell
house, except, with its walls intact and numerous furnishings, it felt alive.

"Do you have anything to identify yourself? A license or something?" the woman said.

Patricia smiled and pulled a copy of her license from
her briefcase after she slipped off her gloves and hat
and stuffed them in her pocket. She was always amazed
by the number of people she encountered who weren't

suspicious enough to ask her for some formal identification. In a way it was refreshing to encounter someone who was.

The woman examined the license and handed it back. "I'm Janet Moyers, Nadine's daughter. I'm sorry if I seem abrupt, but Mom hasn't been feeling well lately. Usually we have a nurse living here with her, but it's her day off, which means I take off from work and come over to take care of Mom." Janet stopped, and smiled sadly. "Sorry. I don't mean to complain."

"That's okay. It sounds like a tough situation. I hope your mother starts feeling better soon."

Janet shook her head. "She's not going to feel better. It's just a matter of time—" She paused, pressed her fist to her mouth, swallowed. "Sorry." Then she laughed halfheartedly. "I seem to say that a lot lately. Well, here, let me take your coat."

Patricia removed her coat and handed it to Janet, who hung it up, saying, "I normally wouldn't let you talk with Mom, but if you want to ask her about Rena Powell, that's okay. She always perks up when people ask her about Rena. Why do you want to talk with her about Rena? You said you work for Carlotta Moses?"

"Yes. I'm checking into some private matters for Carlotta which necessitate me finding out as much as I can about Rena's past," Patricia said. Not strictly true, but it would do.

"There was someone here from the retirement home, a Betty, I think, who was asking about Rena."

"Yes."

"You know, Mom's been talking a lot about Rena for years, but no one's been interested in Rena until lately.

We grew up hearing the story of Rena from the time we could remember, until we grew tired of hearing about it."

"You mean your mother told you about finding Rena after she was attacked?"

Janet shook her head. "Of course not. We heard about that like everyone else does in this town—it's town lore by now. And kids would tease us about our mother being the one who found Rena, and how we lived in a house next to hers, and that no one really lived there, it was haunted. Kids would dare one another to go up to that house at Halloween." Janet gave a little shudder. "No. Mom has stories about Rena from before then. That's what she likes to talk about. If you want to ask about the attack, it won't do you any good. She won't talk about it, or even remember it."

"Did she tell you anything about the attack, after you were older?"

Again Janet shook her head. "Nothing. She never liked being reminded of it. It always made her very sad."

"Did she ever visit Rena?"

"Oh yes. Sometimes we all did. Mom inherited this house from her parents and it's where I grew up, too. So we'd go and visit Rena and Violet Powell. Usually just Mom went. She visited them up until five years ago when she started getting sick. After that, I or my little sister or my brother would check on them every now and then when we came to visit Mom."

"What happened when you'd visit?"

Janet shrugged. "Not much. Violet would serve coffee. Lemonade or milk for my brother and sisters and me. We couldn't wait to leave the house of these strange old ladies, as we thought of them, although Rena is only a few years older than Mom. So mostly we stared at the floor. Violet scared us—she was such an intimidating woman. I don't think I ever saw her smile."

"You found her, later, Betty told me."

Janet shivered. "Yes. She still looked intimidating, even dead. It was . . . horrifying. And poor Rena, wandering the house, unable to leave or to telephone out, and so scared . . ."

"It does sound terrible," Patricia said.

Janet nodded. "Well, you'd best visit Mom before it gets much later. She's usually at her most lucid after lunch. Come on. This way."

Patricia followed Janet up the stairs into a bedroom. A woman appeared to be asleep on the white hospital bed, a book open at her side. The woman was petite, and pale, her dark hair prettily done up on top of her head, its chestnut darkness the only contrast to the white sheets and pillows. Only her shoulders, head, and arms were visible above the top of the white sheets. Her shoulders were thin in the loose gown.

"Mom?" Janet said softly.

The woman's eyes came open slowly. "Is that you, Christie?"

"No, love, it's Janet."

"Oh." Nadine looked up at Janet. "When will I see Christie?"

"Soon, Mom, soon. Were you reading?"

Nadine took a long, labored breath. It shuddered out

of her, and a sharp cough racked her. Janet gave her a glass with a straw, and Nadine took a sip.

"Frost. You know how I love Frost."

"Yes, Mom," Janet said. She took the book, closed it, and put it on a bedside table. Patricia glanced at the book. *Best Loved Poems of Emily Dickinson*, the book's title said.

Janet glanced at Patricia. "Mom taught English at the high school for many years. Pull up a chair alongside the bed so she can see you."

As Patricia did so Janet said, "Mom, this is a friend of Rena Powell's. She wants to hear what you have to say about her." Janet pressed a button and the hospital bed's head elevated.

Nadine looked at Patricia, her gray eyes suddenly focusing. "A friend of Rena's? How is Rena?"

Patricia smiled gently. "She's fine, just fine."

"Is she still singing?"

Patricia was stunned. Singing? It was possible, of course. Before the attack she could talk, so why not sing? And the words *i sing, i sing* on the computer screen . . .

She glanced up at Janet. "Say yes," Janet mouthed at her.

Patricia looked back at Nadine. "Yes," she said. "Yes."

Nadine took another labored breath, then said, smiling, "Oh good. Rena's voice . . . is golden. Beautiful. I could listen to her for hours. I know I'll hear her again, soon. . . ." She grasped Patricia's hand. "Do you think she might come sing for me?"

"I—I don't know—I—"

"You're her friend. Ask her. I'd love to hear her sing again. Why, when I was a child, I'd go to the garden shed behind her house and there she'd be, singing. Singing beautiful songs. Beautiful. Sometimes she made things up to sing. She wanted to compose, she told me. She'd let me listen to the songs she made up. . . ." Nadine's voice trailed off.

"Why did she sing there?"

Nadine's eyes grew wide. "Oh, her aunt Violet. Never liked music. Didn't believe in it. Went to a strict church. Thought music outside the church was worldly and evil. Now, her daddy wasn't that strict . . . but Violet took care of that family, did all the cooking, all the cleaning, so he listened to her, especially after his wife died—his second wife. He did insist it was all right for Rena and Carlotta to sing in the high-school choir, but it made Violet very angry. Rena told me about it. Rena was an only child, you know. Her own mother died from an infection after she was born."

"But then her daddy remarried," Patricia said, gently urging.

"Oh yes. The woman had a daughter, too, but I never got to know her. She kept to herself. The woman brought a phonograph, but Aunt Violet made them get rid of it. I remember that. Rena cried when she told me about it. She was happy about the phonograph, thought maybe music had come to the house finally. The little girl, too . . . what was her name . . . ?"

"Carlotta," Patricia said. "Do you remember Carlotta?"

"Carlotta was sad, too. She sang. I heard her a few times, with Rena. She sang well. Almost as beautifully as Rena—sounded more sophisticated. Learned faster than Rena when they had those lessons . . ."

"Lessons?" Patricia asked, trying to keep her voice level. Maurice Horne had given lessons in the area. "They had a teacher come to the house?"

"Oh no. Their aunt Violet wouldn't have allowed it. They all met in the shed. He taught at school, too. I was in the choir then, when he taught. He gave private lessons, too. For the Powell girls, it was in the shed." Nadine giggled suddenly, an incongruously little-girl sound that shook her thin, aged frame. "It was because he was sweet on Rena. Carlotta would leave, then Rena and the teacher would start kissing. They didn't know I was outside, hearing it all." She suddenly looked embarrassed, her little-girl expression disappearing. "I didn't think I was doing anything wrong. I thought it was all so romantic at the time."

"You weren't doing anything wrong," Patricia said quickly. "Do you remember the teacher, Maurice Horne?"

Nadine closed her eyes, and for a moment Patricia feared she'd slipped into sleep. Then her eyes opened suddenly, widely. "Not much. Just that he would get mad at Rena, something about her lack of technique. But I thought the songs she made up were . . . special. I still hear them. . . . Do you think she would come sing to me?"

Patricia took a deep breath and said quietly, hating herself for it, "No. You found her, remember? She was hurt. . . ."

Nadine looked confused, suddenly wild-eyed. Janet shook her head at Patricia. "Hurt?" Nadine said. "When was Rena hurt? Something hurt her? But I just saw her, in the garden house, she was singing. . . ."

The older woman no longer remembered finding Rena after the attack. Patricia smiled. "I'm sorry, Nadine. I was thinking of someone else."

Nadine's eyes started to clear. "Rena's not hurt, then."

Patricia shook her head. "No. I got confused."

Nadine patted Patricia's hand. "It's okay dear. But if you could ask Rena to come for me. Her voice was so lovely. . . . I think I could rest if she would sing to me."

"Rena's friend has to go now," Janet said.

Patricia stood. "Yes. Thanks for talking to me."

"Oh yes, my dear. And tell Rena to keep singing, no matter what her aunt says. I don't mean disrespect, but she's wrong. Music is God's gift, in church and out."

Patricia nodded. She started out of the room, and heard Nadine say, "Could you hand me my Frost, dear?"

"Is Dickinson okay, Mom?"

"Oh yes, I love Dickinson. . . ."

Patricia waited at the bottom of the steps. Janet came down soon.

"She doesn't remember the attack," Patricia said.

Janet shook her head. "No. She's edited all the bad things from her life. She doesn't remember that Christie, my oldest sister, was killed in a car wreck either. She only knows the good. I suppose that's not such a bad way to leave this life."

Janet handed Patricia her coat and gloves and hat, and as she put them on she said, "Thank you. I hope I didn't disturb your mother too much."

Janet shook her head. "It's okay."

"Good luck."

"Thanks."

Patricia left, and started back to her truck. Unbidden, Lewis's voice came to her, singing, "Rock of Ages . . ." She shook her head, walked faster, but she couldn't escape his voice, or the images of Rena: as a young woman, singing in the garden shed away from her aunt, in love with her teacher, who was most likely Maurice Horne, or at least willing to flirt with him; as an older woman, wandering the Powell house; now, tapping out *i sing, i sing.* The images were all jumbled and disjointed in Patricia's mind, and yet somehow, if she could just sort them out along with everything else she'd learned, she was sure she'd know who killed Lewis.

Chapter 21

Dr. Sara Lamont was waiting for Patricia as she entered the Heartland Retirement Home. The psychologist was younger than Patricia expected. She was nearly as tall as Patricia—unusual, since Patricia was five feet eleven inches. Her dark hair was brushed back into a ponytail, and her pale skin free of makeup. What saved Dr. Lamont from looking severe were large, gold loop earrings and a relaxed smile.

After they introduced themselves, Patricia said, "Betty can't join us today?"

"She's out this afternoon with a cold," Sara said. "But she explained to me before she left what you wanted from this visit. Let's talk in her office before we go down to see Rena. Mine is in the opposite end of the building."

"All right."

In Betty's office, they both took visitors' chairs.

"I understand that in some way you hope to talk with Rena about her past, see what reaction you get," Sara said.

Patricia nodded. "I think I may have pieced together

part of her past. I'm eager to get her reaction, because I think it will tell me if I'm right."

She explained her theory of Rena being Lewis's mother, adding that she had pictures of Rena with a young Lewis and wanted to show them to her.

Sara let out a long slow whistle. "I don't know. Part of me thinks no, we should wait until Rena starts showing signs of wanting to communicate before asking her about this. But another part of me says she hasn't reacted much at all before—except this morning, when Kendra got that computer of hers to somehow let Rena compose music."

"Kendra modified the composition software to work with her mouse pad?"

Sara smiled. "Betty mentioned you use computers in your work."

"Yes. I'm impressed with Kendra's work."

"So are we. All right. Let's go see Rena. We'll take it slowly. But if I cut off the visit, or cut you off, I don't want you to push."

"I understand."

At Rena's door Sara knocked, and after a few seconds Kendra answered.

"Hello," Patricia said. "Remember we met yesterday?"

"Oh, yes," said Kendra. "Come in."

"I've agreed that Patricia can ask Rena a few questions," Sara said.

Sara and Patricia entered. An electronic melody was playing. Despite the poor quality of the sound, not like the sounds which could be produced by some better machines on the market, Patricia could hear the beauty of the phrase. She thought immediately of Nadine's memory of Rena wanting to compose songs.

"Not the best production quality, I know," Kendra said. "But with some help from a computer scientist I know at the university I attend, I got the composition software to work with the mouse pad I've created for Rena. And as soon as I showed her how it worked, she attached herself to it. She's been making melody lines with it all afternoon."

Patricia stood and listened for a long moment, watching Rena, who sat before the computer listening to the music. Then she moved the mouse over the pad, clicked a button with the side of her hand, and a note on the bar across the screen moved down a half note. Then she moved the pointer to the bottom of the screen and clicked again. The melody, adjusted, played again. It was even lovelier than before.

"Incredible," Patricia murmured.

Kendra nodded her agreement.

Patricia looked at Sara. "Should I begin?"

Sara nodded.

"Let me get her attention," Kendra said. She wheeled over to Rena and touched her lightly on the arm. "Rena."

Rena looked reluctantly away from the computer screen. "Do you remember Patricia Delaney?"

Rena turned in her chair and glanced up at Patricia. Then she looked back at Kendra and nodded.

"Patricia wants to talk with you about your past. Is that okay?"

Rena stared at Kendra, totally still for a moment, then nodded.

Kendra wheeled to the other side of the room, and Patricia pulled up a chair in front of Rena.

For a moment Patricia simply looked at her: the scar on her throat; the inscrutable expression; the blue eyes as empty as a winter sky relieved of snow. Today there was no fear, or anxiousness, or reluctance in her face. Today there was simply nothing.

"I talked to an old friend of yours today. Nadine Bender," Patricia said. No response. "Do you remember her?"

No response.

"It's okay, Rena. You can nod or shake your head to Patricia's questions," Sara said.

"Do you remember Nadine?"

Rena nodded slowly.

Patricia looked at her evenly. "She said you sang beautifully, a long time ago."

For a moment Rena was again still. Then she nodded.

"I met someone else I think you may remember." Patricia braced herself, not sure what reaction she would get. Then she said simply, "Lewis."

Rena looked as if struck, then froze. She stared blindly at Patricia.

"I'd like to show you his picture," Patricia said. "It's an old picture of when he was a baby." She got the photo of just Rena and the young Lewis out of her purse and turned it around so Rena could see.

But Rena stared at Patricia and did not look down at the photo.

"Would you like to see it?" Patricia asked again.

No response.

Patricia glanced up at Sara.

Sara shook her head and motioned Patricia away from Rena.

"I can bring it some other time," Patricia said. "If you'd like to see it then."

She still held out the photo. Rena kept staring stiffly beyond her. Sara cleared her throat.

Patricia stood up, moved away, and left the small room. She waited in the hallway and a few seconds later Sara joined her.

"Kendra is with her. I think Rena will be okay. Sorry. But that frozen look—that's how she was when she first got here. I didn't want this mention of Lewis—or seeing his photo—to undo all the work we've done, all the progress we've made, as little as it may seem."

Patricia nodded. "I understand. But I will try to have access to the photos as long as possible so I can keep my promise to show them to Rena if she changes her mind."

"We'll stay in touch, okay?"

"All right," Patricia said.

"I can walk you out."

"That's okay. I know my way."

Before leaving Lebanon, Patricia stopped at Detective John Tate's office and made photocopies of the photos and arrangements to borrow them again, after telling John about her meeting with Rena and the psychologist.

Now she was on her way back to Cincinnati, driving slowly and carefully on a narrow country road. It was

4:00 P.M. and Patricia was hungry and discouraged. What had she really accomplished today? she wondered. She'd managed to upset three older women—not that she was entirely remorseful about upsetting Alma—and she had not really confirmed her theory. Alma was insistent that Carlotta was Lewis's mother. From Nadine she had learned that Rena had sung beautifully, something Violet, the aunt, disapproved of, and that Rena had been enamored with a music teacher, probably Maurice Horne, who had taught at the high school and also taught Rena and Carlotta, privately and secretly. Was it possible, then, that Violet had discovered Rena singing and attacked her violently? If so, how did that explain Carlotta's unwillingness to say Rena was Lewis's mother—assuming Patricia's theory was true. And Rena herself had shown no reaction to Lewis, except to withdraw, which could mean anything or nothing.

The only thing left, Patricia thought, was to talk with Carlotta about her theory and see if at last Carlotta would offer any explanation of Lewis's claim other than saying he was making the whole thing up. But first, Patricia was going to go home and have a nice hot meal.

She flipped on her truck radio.

"Another night of ice and snow and subzero temperatures. Bundle up, people, that last bit of warmth that brought us all that fog is going to be gone for a few days. So stay in tonight unless you have an emergency—temperatures will dip again to seventeen below by midnight. . . ."

Weather information seemed to be all that was on. Patricia flipped off the radio, turned on the tape player, and put in a tape of *Aïda*. That was one opera in which Carlotta Moses had not performed. Somehow, that made it all the more enjoyable right now, Patricia thought tiredly.

Suddenly her truck lurched forward. She had been hit from behind. She glanced in the rearview mirror. A large older American car was right on her tail. The driver was wearing a green-and-red ski mask and a heavy coat.

"Idiot," Patricia muttered. Why did people have to rush in weather like this? She started to ease her truck to the side of the road. Now they'd have to pull over, get out in the bitter cold, inspect the pickup for damage, call the police, give a report.

As she eased onto the berm she was suddenly rammed from behind again. Patricia lost control of the truck, and crashed into a field of frozen corn stubble.

When the pickup came to a stop, Patricia looked out her window back up the road. The car was spinning its wheels on the road's icy edge, where it had come to a stop after ramming her. The driver put the car in reverse and backed up, then lurched into forward gear and started off down the road again.

Patricia scrambled out of her truck and ran, slipping and sliding through the frozen corn stubble toward the road. If she could just get a license-plate number . . .

She was too late. By the time she'd scrambled up to the edge of the road, the car was out of sight.

Patricia cursed. That was no accident. Someone was

trying to run her off the road, and they'd succeeded. But who? Why?

Alma, she thought, or one of her friends or relatives. But would Alma risk Patricia figuring out she was behind the attack, and thus cause further trouble with the police? But who else would be so angry with her . . . ?

Wayne, of course. Wayne must be very angry that she'd embarrassed him the night before.

But why would Wayne bother? His vindication would be a story on *Flash*—that's all he wanted. Or maybe it was someone else, maybe someone hired by Carlotta or Quentin, to scare her away from further contact with Rena.

Back to the truck, Patricia thought; no point in freezing to death while she thought about this. All she really knew was that someone was definitely not pleased with her.

Patricia started back to her truck and slipped. Her left ankle caught on a corn stub as she fell onto the stubble.

Landing on the frozen ground hurt, even in her thick coat. She pushed herself up from the ground, stood, and almost immediately started to collapse again from the sickening, wrenching pain in her ankle. She shifted her weight to her right leg and forced herself to breathe evenly as she hobbled back to her truck.

Inside the truck, she sat for a second with her head down, trying to keep from passing out from the pain in her ankle. If she passed out, she'd freeze to death, and no one would know she was here.

She took several long deep breaths, and then, focusing only on breathing, on keeping conscious, again started up her truck. Then, for the third time since she'd started on this case, she reached for her car phone.

Chapter 22

Joseph came out of the kitchenette carefully carrying a tray loaded with chicken stew, crackers, applesauce, a glass of 7UP, and a cup of hot tea.

Patricia was in her living room, lying on the couch under an afghan, reading *A Tale of Two Cities*. So far it had done nothing to break up the foul mood that had hung over her this entire Sunday.

She had a torn ligament in the left ankle. Which put her left ankle and calf in an air cast and Ace bandages. Which meant, according to the doctor at the emergency clinic in Lebanon, at least two full days on crutches, no weight on the ankle, and two weeks after that on one crutch, using it as sort of a cane, and another six weeks after that of wearing the air cast. Which meant that her dad insisted on hovering over her every minute, to make sure she followed the doctor's orders strictly. Which meant she as at his mercy again whenever she wanted to go somewhere for the next two days. Which meant she wasn't going anywhere, because ever since he'd come to retrieve her in Lebanon the evening before, he'd been lecturing her on taking care of herself, resting, taking it easy.

Which meant she was about to go crazy. Patricia had cases to work on. She wanted to go to the office. Even the dozen yellow roses from Dean, which he brought along with Chinese food for lunch, didn't help her overcome her restlessness. Not even Dickens could make her feel better.

She shut her book and watched her father set the tray on the coffee table. She studied the food on the tray, then looked up at him.

"I don't have the flu, you know," she said. "Why didn't you just heat up the leftover Chinese food?"

Joseph gave her a hurt look and plopped into a chair. " 'Oh, dearest father of mine,' " he said in a falsetto, " 'thank you *so* much for making me my favorite home-made chicken stew. Thank you *so* much for slaving away in the kitchen, trying to come up with something to make me feel better.' "

"I'd feel better if I could get some work done!" Patricia shouted.

Joseph stared at her for a minute, then suddenly lunged at her, grabbed the pillow out from under her foot, and whopped her over the head.

Patricia pulled the pillow away from her face and said incredulously, "Hey! You're supposed to be taking care of me."

"I was. But you're a lousy patient. You're grumpy and ungrateful." He stalked out.

Patricia wiggled to turn around and sit up on the couch and looked again at the tray. Her father only cooked a few dishes. One of them was a wonderful chicken stew made with chicken, cabbage, and spaetzle noodles. She had spent the day napping or engrossed in self-pity or trying to lose herself in Dickens—and hadn't noticed him working in the kitchen. Then she remembered he'd said he was going out to the grocery store while Dean was there.

She picked up the bowl of stew and a spoon and took a bite. It was wonderful—exactly as she remembered it from childhood. She finished it off quickly.

When she looked back up, her father was back in the room, looking at the newspaper.

"I'm sorry," Patricia said. "I am a grump today."

"Apology accepted," Joseph said. "Do you want some more stew?"

Patricia grinned. "Yes."

After she finished eating, Joseph cleaned up and came back into the living room and settled down again with the newspaper. Patricia picked up *A Tale of Two Cities*, but the words didn't really register. She put it down with a bit of a thump on the coffee table and sighed.

Joseph folded up the newspaper, put it down next to Patricia's book, and said, "Do you want to talk about it?"

"About what?"

"I don't know. You're the one who's sighing."

Patricia half laughed. "Yes. I guess I can't stop trying to piece everything together in my mind. I know Lewis's death has to be connected to his claim that Carlotta was his mother. One possibility is he felt guilty over the claim and committed suicide."

"Because he was guilty over making up the story?"

"No, I think Lewis really believed his claim. But taking something so intimately personal on television would have bothered him, and I know I clearly pointed out to him when we visited that Carlotta was distressed about his intentions. I think causing that distress in another would have troubled him."

"Patricia, you can't blame yourself if the man committed suicide—"

"Dad, I'm not." Patricia smiled thinly. She'd lost a lover once long ago to suicide, and had for a long time blamed herself for his death. "I've stopped blaming myself for other people's actions. Besides, I don't believe he committed suicide. I just said it was a possibility not to be ruled out."

"He was murdered, then."

"I think so. If he was going to back out of the show, then Alma, or even Wayne, are suspects. But when I questioned Alma yesterday, she clearly believed he was not going to back out of the show."

"She could be lying. It wouldn't look good for her if she said he was going to back out."

"True," Patricia said. "But I don't think she was lying. Again, it's a possibility that shouldn't be ruled out—I just don't think she was."

"So that leaves someone in Carlotta's family. Any of them would have had reason to wish for Lewis's silence."

Patricia nodded. "I can't get the detective on the case to tell me the autopsy results, or a time for Lewis's death more specific than between five and eight A.M. That would mean someone from the Moses household would have left between four and seven A.M. to get to the Switzer place in time to kill Lewis. I didn't hear anyone stirring at that time. Did you?"

Joseph looked suddenly pale.

"Dad, are you all right?"

Joseph looked down at his hands for a minute, then said quietly, "I was up for much of that night."

"You were? Did you see anything? Hear anything?"

"I went down to the kitchen to get a drink. Carlotta was there."

"She was?"

"Yes. She apologized for being rude when you introduced me. She wanted me to describe my experiences of hearing her perform."

Patricia waited a minute, then said, "So? Go on?"

"So I did. And we talked a long time after that, about music, and so on. And at the time I was so complimented she wanted to talk with me . . ." Joseph's voice trailed off.

"And now?"

"Now I'm wondering if she wasn't up because she was waiting for someone to come back from killing Lewis. If she'd sent Quentin . . ."

"How did she act?"

"Nervous," Joseph admitted. "She kept pacing, looking out the kitchen window."

"What time did you finish talking with her?"

Joseph thought a minute. "I remember the grandfather clock in the hallway outside the kitchen striking five. A little later she said she was tired. She thanked me for talking with her and left the kitchen. A few minutes after that I did, too."

"Did you see anything? Hear anything on your way back to bed?"

Joseph shook his head. "No. I went to bed, and I fell asleep almost immediately."

Patricia thought a minute, then said, "All right. So it's possible she did just want you to keep her company while she waited for whoever she might have sent to kill Lewis to return."

"It is possible she didn't know someone was going from the house to kill Lewis."

Patricia nodded. "That's true. But she's been so reluctant for me to learn anything about her past at the time when Lewis was born, even if it means finding someone, like Maurice Horne, who can verify that Carlotta wasn't pregnant then. Her reluctance makes me think she's hiding something, and that something relates to Lewis's claim."

"Is that why you were in Lebanon yesterday? Trying to figure out that something?"

Patricia nodded, and told her father about her visits with Alma, Nadine, and Rena, and her theory that Rena was Lewis's birth mother.

"But why wouldn't Carlotta just say, then, that Rena was Lewis's mother?" Joseph asked after Patricia finished.

Patricia shrugged. "I don't know. Maybe because my theory is wrong. Maybe because I'm missing some of the pieces about what happened back then. I'm afraid the only people who can tell me are Carlotta and Rena—and possibly Maurice Horne. From what Nadine said, he was more than a teacher to Rena, so if Rena is Lewis's mother, then it is possible that Maurice is his father. I'm trying to locate him, see what he can tell me. Meanwhile Carlotta probably won't tell me anything, and right now Rena doesn't appear like she can." She sighed. "I think I'll check my voice mail service, see if any of the people I've contacted have gotten back to me about Maurice. Maybe that will at least make me feel like I'm doing something."

Joseph gave his daughter a stern look. "You're supposed to be resting, young lady."

"Dad, I'm just checking the voice mail service."

Joseph sighed. "Right. Like I'm going to keep you from working, anyway. Mind if I turn on the evening news while you call?"

Patricia shook her head. "That's fine." She ambulated, as the doctor called walking with crutches, over to her desk. She heard the television coming on in the background as she picked up the telephone.

There were several messages. Two of them related to Maurice Horne. One was from the teacher at Lebanon High School. Maurice was pictured in a yearbook from 1940 with the choir. If Patricia would like to call back with her fax number, the teacher could fax her a photocopy of the picture. Or she was welcome to come look at the yearbook herself.

The next message was from the Piano Technicians Association. A Maurice Horne of Franklin, Ohio, had recently renewed his membership. The young man gave Patricia Maurice's address and telephone number. She jotted down the information, a sense of excitement growing within her, and was starting to dial Maurice's number when she felt her father shaking her gently.

"Patricia—Patricia! Look at the news! Look!"

Patricia turned and looked at the television. It took a few seconds for the words of the television announcer to register. Photos of Carlotta and Howard were blown up larger than life behind the announcer, as if they were staring down at her.

"And today, in other developments, Howard Eismann, local furniture manufacturer and husband of Carlotta Moses, retired opera singer, was found dead in his automobile," the announcer said. "Eismann died of a stroke, police say, and was last seen by his family Wednesday afternoon when he left the family estate. Police are not releasing any further details and Carlotta Moses and other family members are offering no comment. . . ."

Chapter 23

The news of Howard Eismann's death was on every television channel. Patricia watched silently as Joseph pressed the next channel button on the television's remote control. The news story on each channel was the same: Howard Eismann, husband of Carlotta Moses and millionaire furniture manufacturer, was dead at age sixty-nine from stroke, found in his automobile on a country road heading north out of Indian Hills. The coroner had yet to determine if the stroke had killed him instantly, or if it had incapacitated him so that he froze to death. His car was undamaged, pulled over to side of the road, so reporters were theorizing he'd pulled over when he felt poorly, had the stroke, and then . . .

Joseph paused at *Flash*.

"This just in," said the perfectly coiffed, blond announcer. And then she repeated the story.

Joseph shook his head and pressed the next-channel button again.

"Wait, go back," said Patricia. "Normally shows like *Flash* don't report the news as it's happening."

Joseph pressed the previous-channel button, and Wayne Hackman's image flicked onto the screen.

". . . live from Cincinnati. Thanks for letting me break in, Audrey," Wayne said seriously. "Ironically, I was here on behalf of *Flash* investigating a breaking story about a man from this area, Lewis Switzer, who claimed that Carlotta Moses was his birth mother—and had strong evidence to back up his claim." Dramatic pause. Count two three, thought Patricia. He had the dance down well. "And just two days ago Lewis Switzer was found murdered outside his home. Now we learn that Carlotta Moses's second husband has died under suspicious circumstances. Are the incidents related? We're continuing to investigate. For now, let us turn back to the story of Lewis and Carlotta, a strange story that can only be related to us by Lewis's sister—at least, a woman who always believed she was his sister—Alma Switzer."

The camera angle grew wider, taking in Wayne and Alma, and Patricia realized the camera crew was in Alma and Lewis's home. In the background was the *Last Supper*, the case of twelve guns—one gun now missing. The carved wooden animals appeared to have been cleared from the table in the room.

Alma was pale and shaking as she stared into the camera. She wasn't prepared, Patricia realized. Hackman probably hadn't been planning to tape until the next day or so. But Howard's stroke made waiting impossible. Viewers' interest in this story would be diverted by that of Howard's stroke unless Wayne jumped on it quickly.

"I—I loved my brother," Alma said. "So you can imagine how stunned I was when I learned the truth." Voice quivering, she launched into the same story she had told Patricia. But this time she was not gloating. She was so nervous about being on camera that she appeared devastated by the turn of events. Alma ran trembling fingers through her hair as she spoke. Wayne listened sympathetically and played expertly upon her fears until by the end of the segment she was crying.

The final scenes were of Alma crying in the background, Wayne in the foreground, looking solemnly into the camera. "Tomorrow we'll have details of dissension and disagreements in the Moses household, given to us by an insider. And we'll talk to local detectives about the proof of Carlotta and Lewis's relationship, proof being held now as evidence in Lewis's murder, and of course we'll keep you posted on developments in this other bizarre, and possibly related, turn of events—the death of Carlotta Moses's husband, so closely following the death of the son who she rejected, damning him to a life of poverty and anonymity so long ago." Wayne paused, swept a hand to indicate the room in which he stood, his expression carefully balancing sadness and pity at poor Lewis's fate. Alma kept crying, unaware, Patricia supposed, that Lewis's home and family and life were being held up as a pitiable, even contemptible, fate for the descendant of one so rich, so talented, so blessed as Carlotta.

Then Wayne said, "And now, back to you, Audrey."

The scene cut to the announcer, who looked appropriately dismayed at the sadness of the story as she pursed her lips and shook her head. Then she said, "And now we take you to the story of a young tennis player, so determined to win in the sometimes cruelly competitive world of tennis that she was willing to stoop to—"

Joseph flicked off the television. He looked at Patricia. "Well, at least it's a show like that that's putting up Alma's story. If it were one of the reputable news shows . . ."

"They'll pick up on it now, Dad," Patricia said. "With Howard dead, they will. They will be subtle about it, of course. More tasteful. But it will get covered. And Wayne will look like some kind of reporting genius."

Joseph shook his head. "Now what do we do?"

Patricia shrugged, about to say there was nothing for them to do, when her telephone rang. She picked it up. "Delaney residence."

"Quentin Moses here. You've got to come over."

"Quentin. I'm so sorry—I just heard on the news about your stepfather."

"Yes, yes. Terrible. But it's Mother I'm worried about. She's sedated and sleeping now, but the rest of us just saw that terrible *Flash* report. This has gotten so out of hand."

"Yes, well, I'm sorry it has, but I'm afraid Alma was determined to bring the story to the news."

"You've got to help us deal with this. With Howard's death, Mother is devastated. And now we'll have to tell her that this terrible story has come out after all."

"I can appreciate that, Quentin, but I'm not sure how I can help now. I've finished with the case, remember?"

Quentin ignored the question. "You can help because you're the one who talked with Alma and Lewis. You can handle the press's questions, tell them anything you've learned about the Switzers that would discredit their claim—like their need for money. Now, I'd like you to come out here as soon as possible. We've got guards at the front gate—even in this weather the press is already starting to swarm—but I'll let them know. . . ."

Patricia pressed her eyes shut as she listened to Quentin ramble on about his battle plan. He offered no pause for her to say yes, she'd agree to what he was asking, or no, she wouldn't. He just assumed that she'd continue to help his mother.

And Patricia would. Of course she would. She still wanted to know how Lewis was connected to Carlotta; even more, she wanted to know if his death was connected to her. Knowing the truth was all that would enable her to deal with her awful discovery of Lewis's body.

"All right, all right, Quentin," she said when he finally paused. "I'll be over. We'll see what we can work out. But I want you to understand something. In the first place, I'm not going to tell the press anything about the Switzers that I don't know to be absolute fact. I'm not going to insinuate, or allege, or theorize. I'm not going to play Hackman's game. And in the second, I have some questions I have to ask your mother about her relationship with Lewis Switzer. And this time I want some straight answers. Are those conditions understood?"

There was only the slightest of pauses before Quentin answered. "Yes. Yes, certainly."

Patricia hung up the phone. She looked at her father. "Well?" he said.

Patricia sighed. "Gee, Dad, I need a ride. To the Eismann–Moses estate. What do you say?"

* * *

What Joseph Delaney had to say as he drove down the hill toward the Eismann–Moses estate was a muttered string of unkind words. His mutterings were for two reasons, the first being the sheet of ice covering the road. The other reason was that the road, as they got closer to the estate, was crowded with news vans, which didn't make the driving any easier.

Joseph finally did make it to the gate, though, in front of which a large van was parked. A man jumped out of the van and approached the car. The man had on a thick navy-blue jacket that had an emblem in the shape of a shield over the chest pocket.

"Police?" Joseph asked Patricia.

"Rent-a-cop, thanks to Quentin," Patricia said.

Joseph rolled down the window; it screeched in the cold.

"Sorry, sir, no visitors allowed on the Moses premises tonight. . . ." the security guard said, white puffs coming out of his mouth with each word. He held his scarf up near his face in a feeble attempt to stay warm.

"I'm Patricia Delaney. The family's expecting me. Mr. Quentin Moses should have called down."

"I'll need to see identification."

Patricia handed him her driver's license. He examined it closely, then handed it back.

"All right," he said. "You can go. But who is this?"

"My father," Patricia said impatiently. Why was it that about half the security guards she encountered seemed to have something they needed to prove? "He drove me over." She gestured at the crutches in the backseat. "I can't drive anywhere."

"Well, I don't know if I should let him in. Mr. Moses didn't say anything about—"

"Look, Mr. Moses wants me to come in, so I'm coming in," Patricia said. "My father had to drive me over here; he sure isn't going to sit out here in the cold. Now you can let me in, nice like, or I can shove my crutches down your throat and then you can let me in and I'll tell Mr. Moses how uncooperative you're being. Got it?"

The guard coughed. "I'll move my van. You can go."

Joseph rolled up the window, waited for the guard to move his van, then drove through the gate. He glanced in the rearview mirror. "Hey, would you look at that!"

"What?"

"Several of the reporters—I guess they're reporters—tried to run in after us when the guard moved his van."

Patricia sighed. "No one is paying them to be nice."

Joseph parked in front of the door. "Now you wait, I'll come around and help you out."

Patricia waited until her father got out and shut his car door. Then she opened the door and hopped out. She nearly slipped on the ice, but supported herself on the door. She was pulling her crutches out of the back when a young man—not the guard—rushed up to her.

"Are you Patricia Delaney?"

Patricia was taken aback. She didn't know him. How did he know her name? She wasn't that well-known in the area; her clients didn't usually attract this much attention. She saw that the guard was running up to them, and at the same time her father was coming around the front of the truck.

"I don't have any comment," Patricia said.

That she had neither acknowledged nor denied her

name did not seem to register with the reporter. He rushed on, "Can you tell me what you know about this Lewis Switzer we're just now hearing about?"

"Hey, hey! You are not authorized to be on these premises. You are trespassing," the guard warned.

Patricia turned and edged toward the door, gingerly wielding the crutches, which still felt awkward. Time for the rent-a-cop to earn his keep.

Joseph helped her up the steps. After a few seconds Quentin came to the door and ushered them in.

"See," he said as he took their coats. "The press is swarming already." He shook his head.

"How is the family holding up?" Patricia asked.

"What?"

"With the news of Howard's death."

"Oh—yes. Well. Very shocking. But we're holding together. Mother is in the library. She's a little drowsy still; the after-effects of the Valium. She didn't quite sleep it all off. Wallis is with her." Quentin glanced down at Patricia's leg, noticing the bulky air cast for the first time. "What happened?"

"Torn ligaments in the ankle. I fell on the ice."

Wallis and Carlotta were in the library. As she had done the first time Patricia visited, she found Carlotta standing at the window, staring out, impossibly still, immovable, seemingly immutable. Wallis paced, wrenching her hands.

Patricia and Joseph sat down on a sofa, and Quentin went up to his mother. He put his hands gently on her back. "Mother. Patricia is here."

For a long moment Carlotta did not respond. Then she turned slowly, looked at Patricia, but said nothing.

Her gaze was unfocused. She did not even seem to see Patricia. She had, Patricia thought, again drawn a veil between herself and the rest of the world.

"I am sorry about your husband's death," Patricia said.

For a second Carlotta focused. She nodded slowly. "Thank you." She looked at Joseph then, and the dreamy cloudiness came over her again. "Oh! I'm so happy you're here again! My fan!" She looked at Wallis and Quentin. "He's my fan, you know. He comes to all of my performances, I'm sure he does, my fans love me."

Quentin looked pained. "Yes, Mother, we know," he said as Wallis guided Carlotta to a chair and helped her sit down. "Now, Mother, please try to listen. Patricia is going to talk to the press tomorrow, and let them know just what kind of people the Switzers are—"

"Wait a minute," Patricia said. "What do you mean I'm going to talk to the press? And I've already told you I'll say nothing about the Switzers that isn't fact."

"It's a fact that they were desperate for money, right?"

"First things first. What makes you think I'll agree to talk to the press tomorrow?" Patricia asked.

Quentin glanced down at his hands. "I thought we'd call a little press conference. You and I will be there. Answer any questions, make a few statements. A proactive approach. And then you'll need to be at the memorial services of course. There will be a family-only service here at seven tomorrow night for Mother's sake, and then a brief service the next morning at the funeral home, fairly early, at nine A.M. Howard's being cremated, so there's no burial. The Tuesday-morning service is only for family and a few close friends, but there's bound to be press all over the place anyway. So if you could handle the questions there—"

"I'm an investigator, not a PR agency."

"Yes, but you lend authority to our statements," Quentin said, with a small, tight smile. "Besides, I already had the guard circulate a statement that you and I would be giving a press conference tomorrow afternoon at my office at Eismann's Furniture. So you're going to get a lot of questions anyway. You might as well help."

Patricia inhaled sharply. So that was how the reporter had guessed who she was. "I do not appreciate being manipulated," she said. But backing out now would make her involvement look more questionable.

"My apologies," Quentin said with more bemusement than sincerity.

Patricia looked at Carlotta, whose thoughts were elsewhere. Her gaze was again unfocused, her head tilted, her mouth slightly slack. Wallis was holding and patting her hand.

"Carlotta," Patricia said. "Carlotta, I need to ask you some questions."

Carlotta looked at her and smiled weakly. The Valium was helping her stay in a haze, Patricia thought. Well, at least she might be relaxed enough to answer some questions.

"Carlotta, I know you're under a lot of stress right now, but I need to know some things from you. When you first talked with me, you swore you knew nothing about why someone other than Quentin would claim you're his mother."

"I remember," Carlotta said slowly.

"And you've been very reluctant for me to find out anything about the time of Lewis's birth."

Carlotta nodded.

"It's because Darlene Switzer really isn't his mother, as you said."

Carlotta gave a dreamy smile. "Yes."

Wallis gasped. "She doesn't know what she's saying."

Patricia glanced at Wallis. "Oh, yes, Carlotta understands." She looked back at Carlotta. "Darlene and Lewis lived with you in New York, up until he was four, just like he said, until Douglas died, and your stepfamily came to visit you in New York."

Carlotta closed her eyes. She pulled her hand from Wallis. "Yes, yes."

"But Rena is actually Lewis's mother, isn't she, Carlotta?"

Carlotta opened her eyes. She spoke slowly, deliberately, as if it were crucial to her to get her words just right. But her pronunciation lacked its usual preciseness. Her words were slurred.

"Yes. Yes, she is. Rena was discovered to be pregnant while she was in the hospital after her horrible attack. Douglas Powell couldn't stand the humiliation he'd feel if his only daughter were known to have a child out of wedlock. But he couldn't stand the thought of never knowing his only grandchild either. So we made a deal. I'd go off and pretend to have the child, pretend the child was mine. He'd pay for us to go to

New York, and for Darlene as well. What I got out of it was escape from that terrible house, a chance to go to New York, some money to study with some decent teachers. And so I agreed. Really, I had little choice. If I'd stayed in that small town, I'd have suffocated. And with my own mother dead, living with her husband's family—I knew they didn't want me around. But Violet never liked the arrangement. After Douglas died, she asked me to ask Darlene to take the boy, for a price, of course. I did and Darlene agreed." Carlotta smiled. "Of course, it was a heartbreaking situation. And you can see why I wouldn't want it known. For my sake or for Rena's."

"And the father? Maurice Horne?"

Carlotta frowned. "Yes. He taught us each voice, privately, in the garden shed. But to Rena he was a great deal more than a teacher. He was Rena's lover, and undoubtedly the father of her child."

"What did he think of this deal?" Patricia asked, more roughly than she intended.

Carlotta shook her head. "He never knew."

"But at your debut—"

"Maurice wanted credit for my success. That's all."

Carlotta closed her eyes then, and pressed her hands to her temple. "I need to lie down now," she said.

Wallis led her from the room.

After they left, Patricia looked at Quentin. He sank into his chair. "My God. My God."

"We're going to have to tell the truth about this to the press tomorrow," Patricia said.

Quentin shook his head. "We can't. If people found out Mother agreed to a deal like that . . ."

Patricia sighed. "She was young. She had few choices. We can present it like that. Look, Wayne's already publicized Lewis's story as he believed it. People will believe it, too, as long as Wayne keeps repeating it. And he will. The truth can't be any worse."

Quentin nodded. "You're right, of course. We'll make a statement tomorrow afternoon at the press conference."

The press conference the next afternoon was a nightmare. At least twenty reporters—including Wayne Hackman, Patricia noticed—were crammed into Quentin's office, some of them from the local press, some from the national media. And they had numerous questions after Patricia read the statement that explained Carlotta's connection with Lewis. Most of the questions neither she nor Quentin would answer—such as the name of the stepsister, and where she lived or the name of the father. But it would only be a matter of days, Patricia thought, before they figured it out. Quentin had already made arrangements to have Rena moved the next day, after the morning service for Howard.

The only bright spot of the conference for Patricia was knowing that Carlotta's statement would take some of the focus off Wayne. She made sure she caught Wayne's eye and then she smiled at him.

She had expected him to scowl back at her. Instead, Wayne gave her a sly, knowing smile, which startled her. Was he just toying with her, she wondered, or did he truly know something she'd missed, something he was holding back for an opportune moment?

* * *

That evening, Patricia was clearing off her desk at home when she found the paper on which she'd written Maurice Horne's address and telephone number. With the shock of Howard's death and its aftermath, she had forgotten about them. Now she wondered if it mattered whether she talked to Maurice. Carlotta had already explained about Lewis's parentage.

But some things still bothered her. She could understand why Carlotta would not want the world to know about Lewis and her role in keeping him from his parents. But why hadn't Carlotta told her, when she had trusted her enough to hire her in the first place? It would have simplified her work.

Perhaps the diva was not telling all she knew, even now. Patricia decided to talk with Maurice, see if he knew anything that would confirm Carlotta's statement. She planned to ask her questions carefully, without telling him that Lewis was his son. After all these years, and given Lewis's death, that seemed an unnecessary cruelty.

A woman answered Maurice's number on the third ring.

"May I please speak with Maurice Horne," Patricia asked.

"Who is this?" The woman's tone was alarmed, suspicious.

"I'm Patricia Delaney, an investigative consultant. I've been hired by Carlotta Moses to look into some matters from her past, which I think may also concern Mr. Horne."

There was a long silence. Finally, Patricia said, "Hello?"

"I'm still here," the woman said gruffly. "I was just trying to think. You say you work for Carlotta Moses?"

"I work for myself, actually, but Ms. Moses is one of my clients. I'd really rather discuss this with Mr. Horne if he's there—"

"Oh, no, he's not here," the woman replied her voice shaking with anger and grief. "I'm his daughter. You tell the high-and-mighty Carlotta Moses you spoke with his daughter. And that if she'd have given my father any of the recognition he deserved for what he taught her, his life would have been much better. So would have my mother's. And mine. As it was, his bitterness over her denying him—"

"Ma'am, I'm sorry you're so upset, but I'd really rather discuss this with your father."

Another silence. Then the woman's voice became coldly composed. "You don't know what's happened, do you? My father is dead. He was murdered. You tell your precious Carlotta that when he was found, he was holding a program from her debut. See how she likes that image. I don't know how she can live with herself."

Patricia tuned out the woman's railing against Carlotta as she tried to think. She felt cold with shock. "When was your father murdered?"

"Last Wednesday afternoon, that's what the police are saying. I tried calling him that night, and when I didn't reach him I got worried and called the police. Why are you asking?"

Last Wednesday afternoon, thought Patricia, her mind reeling. After her initial visit with Carlotta and her family. Just about the time Howard went missing . . . suddenly she was desperate for more information.

"Do you know how he was killed?"

"He was shot."

"Do you know the kind of bullet or gun used? Did the police tell you that?"

There was a long silence. Finally, the woman said grimly, "You're a creep, you know that? A creep."

Then Maurice Horne's daughter hung up on Patricia.

Chapter 24

One never sees fog begin, thought Patricia.

The morning of Howard Eismann's memorial service was dense with fog. As she sat in the back of the room at the funeral home, Patricia thought about the fog. It had been dangerous, haunting, and yet somehow comforting, as if it were a live being curling itself around the truck as she drove to the funeral home that morning, and then around her as she walked carefully—needing just one crutch now—from her truck to the funeral home.

Patricia had insisted upon driving herself, getting to the funeral home well before the press, or even Quentin and Wallis, arrived. Now the mourners were all assembled, all except Carlotta, who was at home in the care of Ashley and Marcy. Carlotta had specifically asked that Ashley stay with her, Quentin explained.

The organist began to play, each chord hovering tremulously before dissolving away for the next. Patricia closed her eyes and concentrated on the music. It was a relief to have the service begin; a brief respite from the press gathered outside the funeral parlor.

Wayne Hackman, Patricia had noted, was not with his fellow reporters.

But now she did not care what became of Wayne and his pursuit of Carlotta. He didn't have much of a story left; maybe that had been enough to send him back to Los Angeles. Patricia was nearly done with the case herself. She had called Detective John Tate the night before, telling him what she'd learned about Maurice Horne's death. He'd thanked her grimly for the information.

Patricia then told her father about Maurice's death, and they stayed up much of the night working out its probable aftermath. John would contact the Franklin Police Department. Then detectives from both jurisdictions would compare notes, probably discover that the bullets used to kill both Maurice and Lewis were from the same gun, link both murders back to Howard, who had undoubtedly acted to remove anyone from Carlotta's past who could harm her. Rena was lucky he hadn't gotten to her.

Now Patricia just had the service to endure, and then more questions from the press as Carlotta's family escaped to the sanctuary of the estate. And then, just as the fog would eventually do, the press would dissipate, and Patricia could go home. This case, for her, would finally be over.

And then, she thought, perhaps the personal fog she felt she'd been living in for the past twenty-four hours would dissipate as well. She had done nothing but answer questions from the press as a representative of the Moses family, attempting to shield them from the publicity. It was not a role with which she was comfortable, or for which she felt particularly well suited.

Someone sat next to her and whispered her name. Patricia opened her eyes and looked over. Her father had slid in next to her in the pew. He squeezed her hand; she smiled and closed her eyes again.

Her mind drifted back to the morning fog, as if drawn somehow by it. But for what purpose? One cannot grasp fog, or attain it, or touch it, Patricia thought. Fog only swirls around one, an untouchable mist obscuring what would otherwise be obvious.

Thought of the fog turned her mind to Lewis. His funeral service was also being held today. How ironic for poor Lewis Switzer, she thought. He had died on a morning much like this, his killer approaching the humble Switzer home shrouded in fog. . . .

Patricia opened her eyes suddenly. "Oh my God," she muttered. Several people in the pew in front of her turned around and stared at her.

Patricia stood up and started hobbling out on her crutch. "Where are you going?" Joseph whispered, frowning.

She stopped. By now several other people were frowning at her as well, and a murmur was going through the crowd. Where was she going, indeed? She couldn't escape the media without a diversion. "Come with me," she whispered.

Outside the funeral parlor, the media people immediately started toward them.

"Please, please, I'm going to be sick," Patricia said. She waved the press away.

"Out of my way," Joseph said. "I've got to get my daughter to a ladies' room!"

They ducked into the women's rest room. Some of the press started to follow, and Patricia began making retching sounds. The press backed off. In the rest room Joseph looked around.

"Well," he whispered. "I've always wondered. You all get nicer wallpaper than we do. All right, Patricia. What is this all about? Are you okay?"

"Listen. Remember we worked it out that Howard probably killed both Maurice and Lewis?"

"Yes."

"What if he only got to Maurice? Remember, the news reports said Howard was found north of Indian Hills—not near Lebanon. Why would he return to Franklin after killing Maurice? And given the frozen state of his body, he could have been dead for several days. And besides, he wasn't around when I revealed Lewis's identity to Carlotta and the others."

"But maybe his going missing was a ruse, and Carlotta called him somewhere with the information—"

Patricia shook her head. "Why do that? And as good an actress as Carlotta can be, I don't think she was faking the shock she felt upon learning that Howard was missing."

"So what are you suggesting?"

"I think Carlotta killed Lewis. And I think maybe she is going to kill Rena right now."

"What? Are you crazy? Carlotta is agoraphobic, Patricia. She hasn't left her house in years . . . you know that, everyone knows that. . . ."

"The fog, Dad. The fog."

Joseph stared at her a long moment, then moaned as he went pale. "Oh my God. The night we stayed up talking . . . I told you she kept glancing out the kitchen window. What if she wasn't looking for someone to return. What if she was waiting for the fog to get thick enough . . ." Then he shook his head. "No, Patricia. I just can't believe . . ."

"Listen. I want you to make a diversion for me so I can get past the media to my truck. Give me a few minutes."

"Then what are you going to do?"

"Find out if I'm right. It's just possible that the fog, and the therapy Carlotta's been getting for her agoraphobia, and her tranquilizers, and a strong motive would have been enough to get her out of that house."

"But why would Carlotta want to kill Rena?"

"Someone attacked Rena, years ago, taking away her voice. And Nadine, the Powells' neighbor, told me Rena was a good singer. Carlotta could have been jealous, and attacked Rena. And maybe she thought she was safe from Rena telling the truth as long as Rena couldn't communicate, but now . . ." Patricia stopped. "Look, I know I'm going partly on instinct here. If I'm wrong, you can be irritated at me the rest of my life, okay?"

"If you're right, you could be putting yourself in danger."

"Dad, trust me. I think I know what I'm doing."

Joseph stared at her for a long moment. "You'd better," he said finally, then left the ladies' room.

Patricia waited a few seconds, then hobbled as quietly as she could from the ladies' room. Members of the press were gathered around her father just outside the funeral parlor.

She found a side door, exited, and worked her way to her truck. She got in and started toward Lebanon.

It was half an hour to Lebanon from the funeral home in semidecent weather, she calculated. The fog was starting to dissipate, but was still thick enough to slow anyone down. She picked up her car phone and dialed the Moses estate. On the third ring, Marcy answered.

"Marcy, this is Patricia Delaney. I need you to check right now on Carlotta."

"I'm sorry," Marcy said, "but she left me with strict instructions not to disturb her. She's resting in her room."

"Marcy, listen. This is important. I want you to check on Carlotta."

"I have my orders—"

"And I know you've been working with Wayne Hackman," Patricia said. There was a long silence that told her her guess was right. Patricia had realized that this was probably the case when she heard Wayne on the other night's *Flash* refer to an insider's revelation of dissension in Carlotta's household. She knew that Wallis was unhappy enough with Marcy that she stood a good chance of losing her job; Marcy had little to lose by helping Wayne.

"Yes," Marcy said, drawing the syllable out as a sob.

"Right. So go to Carlotta's room, come back, and tell me if she's there."

Minutes passed as Patricia maneuvered her truck along the winding roads through the fog, waiting for Marcy to return. Finally Marcy's voice came back, crackling on the phone as the distance increased between Patricia's truck and the Moses estate.

"She's not there, Patricia. I can't find Carlotta anywhere . . . and Ashley's gone, too. I knew she was leaving; she told me she was going to move Carlotta's stepsister from the retirement home."

Ashley couldn't do that, Patricia thought. She was too young. But Carlotta would be unable to drive—she hadn't driven in years. Ashley could be driving her to the retirement home now; had she also driven her to the Switzers'? If Carlotta was going to get Rena, where would she take her? The Powell house, Patricia thought; that was the first place to look.

Marcy was saying something.

"I can't hear you; speak up, Marcy."

"I said I called Wayne Hackman after Ashley left and told him where she was going. He wanted me to let him know of anything that happened at the house today."

"When was this?"

"About an hour ago."

That explained why Wayne wasn't at the funeral home. And by now Ashley and Carlotta would have already reached the Heartland Retirement Home and gotten Rena.

"Listen, Marcy," Patricia shouted into her phone. "Call the police. Tell them to get the Lebanon police out to the old Powell house. Tell them it's an emergency—lives may be at stake. Marcy? Do you hear me?"

There was no answer. Patricia put down the car phone, hoping Marcy had heard her, and focused on driving as fast as she could to the Powell house.

* * *

A Mercedes was parked in front. Patricia parked behind it, exited her truck, not bothering with her crutch, and hobbled as quickly as she could to the back. Rena had been attacked so many years ago in the garden shed; perhaps if Carlotta was the attacker then, she'd bring Rena here now?

No one was in the shed. Patricia hurried to the kitchen door; it was locked. She slipped out her credit card and picked the lock.

She heard Carlotta as soon as she entered. She was singing an aria, her voice wavering and off-key, a pathetic mimicry of the beauty it had once possessed. The bits of singing were broken by panicked laughter and by her speaking.

Patricia followed Carlotta's voice up to the front room. Carlotta stood over Rena, who knelt on the floor, her club hands pushed over her ears. Carlotta held a gun to her head. Ashley cowered in the corner, crying, and gave a little mew of surprise when she saw Patricia, who put her fingers to her lips. Carlotta had not seen her yet; Patricia wanted a few seconds to decide what to do.

"I heard you, I started hearing you again after I retired, after I came to Cincinnati to live with Howard. That was the only terrible thing about being married to Howard; it was so close to this awful town, so close to you. I thought I could handle it, but I was wrong. Anytime I left my home I heard your voice . . . singing, singing. . . . So I couldn't leave. At the time I thought you were better than me, but of course you weren't—

but I didn't know that then, didn't believe you really just wanted to compose songs."

"Carlotta," Patricia said softly. Her only hope was to keep Carlotta from shooting Rena, or anyone else, before the police came—assuming Marcy heard and had followed Patricia's instructions.

Carlotta's head jerked up as she looked at Patricia. "Ah. Patricia. Well, you figured it out."

"Not all of it. I figure you killed Lewis."

Rena jerked up at that, stared wild-eyed at Patricia.

"Yes, your precious little son. I killed him." Carlotta was addressing Rena. "Ashley drove me, of course. She was so stunned that I would leave the house that she didn't question . . . I hadn't driven in years. . . . The fog, the fog made it simple. I didn't let her know what I'd done, of course. I was going to come after you after that, but then the fog was breaking up, and I panicked and had Ashley take me home."

Carlotta stared down at Rena. "For years, I have lived for fog. I wander out into it. I can leave then, and not hear you."

"How did you get Lewis outside?" Patricia said. Keep Carlotta talking, keep her distracted, she thought.

"Oh, that was simple." Carlotta looked up at her. "I told him who I was. He apologized so profusely for upsetting me. It was sad; he was so sincere. I told him I wanted him to go outside, wait for me outside. He went out, didn't bother with a coat, just held on to this little wooden thing he had when he came to the door. I simply got down a gun from the rack inside, although I'd brought this gun with me. It's just a twenty-two we keep around the house for protection. Quentin's idea. I shot him with my gun, and left his gun outside to make it look like suicide. I had planned to kill his sister, too, but she wasn't there. But then I thought, if it looks like Lewis committed suicide, surely she'd be too devastated to go on with *Flash* anyway."

"That won't work," Patricia said. "The police will know the bullet that killed Lewis came from a different gun than his."

Carlotta sighed. "I'm not experienced at this, you know. Howard was supposed to take care of all of it for me. Kill Maurice first. That's who I thought must be contacting *Flash*. I didn't want to hire you, Patricia. That was Quentin's idea, and I thought it best to go along with it. When I learned someone had contacted *Flash*, I assumed it had to be Maurice. I lied to you before. He'd visited me in New York, seen Lewis. I'd told him he was a neighbor boy, but I always knew he didn't believe me, might guess the truth. I told Howard everything, and he went to kill Maurice for me. Then, after we learned Rena was learning to communicate, Howard was supposed to get her and bring her back to our house, where we could keep control of her. But poor Howard never made it to Rena. He came home to tell me he'd killed Maurice—then after that, I never heard from him again." Her voice caught on a sob. "The stress of it—I'm sure that's what caused his stroke. And when I learned that it was actually Lewis who had contacted *Flash*, I had to take matters into my own hands."

"Why, Carlotta? Why did you and Howard have to do all this? Was it you who attacked Rena all those years ago?"

Carlotta looked surprised at the question. "Oh, no.

Maurice was the one who attacked her. I saw it happen, and I didn't try to stop it. Maurice did not see me; I hid behind the bushes growing by the garden shed. I heard the whole thing. Rena was pregnant, in love with Maurice, wanted him to marry her. But he was already engaged to someone else. When she threatened to tell everyone, he panicked. He grabbed a hoe and hit her, cutting her throat. Then he ran. I left her there to die. I left her there. I was so jealous; I thought at the time she had a better voice than mine, and that because she was Maurice's lover, he might help her with a musical career. I didn't know enough at the time to realize mine was the greater talent. I just knew I wanted a singing career, and that I didn't want her to compete with me. I thought if she died, she'd be out of my way. So after Maurice left the shed, I left, too. But the neighbor girl found her a few minutes later. It was pure luck."

"And ever since then, you've felt guilty, haven't you, Carlotta? You left Rena to die, and when she didn't die, you didn't identify her attacker, because then everyone would know you'd left her to die. Then you agreed to a conspiracy to take away her son, and you let Violet keep her locked away in this house, away from anyone who might help her, because you feared she might learn to communicate, to tell the truth about what you'd done, and then the world wouldn't love you quite so much. But running from what you did hasn't really helped you, Carlotta. It hasn't made you happy. And this won't work now. Rena's not the source of the guilt you feel. You are. You have to face your guilt alone," Patricia said. Carlotta had never had the courage to walk alone;

she'd always required the spotlight, the comfort of being surrounded by adoring fans.

"Yes, yes, it will work. I've paid enough, haven't I? The guilt all these years? Killing Lewis—don't think I liked that. I just felt it was necessary ... so much at stake ... And Howard, poor Howard was so upset. ... What I asked him to do for me killed him. And he's the only person I've ever really trusted, ever fully loved."

Carlotta looked up at Patricia, tears glistening in her eyes. "I'm sorry, dear. You've been so helpful, and I really like your father. But I'm going to have to kill you, too. After I kill Rena. Or maybe before. Yes, before, because of course she's helpless and you'll try to rescue her. Of course. That's why you're here."

"What about Ashley?" Patricia said quietly. "You can't let her see you like this; you have to give me the gun."

"But I'm doing this *for* Ashley." Carlotta looked confused. "I'm doing this for her. Don't you see? Ashley understands; I told her to bring me to the Heartland Retirement Home and we got Rena and brought her here."

"Ashley didn't know you were going to do this, did you, Ashley?"

"No, I—Grandmama—I—" Ashley's voice came out in a squeak. The young woman was shaking and crying. "Please listen to Patricia, Grandmama. Give the gun to Patricia, please—"

"But for you, Ashley, I'm doing this for you. If people know what I did then, your future ... they'll shun you. ... It's over for me now, but for you ..."

"Grandmama, please—"

Suddenly a new voice barked out. "Oh, come on,

you're not doing this for dear Ashley. You're doing this to preserve your wonderful reputation. You couldn't stand to have your adoring fans hate you."

Patricia started, and turned. Wayne Hackman stood in the doorway, grinning. He, too, had a gun. "I have it all here on tape, Carlotta, your every word. It's going to make a lovely story. Now drop the gun, and I can be a hero, too. Rescuing poor Rena and Ashley and Patricia—"

"Wayne, you idiot!" Patricia cried.

Carlotta turned her own gun on him and shot. Patricia fell to the floor. Carlotta was turning the gun on her. Rena's face suddenly filled with the fury that Patricia had observed flickering briefly during her first visit with her. Rena lurched, knocking Carlotta over. Patricia scrambled across the floor and took the gun from Carlotta, who struggled for a few seconds, then collapsed, sobbing. Ashley rushed over and held her grandmother in her arms. Rena backed away, then suddenly collapsed, lost again to some internal trance.

Wayne was moaning on the floor. "Oh my God, I'm shot, I'm shot. . . ."

Patricia looked over at him. "Oh, shut up," she said, "It's just a shoulder wound. She barely grazed you. I ought to finish you off for her. For the rest of us. What's the idea, coming in like that?"

"The story," Wayne winced. "I wanted to get the story. You've got to get me some help."

Patricia walked over to Wayne, picked up his gun and tape recorder, and trained the gun on him.

"Remember the toast you asked me to give you? May you be in heaven an hour before the devil knows you're dead? For you, God may have a messenger to let the devil know you're on your way. . . ."

"Patricia, no, you wouldn't. . . ."

"I wouldn't? Really, I wouldn't? Don't test me, Hackman. Answer some questions, and then I'll think about calling nine-one-one for you. Where'd you get this gun?"

"My brother." Wayne winced. "He lives near Cincinnati—"

"I know, I know. Is he the jerk who ran my truck off the road?"

"Yes. I just wanted to scare you."

"And you asked him to do so?"

"Yes."

"Wayne, buddy, I hope you know your tape is still running, and I'm going to give it to the police right after I file a complaint against you and your brother. . . ."

Wayne gave a grimacing smile. "Patricia, no, my story, my career . . ." He started to get up, and moaned again.

"Oh, Sweet Saint Peter," Patricia said. "What would old Shelly from Cheviot High days say if she could see you now, you football star you?"

Wayne moaned.

Patricia started laughing, just on the edge of hysteria. She was still laughing when the front door burst open and Detective John Tate and several other officers rushed in.

"What the hell—" John started.

"Welcome," Patricia said, "to the Carlotta Moses Opera Museum."

Chapter 25

Two days later Joseph Delaney had his violin and his few purchases sitting by his daughter's front door. He was ready to say good-bye to Patricia and start home to Maine.

"Are you sure you're going to be all right, still needing a crutch?" Joseph asked.

"Yes, Dad, yes, for the zillionth time. I only need to use it for a few more days, then I just have to put up with this ankle brace for a while. I'll be fine."

Joseph pouted. "A father has a right to worry, you know, especially when his youngest daughter is so bullheaded."

"Dad—" Patricia glanced at her watch. She had two hours before Dean came over.

"Okay, I'm going. I know you've got plans this evening."

Patricia arched an eyebrow. "What, did Dean call you and discuss them?" Dean was leaving his tavern in the care of the bartender that night and taking Patricia out for dinner.

Joseph wrinkled up his nose. "No. But you already smell like a field of flowers. And why did you get such a heavy scent? If you keep spritzing that stuff on every half hour, by the time he gets here—"

"Dad."

"Yes?"

"You got me the perfume at Christmas. Goes with the liquid soap."

"Oh."

Patricia laughed. "You know, I've actually enjoyed your company—for the most part. How long has it been since we've done anything together, just the two of us?"

"Too long." Joseph's eyebrows arched. "And too long since we've played our duet."

"Oh, Dad."

"C'mon now, Patricia."

Patricia sighed. She went back to the spare room and got out her violin. When she came back to her living room, her father already held his violin and was tuning it.

"Mine's not in the best shape," Patricia said.

"Just give it a tuning and it will be fine."

After a few minutes Patricia and Joseph started in on the duet they had been trying to play with each other for years, an Irish jig Joseph had transposed into a duet for violins. As usual, they whisked through the merry tune—until they got to the second-to-last bar, at which point the melody and harmony broke apart and they both stopped and glared at each other.

"Now, you always do that, Patricia. That note is an accidental sharp, you know."

"It doesn't sound right to me to play it that way. You're deliberately taking a traditional melody and breaking the sound that has made it beloved all these years."

"No, I've told you, I want that note played sharp to draw the listener's attention to—"

Joseph started laughing. After a few seconds Patricia started laughing as well.

"I hope," Joseph said, starting to put his violin away, "that my new student back in Maine listens better than you do."

Patricia smiled at that, suppressing a whoop of joy at her father's words. "I hope so, too," she said. She put her violin aside.

Joseph and Patricia hugged for a long moment, then Joseph patted Patricia on the back and pulled away. "I'd best be on my way. I'd like to get back home before nightfall tomorrow." He stroked Patricia's cheek, then held his thumb under her chin for a moment. "Thanks, Patricia."

Patricia nodded. "You're welcome, Dad."

One week and three days later Patricia was off her crutch.

The telephone calls from the media following Carlotta's arrest started trailing off when the reporters realized that Patricia was not going to tell them any more than what they could get from the police and lawyers involved in the case.

Wayne Hackman, of course, was on *Flash* every night with any tidbit he could find about the case, a self-proclaimed hero for tracking down Carlotta and capturing her confession on tape, and for putting himself in danger—even getting shot—in the process of upholding the public's right to know anything it wanted about its heroes.

He did not, of course, mention that Patricia was prosecuting him and his brother. No other media people seemed interested in airing that part of the story either.

Two weeks later Patricia settled out of court with the Hackman brothers. Hackman's lawyer had pointed out that Wayne had confessed under duress—she had been holding a gun on him. Jay, her lawyer, reluctantly agreed that Hackman's lawyer was right, and counseled her to settle. She did, and donated the modest settlement to the Lebanon Baptist Church, as the Lewis Switzer Fund, to be used for charitable works in his name.

Four weeks later several events occurred to let Patricia know that spring would actually arrive.

The snow started to melt.

Patricia got off her air cast.

It was Saint Patrick's Day and Dean's Tavern was serving green beer, but Patricia opted for her favorite, iced coffee and bourbon, to wash down her corned beef and cabbage at lunch.

Patricia called her parents from Dean's office to wish them a happy Saint Patrick's Day. Her parents were happy that she was out of her air cast. Dad was teaching violin to two kids now. Mom was in charge of a charity auction. Maureen, one of Patricia's sisters, had asked them for money again. Kelly, her other sister, was worried that Patricia hadn't taken good enough care of her ankle. . . .

Patricia hung up after the call, and laughed. Families.

That afternoon, she went to the Heartland Retirement Home to keep her appointment with Rena. This would be her second visit since Rena had returned to the home; on the first visit Rena had barely seemed to recognize her. Patricia had requested the first visit. Rena had requested the second, spelling out the request on the computer, according to Betty, who had made the appointment on Rena's behalf with Patricia.

At the home, Patricia asked Betty how Rena was doing.

"Better. She's starting to communicate. The ability to make music seems to be the best therapy for her. She specifically wanted to talk with you, though. I'll be in the room in case she gets upset."

In the room, Rena turned and looked at Patricia. Then she moved the mouse up on the screen and posted a request for Patricia to see: *Tell me about my son.*

Rena looked up at Patricia, waiting.

Patricia took a deep breath. "He was a gentle man. I liked him, even though I only met him once. And he could sing. Beautifully. He sang hymns. I'll never forget hearing him sing. . . ."

SHARON GWYN SHORT

Published by Fawcett Books.
Available in your local bookstore.